What the critics are saying…

SUMMER PLEASURES: THE CAPTURE

"The sex scenes are some of the hottest I've read. Ms.Bast has done an amazing job of exploring women's sexual fantasies in this series...." ~ *Five Stars Just Erotic Romance Reviews*

"Ms. Bast story telling ability once again astounds me!! Her depiction of emotion just overwhelms me." ~ *Five Stars Just Erotic Romance Reviews*

"Anya Bast has penned a superb fantasy with the perfect hero." ~ *Five Roses A Romance Review*

AUTUMN PLEASURES: THE UNION

"Anya Bast delivers the perfect combination of intrigue, romance and erotic encounters..." ~ *Four Stars Romantic Times BookClub*

"....an enjoyable and pleasing end to what has proven to be an immensely satisfying erotic fantasy series." ~ *Romance Reviews Today*

"For a heart wrenching good read grab this book with both hands and hold on tight!!!!" ~ *Five Stars Just Erotic Romance Reviews*

Anya Bast

SEASONS OF PLEASURE
Winter and Spring

ELLORA'S CAVE
ROMANTICA PUBLISHING

An Ellora's Cave Romantica Publication

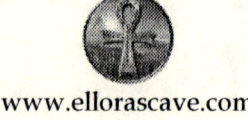

www.ellorascave.com

Seasons of Pleasure: Summer and Autumn

ISBN #1419950908
ALL RIGHTS RESERVED.
Summer of Pleasure: The Capture
Copyright© 2004 Anya Bast
Electronic book Publication: January, 2004

Autumn Pleasure: The Union
Copyright© 2004 Anya Bast
Electronic book Publication: June, 2004

Edited by: Briana St. James

Seasons of Pleasure: Summer and Autumn
Trade paperback Publication: May, 2005
Cover art by: Syneca

Excerpt from *Ordinary Charm* Copyright © Anya Bast, 2004
Excerpt from *Blood of an Angel* Copyright © Anya Bast, 2005

With the exception of quotes used in reviews, this book may not be reproduced or used in whole or in part by any means existing without written permission from the publisher, Ellora's Cave Publishing, Inc.® 1056 Home Avenue, Akron OH 44310-3502.

This book is a work of fiction and any resemblance to persons, living or dead, or places, events or locales is purely coincidental. The characters are productions of the authors' imagination and used fictitiously.

Warning:

The following material contains graphic sexual content meant for mature readers. *Seasons of Pleasure: Summer and Autumn* has been rated *E-rotic* by a minimum of three independent reviewers.

Ellora's Cave Publishing offers three levels of Romantica™ reading entertainment: S (S-ensuous), E (E-rotic), and X (X-treme).

S-*ensuous* love scenes are explicit and leave nothing to the imagination.

E-*rotic* love scenes are explicit, leave nothing to the imagination, and are high in volume per the overall word count. In addition, some E-rated titles might contain fantasy material that some readers find objectionable, such as bondage, submission, same sex encounters, forced seductions, etc. E-rated titles are the most graphic titles we carry; it is common, for instance, for an author to use words such as "fucking", "cock", "pussy", etc., within their work of literature.

X-*treme* titles differ from E-rated titles only in plot premise and storyline execution. Unlike E-rated titles, stories designated with the letter X tend to contain controversial subject matter not for the faint of heart.

Also by Anya Bast:

Blood Of The Rose
Spring Pleasures: The Transformation
Winter Pleasures: The Training
Ellora's Cavemen: Tales from the Temple III
The Embraced: Blood of the Raven
Ordinary Charm
The Embraced: Blood of an Angel

Contents

The Capture
Summer Pleasure
~11~

The Union
Autumn Pleasure
~145~

The Capture
Summer Pleasure

Chapter One

Lilane pulled the hood of her thin, black *Anotte* a bit further over her head and took a bite of bread and cheese. She closed her eyes in rapture as the first food she'd had in two days slid past her taste buds.

The Crow's Inn was packed with men and women who all sat at long tables, laughing and talking. Candles guttered, sputtering light and casting shadows over the rough-hewn wood walls and tables. Acrid smoke from the kitchen's cook fire soured the air and made her eyes burn. It was hot outside and even hotter inside. She ran her fingertips over her moist brow.

After taking a careful sip of her room temperature ale, she watched her quarry over the rim of the tankard. A full week of tracking him had brought her close to where she didn't want to go—the Sudhraian-Nordanese border. She'd seen him leave Marken's Lorddom three weeks ago almost to the day. A Goddess-bedamned Sudhraian, he was. She'd suspected it the first time she'd seen him because he'd had the coloring and clothing of one. Then she'd heard him speak Nordanese with a heavy Sudhraian accent, and she'd known for sure.

Her brow furrowed. He was also some other sort of foreign creature, but what she knew not. The first time she'd seen him he'd been flying...with his very own *wings*. Before she'd left, she'd heard whispers in Marken's Lorddom about a mystical race called the Aviat, long thought only a myth, living and breeding in Sudhra. But that mattered naught to her. It was the Sudhraian part of this man that mattered and nothing else.

"Honored *Anottie*, would you like something else?" The barmaid set the steaming meat pie Lilane had ordered on the table in front of her. The young woman bobbed in a deep curtsy out of respect for Lilane's costume. Guilt flickered through Lilane for the deception. Though dishonest, taking the guise of a Sudhraian *Anottie* had been necessary this close to Sudhra. It was the only thing keeping her safe. Besides, the robe was voluminous enough to conceal all kinds of useful items, like a sword and a dagger. Very necessary for a woman this close to the border—this she knew well.

Lilane glanced at the barmaid and answered with her best Sudhraian accent. "No, blessed female, that will be all."

The words set Lilane's teeth on edge. *Blessed female.* The Sudhraian required women to always be called so, to distinguish them from the superior sex—men. According to Sudhraian custom, had the waitress been a waiter, Lilane would have received no physical or verbal mark of respect, and she would not have been allowed to meet his gaze, even though the *Anottie* were the Sudhraian God's holy order, counterpart to the male Priests of *Anot*.

The waitress bobbed once more and left the table. Lilane fell to her meat pie voraciously at first, then realizing she drew attention to herself, slowed and ate as a proper *Anottie* would. The salty meat and vegetables tasted better than anything she could imagine. She ate the entire pie and still her stomach felt empty. But no amount of food would ever fill the hole she had within her. Only Sudhraian blood spilled on the ground by the edge of her blade could ever do that.

And she had strong intentions of doing just that.

She could not sleep, either. She'd had damned little rest in the three weeks since she'd left her village. Being hungry and completely exhausted was a bad combination. She couldn't think straight anymore.

Her eyes narrowed on the Sudhraian male, her hunted. A sexual jolt went through her every time she looked at him. It only made her detest him more, and herself as well. How could she feel attraction for this Sudhraian? She shivered. She must be sick and twisted to find him attractive, though he was undeniably good looking. His face was hewn from a masculine hunk of granite and one could see the exceptionally light blue of his eyes at twenty paces. His body was a work of masculine art, with long, strong limbs.

His musculature was perfect—lean and hard. His hair was a shade close to golden as her own and clipped close to his head. His usually unshaven chin was clefted and his lips full and well shaped, and nearly always quirked in a sexy little smile that made her wonder what he was thinking.

She'd watched him one hot evening from a distance as he'd chopped deadwood without his shirt for a cookfire. The sight had thrummed somewhere low within her, made her wet with need.

Anger rose up within Lilane. It only made her want to kill him more. She had fought against men such as he for her entire life.

Her hunted tipped back his tankard and drained the last of his ale. Then he fished a few coins from the pocket of his buttery leather pants, stood and walked out the door.

Lilane measured the space of ten heartbeats, located her coins and tossed them on the table in a shower of clinks, then stood and followed him.

She breached the exit and entered the hot, darkness-swathed night. Lilane itched to flip back her hood to cool herself, but she dared not. Her pale hair would be visible in the darkness. The black material of her robe was another advantage of traveling as an *Anottie* because it camouflaged her so well.

She walked toward her horse that was tied to a tree some distance into the woods. Her quarry had already traveled down the road leading away from The Crow's Inn, toward Sudhra. She had to take him tonight, before he crossed into Sudhra proper. If he did that, she would not be able to follow.

Goddess-bedamned man always slept outside in the forest, never between walls. Her back ached from doing the same. Though it was true her flourentimes were quickly disappearing and camping in the woods cost no coin.

A tall, heavyset man with black hair stepped out of the darkness in front of her, blocking her path. Lilane stilled. Her body became alert and ready. A thin man with sand-colored hair appeared beside the first. Discreetly, she drew her hand through the hole she'd created in the pocket of her *Anotte*, and wrapped her hand around the handle of her dagger.

The beefy one smiled. "Well, what do we have here? An *Anottie* of Sudhra?" he asked in Sudhraian. He reached out and ripped her hood back. "Tch, tch. Far too pretty a woman to sacrifice herself to Anot, wouldn't you say, Hap?"

Hap's eyes glittered in the moonlight. "Far too pretty, indeed, Crag, and bold, too. Look how she meets our eyes."

She quickly averted her gaze. *Blood of the Goddess*, she kept forgetting that part. She stared at the etched leather grip of Crag's sword, instead. Lucent Priestdom. She recognized the mark of the eagle.

"Shall we keep her?" asked Hap. She heard the greed in his voice. "She'd catch an excellent price, don't you think?"

Slavers. In Sudhra they impressed many women into sexual slavery. The slavers made regular runs over the border into her village that lay just inside Nordan. Lilane had fought the bastards since she'd been old enough to catch their attention.

She replied in Sudhraian. "I am a member of the sacred order of *Anot*. To force me into slavery will put a blight upon your soul."

They laughed. "I'm just quivering in my boots, *honored Anottie*," Crag mocked. He reached out to grab her upper arm and Lilane moved. Pulling her dagger out of her pocket and spinning to the side, she lashed out. The tip of it bit into Crag's upper arm and he bellowed in surprise and outrage.

She backed away and stood her ground. Running at this point would do her no good. She was fleet of foot, but the time it took to mount her horse would allow them to overtake her.

She put some distance between herself and the men, dropped her dagger in the weeds nearby, and found her sword beneath the folds of her *Anotte*. She struggled with the garment for several precious heartbeats before finally drawing it. She was thankful that at least her hair was plaited securely and wouldn't impede her. A ringing hiss filled the air and she stood in battle stance.

Luckily, both men had been too shocked by her sudden transformation to rush her. That luck wouldn't hold long.

"Wha' tha?" muttered Hap. Both men looked stunned. Crag had one hand clamped over his right arm and blood stained his shirtsleeve dark. Lilane noted the sword sheathed on his left side. Aye, she'd wounded the bastard's sword arm as she'd planned.

Hap's surprise quickly faded to rage. "You bitch," he said as he came toward her. "You better know how to use that weapon."

She raised an eyebrow. "Draw and find out."

He drew and came at her. Their swords clashed in the air and Lilane spun around fast, keeping her eye on Crag, who'd also drawn his blade, despite his wound.

She'd trained her whole life to fight sword-to-sword and one of the first things she'd learned was that men always underestimated her skill because she was a woman. Her one rule for fighting the opposite sex was to keep moving, to dodge in and out, never allowing her opponent to bring his superior weight and strength down upon her. Be fleet of feet. Do that and she gained an advantage.

Hap's mouth spread in a sick smile, revealing rotten teeth. "We'll have fun breaking you, girl." He came at her and she blocked his blade. She spun around fast, kicking one leg wide and bringing her booted heel as hard as she could into his groin. Hap gave a shrill cry and dropped to the ground, his sword forgotten as he nursed his injured privates.

Crag glanced at his friend and growled. His sword arced through the air toward her. She met Crag's blade and the force of the blow nearly bowed her in half. She let loose a cry, desperately trying to keep her muscles from failing. He was surprisingly strong even with his arm injured. He pushed her back with a burst of force she couldn't dodge. She staggered, tripped over Hap, and fell to the ground. Silver caught the moonlight above her and she rolled to the side, narrowly missing Crag's sword as it arced through the air and the tip pierced the dirt to her immediate left.

She tried to jump to her feet, but the folds of her *Anotte* got tangled around her legs. She tripped, and Crag laughed. "Having trouble, woman?"

She steadied herself and circled Crag warily. She didn't have time to play. She had to get out of there before Hap recovered and came back in a vicious rage.

"Not at all," she taunted. "Fighting someone with as little skill as you doesn't require much effort."

In a fit of impatience and rage, Crag charged her. She deflected his blow and spun around, bringing the full length of her blade to bear against his exposed side. The edge of her sword cut through flesh and he went down like a tree hewn by an axe.

Lilane ripped the *Anotte* off, cursing under her breath. It was a good disguise, but it hindered her fighting ability. She discarded the garment and quickly sheathed her sword. Then she picked up Crag's blade by the grip. It was a man's sword, heavy and cumbersome, not like her blade that had been fashioned for her especially by her now dead fiancé, Dal. She dragged it over to Hap in order to also collect his weapon.

Hap's face was an interesting shade of white. "Nordanese whore," he gasped in a pained voice. With the hand that wasn't gripping his privates, he reached out and grabbed her arm.

"Goddess-forsaken slaver," she cursed. "You made me late." Lilane elbowed him in the nose *hard*. He bellowed in pain, collapsed to the ground and went still.

Lilane hesitated a moment, her finger rubbing over the grip of Crag's sword. She should lop his head off. She should lop both their heads off. Two less slavers in the world. Two less men to humiliate, rape, and enslave innocent women. Aran would be better off for her action.

She stared down at him. But she couldn't do it. Not like this. In a fair fight, in a battle for her life, yes, but not when they were unconscious like this.

Of course, that begged the question; what was she planning to do with her hunted? Did she really think she could best him in a fair fight? She'd been driven this far by rage, pure and simple.

The Sudhraians had killed her family and her fiancée, Dal, just three weeks ago. They'd destroyed her village and forced her people to find refuge in Marken's Lorddom. She wanted Sudhraian blood on her blade for that and her hunted had been the first Sudhraian she'd laid eyes on.

Reckless rage had brought her this far, nothing more. Certainly not clear thought—not in the cloud of grief she'd been in recently.

She picked up Hap's sword by the grip and dragged both of the heavy weapons to her horse. Perhaps she should reconsider her actions. Perhaps she should consider letting her hunted go.

Someone clapped from the tree line. "Nice job," drawled out a low, masculine voice. She instantly recognized her hunted's smooth tone and Sudhraian accent.

Lilane dropped the two swords to the ground with a clatter and drew her blade once more. She turned to face him. No time for reconsideration now. Her actions had just caught up with her. He leaned against the trunk of a tree causally, one long, well-muscled leg bent, his strong arms folded across his broad chest. Shadow swathed his face. "I wonder what tricks you'll pull during a second performance." His baritone voice had a teasing lilt.

This situation made her nervous. Crag was wounded badly, but Hap could recover. She could fight men like Crag and Hap, but this man she hunted, he was different. She'd watched him over the last week and had seen his skill with a sword. He'd be a powerful match for her, and she didn't think she could fight her hunted and Hap both at once and come out the victor.

She widened her battle stance. "Come out here where I can see you, dark lord."

"Anything for a lady."

He stepped away from the tree and walked a couple paces into the moonlight. The silver light limned his square jaw and well-defined mouth. It seemed a pity to damage such a glorious male form. But damage it she would, if she could.

"You've been following me for the last week," he said. "Why?"

She stiffened. How had he known? She'd stayed far away from him, only following his trail. Lilane leveled her gaze at him. "To kill you."

"Really. Why would you want to do that?"

She stuck her chin out. "I have my reasons, *Sudhraian*."

"Ah. So, you're waging your own private little war, are you? You realize that there's a bigger one going on all around you. Why don't you join that one?"

Lilane ground her teeth. She knew first-hand about the war between Sudhra and Nordan. Her family and fiancée had been killed in one of the first raids on the Nordanese border. "I'm a woman," she replied.

He went silent and looked her leisurely up and down. "Yes." He smiled slowly. "I noticed that. The Nordanese let their women help. They're scouts and messengers—"

"Scouts, messengers." She snorted. "I need blood on my blade."

He indicated the men on the ground behind her. "Well, looks like you got it. Feel better?"

She narrowed her eyes. No, she felt worse, but *he* didn't have to know that. "We're talking too much, *Sudhraian*, and not fighting enough."

"My name is Lord Rue d'Ange, not *Sudhraian*."

"I don't care what your name is."

"You just want to kill me without even knowing my name? That's a little cold blooded, don't you think?"

Behind her, Hap groaned. She closed her eyes and gave a prayer to the Goddess. She had no choice but to fight him. Worse, she had to hurry or she'd be trapped. She opened her eyes, let free a battle cry, and ran for Rue.

He drew his sword and met her first maneuver with ease, squarely blocking her. The impact of his sword against her blade reverberated down her arm and made her teeth vibrate. Quickly avoiding the full power of his blow, she dodged to the right and spun around, coming up behind him. He pivoted, following her movement without effort and blocking her second blow.

Rue advanced on her before she could twist away, forcing her into the defensive. As he pressed her back toward the trees, she realized how badly she was breaking her rule. He slowly brought all his strength to bear upon her and she had nowhere to move.

His blade kissed along the length of hers and locked at the guard. Step-by-step he pushed her back. This time dodging meant death. She couldn't spin away from him, if she tried that now he'd kill her.

A hiss of breath escaped from between her pursed lips. She could tell he was putting barely any effort into this while her muscles strained in protest. He merely played with her now. She concentrated all her power onto her sword and still he pushed her back. She cried out in agony and frustration. Her arms shook with the effort of keeping him at bay.

A hard rough object halted her backward progression — the trunk of a large oak.

"You're trapped now, my lady," said Rue. He didn't even sound winded.

She couldn't reply. Instead she focused all her attention and will on keeping his blade as far away from her throat as possible.

He leaned into her, staring into her eyes. Their gazes locked and Rue's face went carefully blank and his body still.

Her brow furrowed. What did he see in her that seemed to stun him so?

No matter. Scenting opportunity, she focused her last bit of energy and desperate urge to live in a burst toward him. He staggered back and she whirled away, finally out from under his weight. He seemed shocked and she took advantage by swinging her blade viciously at him. He recovered at the last moment and leapt back. Still, she caught him with the very tip of her sword, tearing through the fabric and drawing a thin line of blood from his chest.

He looked down at his chest, then up at her. His eyes were dark now, hooded and dangerous looking. "I'm through playing, my lady Nordanese."

His hard gaze alone had her stepping back. She stopped herself and held her ground. The bushes beside her rustled and Hap emerged, holding the sword that had been on the ground near him.

Lilane jumped away from him. Her gaze flicked between Hap and Rue, calculating how best to handle the situation now that she was forced into it.

Hap's eyes narrowed. "You're going to pay for what you did, whore, right here and now by easing my cock within you," he growled at her. "We can both take her, my lord," he said to Rue. "Then we can kill her...*slow*."

Rue smiled coldly. "I don't share."

Hap stared at Rue, a snarl trickling from his fat lips. He hefted his sword and Rue took the man's invitation. They engaged.

Lilane stepped out of the way, shocked by Rue's action. With several fast and well-placed blows, he defeated Hap.

Rue turned to her. His shoulders were hunched like a wolf's raised hackles and his face was bathed by the shadows. "You're mine and no one else's," he stated.

Lilane whirled and ran, her feet pounding against the earth in a desperate attempt to make it to her mount. Goddess, why hadn't she fled when she'd had the chance? Like an idiot, she'd just stood there in awe of his fighting ability.

Strong arms came around her waist from behind, toppling her to the ground. She kicked, bit and screamed at him. He merely covered her body tolerantly. She felt tiny and fragile pinned down by him. Hot blood from the gash she'd made on his stomach soaked through her shirt at the small of her back. With infinite patience, he let her rail against him until she realized she merely tired herself out. She went still, breathing heavy. A strand of hair blew in and out of her mouth.

He pried the sword from her fingers and eased his weight up. "Take it easy now. I'm not going to hurt you. That's more than *you* could say."

He flipped her. She brought her fisted hands up to strike at his tender throat and eyes, but he had her wrists in a flash and pressed them to the ground on either side of her head.

With a gasp she realized the hard length of his cock pressed up against her pubic bone where he straddled her...*hard* being the most alarming realization. "Wha...what are you going to do with me, Lord Rue?" she choked out.

He leaned down and nuzzled her throat. A thrill went through her at the feel of his hot breath on her skin and his full lips brushing against her. What was wrong with her? Was she some twisted woman to enjoy a man's mastery over her? And at the hands of a Sudhraian male no less?

"Anything I want, my lady," he murmured. "You stalked me, intended to kill me. Indeed, you made every effort to do so. By all rights I could kill you now, but I will not. Therefore, your life is mine. You're my prisoner, to do with as I see fit. My possession."

She shivered and it had little to do with fear. Blood of the Goddess! What was wrong with her? She blinked against the wetness that suddenly filled her eyes as she tried to deal with the slickness coating her sex. "Will you take me unwilling?"

He nibbled at her earlobe, and then trailed his tongue down over her skin to nip in a proprietary way at the place where her shoulder and throat met.

"I have a heightened sense of smell, my lady, far better than most," he murmured against her skin. "I can smell that you're not unwilling. You can't tell me if I pulled those trews down now you wouldn't be hot and wet. If I slid my cock into your undoubtedly pretty little pussy, you wouldn't welcome me? I could even make your mind willing, as well as your body, if you gave me a little time to...*convince* you."

She squeezed her eyes shut, wanting to deny it and failing.

"But no, of course I would not take you while you were unwilling," he said, releasing her wrists. "*When* I take you, it will because you begged for it." He stood and fished something from the back pocket of his trews.

Her eyes widened as she glimpsed a pair of wrist shackles. The sight of them stole the indignant response that had been burbling up from her throat. She hadn't thought her hunted was a slaver, but perhaps she'd been wrong. "Who are you? Why do you have those?"

He knelt, grabbed both her wrists and held them easily with one hand while he snapped the shackles in place. "That's far too many questions for a captive, don't you think? In any case, as to the question of who I am—you should've sought the answer to that *before* you stalked and tried to kill me."

He stood and helped her up. She shot him a look of scorn. "I'll find a way to escape, you know."

His gorgeous mouth parted in a slow, easy smile. He smoothed a strand of hair away from her face. "Well, then maybe I'll find a way to entertain you while you're in my care. Maybe you won't want to escape then, hmmm? You smell ripe for the plucking. Maybe I should take a taste and find out for sure."

His mouth came down over hers and took her breath. His lips skimmed hers, touching, tasting. Then he parted her lips with his tongue and slid inside, branding the inside of her mouth with skillful swipes. Lilane stiffened and then melted as his tongue wove magic within her mouth. He kissed her hard, possessively, and it sent a thrill of lust straight down her spine to her already aroused pussy.

He pulled away, his light blue eyes surprisingly dark, desire gleaming in their depths. "Ready to be consumed whole. You're mine now, my lady. Make yourself ready to pay for your transgressions."

Chapter Two

Thick cloud cover masked the moon by the time Rue finally got the woman to his campsite just beyond the Nordanese-Sudhraian border. It was one of many stopovers he had. A roof made of tree branches sheltered this one. He kept a cottage nearby, but it was just far enough away that it would be dangerous to risk traveling to this eve. Sudhraian soldiers prowled the forests this night. The air was heavy with the scent of rain and this shelter would keep them dry.

He halted his horse and lifted his captive down. He'd tied a rope to her manacles so she couldn't go far if she slipped off the back of his horse.

He dismounted carefully. Sweet God, he'd been hard since the first time he'd looked into her green eyes, smelled the luscious scent of her arousal. Having her succulent body against him on the horse—every movement had brushed her sweet ass against his shaft—had been pure torture. He wasn't sure why *this* woman of all women aroused him like he was some youth without control, but she did. His cock ached to sink into her, piston in and out of her tight, wet heat until she came apart in climax beneath him.

Was there such a thing as lust at first sight? Rue didn't know for certain, but he did know that the woman also felt whatever strange, sexual spell had woven between them. She fought her impulses, but they were definitely there.

Though what he'd seen in her eyes had given him pause. He needed to be sure about *that*.

He had to remember that even though he wanted her badly, the wench had stalked him, followed him, and plotted his death.

The pain of the shallow gash on his stomach was proof enough of that.

Was that why he wanted her body writhing under his? Did he wish to dominate her somehow, put her in her place? No, it went beyond that. He stifled a groan. No matter the reason behind his desire, the best place for her was pressed against him, naked and at his mercy, her legs spread as wide as they could go.

He led both the horses and the woman over to the tree line. He tied the horses to a tree, leaving them enough rope to pull up grass, and unhooked the saddlebag that held his provisions.

He glanced at her as he led her to his burned out campfire. "What's your name?"

Silence.

Rue set his bag down near the small fire pit and led her to a large tree. "Tell me your name, woman." He picked up the length of her makeshift leash and tied it to a high tree limb so that her arms were extended straight up.

"You're not going to leave me here like this all night, I hope," she snapped.

He smiled at her. "You're not in a position to dictate how I treat you."

"At least be humane!"

He looked her up and down. The position she was in stretched her trews over the gentle flare of her hips and accentuated the luscious line of her ass. Her shirt, with all its little buttons running down the front, was pulled tight across her small breasts. He could see the outline of them as they thrust outward, and saw clearly how hard her dark pink nipples were, such a telling sign on this heated summer night.

Though he didn't need any other indicators of her body's state of need, since he smelled her sweet perfume wafting on the air. She was wet for him. He'd bet anything. He'd love to taste her and find out how much wetter she could get.

He closed the distance between them and slid a hand around her waist. Her breasts brushed against his chest and he made sure he rubbed her nipples just the right way through her shirt. God, his fingers ached to undo those buttons one-by-one-by-one.

He dipped his head to her ear and whispered, "I can be very, very *humane*. Would like to see a demonstration?"

She shivered and he absorbed it with pleasure. "Stay away from me," she warned.

He tapped his nose. "Again, your sex betrays your tongue. You don't want me to stay away." He laid a gentle kiss on her collarbone. "Now what's your name?"

"I won't tell you my name until you've answered my questions."

He sighed. "Fair enough."

"You are a Sudhraian, correct?"

"Yes."

"Are you spying on my country for yours? I saw you at Lord Marken's Lorddom. Then you left and traveled south into Sudhra, then back into Nordan and now you're headed to Sudhra again."

"No, Lilane. You've presumed wrong. Though at first glance, your reasoning would appear solid. I am Sudhraian, yes. I was raised in that culture. But I am an Aviat, first and a Sudhraian second. Do you understand? Do you know what an Aviat is?"

She nodded slowly. "I think so. I saw you…your…uh…wings back at the lorddom."

"Lord Marken and I have an arrangement. If I help him complete a certain…*project,* he will provide my people with a safe place to live. He says he will do this regardless of my aid, but I intend to hold it as leverage against him, insurance, you could say. So, I'm working for the Nordanese now, not the Sudhraians. You were plotting to kill someone on your side, love, someone whose mission might just mean the failure or the success of the Nordanese in this war."

Her eyes glittered wildly. "Why should I believe what you tell me?"

He shrugged. "You're the one who asked. I merely answered. Just because you don't believe it doesn't make it any less true."

Her eyes narrowed. "What is the mission?"

He laughed. "Don't push your luck." He fingered her manacles. "You're not in a position to. Now what's your name?"

She sighed almost in defeat. "Lilane. My name is Lilane."

"Lilane." He tested the name out on his tongue and found it tasted just right. "Lilane," he breathed against the skin of her throat. She shivered again. "You should know by now I'm not a Sudhraian slaver, Lilane, and I won't sell you to one, or rape you. You've got my promises on those two counts."

Her body relaxed against him. "Thank you," she breathed.

His hand found the waistband of her trews and she stiffened again. "But I want you. Make no mistake. I will have you. If you say no, I'll stop instantly, but until you do...." He slipped a hand beneath her shirt and rubbed a hard, pink nipple back and forth with the calloused pad of his thumb. She gasped.

"Does that feel good, Lilane?" he purred into her ear. "Are you going to let me play with your body? Remember, you can say no." He held his breath, hoping she wouldn't.

She only whimpered in response.

He palmed her breast, holding its slight weight in his hand and flicking the nipple back and forth teasingly. The scent of her arousal intensified, perfuming the air and tightening his shaft.

He stepped away from her. He wanted her naked. With deft fingers he undid the braid down her back and spread her long, blond hair around her shoulders. It fell nearly to her waist in thick, curling waves. He ran his fingers through the silky length, taking his time and indulging himself in the sensuality of it. He wondered how it would feel to have that hair loose and brushing over him as she sucked on his cock. He groaned at the thought and his hands tightened in her hair.

His hands found the top button on her shirt and undid it. She looked away and he cupped her chin, forcing her pretty green gaze to his. "Watch me as I undress you."

Her gaze flicked away, back, and then steadied. Even her eyes betrayed her lust.

One-by-one he undid the buttons. He held her gaze the entire time. Her tongue darted out to lick her lips, her pupils dilated, and his confidence grew.

"It's very arousing to see you bound and waiting for me to take you. I'm going to spread those pretty thighs, my lady, and thrust my cock into you. I'm going to take you slow. Slow enough to keep you and me on the edge for a long, long time. I'm going to shaft you so slow and easy, it's going to feel like torture. You will break apart beneath me, crying out my name. Do you want to say no?"

Her breathing quickened and her lips parted, but she didn't look away and she didn't say no. He reached the last button and looked down. A narrow swath of pale skin between her breasts was revealed, along with the gentle curve of each luscious mound. He could see her nipples through the material that lay lightly over them. They were thrust up hard, demanding attention.

He bent and removed her boots, then made quick work of the belt of her trews. He slid her leggings down and off, taking her small scrap of damp undergarment along with them. He extracted his dagger from his belt to cut the shirt from her body.

She gasped at the sight of the blade.

"Easy, Lilane. I said I wouldn't hurt you." He made quick work of the shirt.

Now that his handiwork was done, he stepped back to admire the results.

Dear God, she was incredible. Her small breasts were full and firm, begging for his touch. Her stomach was flat and her hips flared. He fisted his hands in an effort not to jump on her and rut with her like an animal.

He drew a breath and fought for calm. Rue walked around her, like a wolf on the prowl, drinking his fill of her body.

There was heaven in the perfectly rounded cheeks of her ass. His hands itched to redden it and he wouldn't deny himself. He understood that a little bit of pain heightened sexual pleasure. He also knew how much pain to give without hurting.

He laid a smart slap to one cheek and his cock twitched when it flushed red and she cried out in surprise. The air perfumed with a sudden rush of her cream and he knew for certain then that she did enjoy being under a man's sexual control.

He pulled her up so her back was against his chest. "I'll never hurt you, Lilane. Understand?"

She nodded.

"That doesn't mean I won't punish you." He laid another stinging slap to her ass and she moaned. "Like that, do we, love? Do you like it? Tell me," he commanded.

Thunder rolling in the distance was the only sound.

He delivered another smack to her ass and he nearly echoed the low moan that it elicited from her. "Tell me. Do you like it?" he growled. He rubbed her cheek with the flat of his hand, promising without words retribution if she dared not answer.

"I...I like it," she said under her breath.

He circled around to stand in front of her. He ran his hands over her breasts, then bent his head and licked and sucked on one as though it were a piece of rock candy. He rolled the other nipple between his fingers. He felt Lilane's body tense and her heart rate and breathing up their tempos.

He knelt, kissing along her stomach, and headed down, straight for the honey pot. "Let it go, Lilane," he murmured against her skin. "You're Nordanese, you should be at ease with your sexuality. There is no shame here."

"But there is," she blurted.

He stilled and looked up her.

She glanced away. "I—I've fought my whole life against men who sexually dominate women—slavers from Sudhra."

He laid a hand on her thigh and moved it up toward her sex inch-by-inch. "There is a difference in this, Lilane. You fought against slavery and *unwillingness*." He dipped a finger through her wet folds, and put his finger into his mouth. He groaned as the flavor of her arousal spread over his tongue. "And this, Lilane, is nothing but beautiful, unrestrained, *willingness*."

His finger circled her clit, using her own moisture as a lubricant, and her head fell back on a moan. Her clit was full, swollen, and ready for a climax. With his other hand, he slipped a finger inside her. Encountering no virginal barrier, he inserted another finger and slowly fucked her with both while circling her clit.

Lilane panted and purred.

"So very willing," he murmured. "And so very wet. All I want to do is slide my cock inside you." In truth, he was ready to explode. He felt her vaginal muscles tensing around his fingers, her body readying itself for the impending explosion. It took a supreme act of will power to pull away from her and stand. He leisurely licked every luscious drop of her warm body's essence from his fingers, groaning at the taste of it and wanting more.

Rue turned and walked away. "Punishment, my lady," he called over his shoulder.

"No!" she cried.

He knelt beside the burned out fire and contemplated how to get it going again, and at the same time trying to tamp down the raging one in his body. "Doesn't work that way, Lilane. You say 'no' when you want me to stop, not when you want me to continue."

She pulled on her bonds, causing the limb to which her rope was tied to swing and rain leaves. "You bastard!" she cried. "Finish what you started, at least!"

Thunder boomed once more in the distance. He leaned back against a log and looked up at her with feigned nonchalance. His body burned to take her. He waved a hand noncommittally. "Oh, I will. *Later.*"

He smiled as she huffed out an angry breath. She was even prettier when she was spitting mad.

Rue removed his shirt and looked down at the band of red that coated his abdomen. The wound itself was shallow, but still sore. He winced. It ran parallel to the white, mottled scar that marked him from shoulder to hip. Yet another decoration for his chest, it seemed.

He treated the wound with ointment from his saddlebag and put his shirt back on. Then he gathered some wood, and caught a rabbit.

By the time he had the rabbit roasting a light rain fell. He untied her and brought her under the canopy. She sat beside the fire with her bound hands in her lap. Rue laid a blanket over her and tucked it around her.

"Better?" he asked.

She merely shrugged in reply. "Can I have some clothes?"

"No. I like you much better without them."

She sighed.

"Are you hungry?"

She'd been watching the rabbit cook with a covetous gaze. He knew well she was half-starved. She affected a bored look. "I could eat." She moved her hands in her lap and the manacles clanked. "Guess you'll have to release me."

"Sure, and I should probably give you your dagger too, right? So you can spear the meat?"

She glowered at him.

He pulled the rabbit from the spit and sat down by her. Tearing a bit of meat from it, he set it to her mouth. Soft pink lips parted and small white teeth nipped. Her tongue brushed his finger and Rue's cock stirred. She moaned and closed her eyes as she chewed. She probably had no idea what a seductive image she presented. Rue's cock grew hard.

Bit by bit, he fed her the meat and she took every morsel ravenously. "Do you not eat?" she asked.

He put a morsel between his teeth and nudged the protruding piece against her lips. She bit it, her lips brushing his. He crushed his mouth to hers, tasting the rabbit and nibbling at her lips, which were even more tender and delicious.

He pulled away, looking into her wide, somewhat stunned eyes. "I ate at the inn. You, however, did not eat enough. I saw that."

"How did you know I was following you?"

He laughed and set the rabbit caress aside. "It's not easy to track a tracker or hunt a hunter. Especially not one with special skills."

He laid her down on the soft, clean bedding that made up the floor of his shelter. Her pretty green eyes sported dark circles beneath them. Rue knew it would not be long before she slept, especially with a stomach full of warm rabbit.

"What kind of special skills?" Her voice grew quiet. "Does it have to do with you being an Aviat?"

"Yes. I saw you that day at Marken's Lorddom, too, Lilane. You're the woman who led the people in from Gadstone Village, are you not?"

Her eyes drooped in fatigue. "Yes."

"I heard about that attack. I'm sorry. Did you lose anyone close to you?"

She went silent for several moments before finally speaking. She closed her eyes all the way and snuggled into the bedding. "My parents and my fiancé, Dal." Sorrow hung on every syllable.

Rue scooped up some dirt and began smothering the fire. Guilt rocketed through him. She was in grief and he'd taken advantage of her. "I'm sorry. I did not know you were hard on the heels of such loss, especially a romantic loss. I never would've—"

"I didn't love Dal that way," she murmured, near sleep. "He was my best friend, and I owed him much. I felt compelled to agree when he asked me to marry him, but it was not a love match, at least not that way."

Several more moments had Lilane breathing the breath of deep sleep.

Rue covered the fire over. It was far too hot a night to keep it going. A light rain still fell, but the clouds had parted now and he could see by the moonlight that Lilane had kicked her blanket away. Moonlight swathed her delicious curves and Rue couldn't help but go to his knees beside her.

He wound a hand gently under her hair to the curve of her neck and pressed two fingers to her nape. No tell tale vibration met his touch and he knew for certain she was not Aviat, though he had reason to suspect the blood ran through her veins somewhere far down her hereditary line. He had not expected her to be full-blooded. Purebloods of his race were extremely rare to find. Hopefully, one day, such would not be the case.

She sighed in her sleep at his touch and he bent over her, taking one nipple into his mouth and sucking on it. God, but she was sweet. He laved and sucked both her nipples to hard little points as she slept. She sighed and moaned softly, seductively as he did it. He could not keep his hands from her. It was simply impossible.

With care not to wake her, he spread her legs and brushed his knuckles against her slick, swollen flesh. She whimpered and moved her hips in unconscious invitation for additional ministrations. He lay down between her legs and blew gently on her pussy, eliciting a low moan from her. He wondered what she dreamt now. Did she dream of him, or her dead fiancé? It didn't matter. He had to taste her.

Rue ran his tongue over her folds, licking up her moisture. He flicked her swollen woman's bud with the very tip of his tongue and she shuddered beneath him. He brought her to the very edge, but did not allow her release.

He eased back and away from her, his brow sweating from the cruel self-torture of it. His cock ached to be thrust within her, but he wanted to tease her first, make her beg for him to take her on the morrow. It was anguish now, but the release would be so very sweet. It was good training for what he had planned for her.

The best was to pair climax with sex acts women feared; in order for them to learn that it was enjoyable. That was one of the things he'd done long ago, in another life in Sudhra.

Rue stood and looked down at her. She looked so innocent in her sleep, and seductive at the same time. She turned and brought her knees up to her chest, exposing the perfect curve of her ass to his view. A woman had not riled him this much in a long, long time.

Another, more honorable man than he would release her, not seduce her body to the dark pleasures he had planned for her. He, however, was neither another man, nor honorable.

His fists clenched as she moaned low in her sleep. No, he'd keep her. Lilane was his now.

Chapter Three

Lilane woke hot, wet between her thighs, and moaning. She looked down to find the morning sunlight glinting off the golden strands of Rue's hair as he covered her nipple with his mouth, pulling on it with long, sensual strokes. His hands were on her hips and he rested between her spread legs. The head of his very large, very *hard* cock pressed her intimate flesh through his trews.

He moved his hips, brushing against her in just the right way to make her gasp. The movement, calculated on his part, she felt sure, brought her to the farthest edge of the climax her body had flirted with since yesterday.

She closed her eyes and clenched her hands in her manacles. "You're killing me, Rue," she said. "This is a merciless punishment you've devised."

He released her nipple, scooped her up in his arms and stood. "It's not easy on me, either."

Lilane tried desperately to ignore how good his body felt against hers and how comforting his arms were around her. She tried to hate him, but couldn't. "Then why do it?"

He carried her into the woods and she noticed for the first time the rope tied to the manacles. "I have my reasons," he answered simply. "Did you sleep well? It looked like you were."

She tensed, realizing she *had* slept well...very, *very* well. How could she have slept so well while in the care of her abductor—bound, no less? A part of her did acknowledge that on some level, despite everything, she felt safe with Rue. Had that been the reason?

"I didn't sleep a wink having you naked beside me," he growled.

He set her on her feet near a tree and pushed her against it gently. He ran his lips from her cheekbone to her chin, making her heart skip a beat.

She closed her eyes and fought the rising arousal of her body...but it was impossible to stop a tidal wave.

He nipped at her jaw line. "Your skin is so soft," he rasped. "I want to kiss you all over. Can I?"

"My body obeys your demands now, not my own," she answered breathlessly. "I have no say in it."

She felt his lips against the skin of her throat. "Good," he purred. "You can trust your body to me, Lilane. I'll make sure it's very happy."

"And what about my mind, Lord Rue? You're keeping me against my will. If you set me free right now I'd run away from you, find my sword, then come back and lop off your head in your sleep." The latter was a lie, but not the former. If she had the chance, she'd run far and hard away from this man, her enemy, who played her body like a Nordanese flute and made her face her darkest, most uncomfortable desires. "How will you keep my mind happy?"

He bit the tender flesh where her throat and shoulder met and she shivered with pleasure. The bite was an act of dominance, she knew, of possession. It should have enraged her, made her lash out, kick him. Instead a new flood coursed between her thighs.

"Hopefully, soon your mind will catch up to your body," he said. "Your body knows this is a good thing, Lilane. Just give in to it."

"I don't understand the power you wield over me," she said softly.

"And I don't understand why you, in particular, make me want to wield it," he answered. "I haven't wanted to in a long time...not like this."

He nibbled on her neck until she was near boneless and completely breathless and then he stepped away. "Do you need to go to the bathroom?" he asked.

She looked up at him, dazed. "Uh, yes."

He pointed at the bushes and swung the rope back and forth. "Go ahead."

She went into the bushes and when she came back, he crooked a finger at her. He led her through the trees to a small spring. Some toweling, a hunk of homemade soap, and a razor sat on a rock near the water. "Wade in," he said.

She stepped into the water, warmed by the long, hot summer days, and waded in deeper. Smooth, flat rock formed the bottom of the forest spring. The water lapped at the juncture of her thighs, licking at her clit.

Rue pulled off his boots, then his shirt. Lilane fought not to stare at him and failed. His chest was lovely, though scarred by a long mark running parallel to the fresh one she'd made the eve before. Muscles corded his shoulders, arms, and stomach and a thin trail of hair slightly darker than what graced his head led past the waistband of his trews to his aroused sex. He dropped his trews, and she drank in the sight of his hard cock. Long and thick, with a broad plum-shaped head, it sprung from a nest of dark blond curls. It was bigger than Dal's, bigger than she'd ever seen. Her pussy watered at the mere thought of it plumbing her depths. She knew then, for certain, that she'd lost her mind.

He went still and she looked up from his cock to the self-satisfied grin on his face, and she blushed…hard. Had her mouth been open? Had she been drooling? Good Goddess, she had to get away from this man before she lost more than her body to him. She had a feeling she could lose herself completely to him and not bat an eyelash.

Confidence showed on his face—though confidence didn't seem to be a problem for this man—as he waded into the water, holding the other end of her makeshift leash. He picked up the soap and walked toward her, heat lighting his blue eyes.

He yanked gently on her bonds and she walked to him. He lathered the soap and worked it over her shoulders and breasts with strong hands. His fingers worked the muscles of her back skillfully; releasing all the tension she'd been holding. She fought the groan of pleasure that rose in her throat.

He gripped her around the middle and sat her on a flat rock at the edge of the spring. He washed her from her feet up and worked his lathered fingers around her pussy and anus. Sensations flooded her, drawing small sounds from her throat.

Then he took up the razor. "Spread your thighs apart further," he said.

She glanced at the razor warily.

"Lilane, I told you I would never hurt you and I meant it. Please, spread your thighs."

She did so and he set the razor to her intimate flesh.

"Pity to shave off all these beautiful blond curls," he murmured. "But I want you bare to my touch and gaze."

She marveled at how efficiently and quickly he shaved off the hair surrounding her clit and pussy. All the while, his powerful male hands worked on her flesh, careful not to nick her. The gentleness he displayed now seemed so at odds with the rough, dominant exterior of the man.

"You seem like you've done this often," she probed.

"I have," came his short answer, revealing nothing.

He set the razor aside and lowered her into the water. His cock brushed her thigh and she felt how achingly rigid he was. With her manacled hands, she picked up the chunk of soap. "Allow me to wash you?"

"I want your hands on me more than anything."

Lilane wet his shaft with a cupped hand; no simple feat with bound wrists and took the soap to him. Once she had him lathered, she set the chunk aside and rubbed his cock, drawing the foreskin back and stroking his length. It was so large she could not even close her hand around him. It didn't seem to matter. He let his head drop back, and his Adam's Apple moved as he groaned.

A thrill went through her knowing that at this moment, it was she that held all the power and the control. "Like that, do you, love?" she echoed his words back to him.

"It's heaven," he breathed.

A pearl of his come beaded at the tip of his cock and her mouth watered to lick it away. She would not deny herself. "Then this should be ecstasy." She went her knees in the water. It lapped at her chin as she licked the head of his shaft, causing him to jerk and groan again. She licked the bead away, loving the taste of him against her tongue and took him into the warm recesses of her mouth.

"Yes, Lilane. That's so good," he groaned.

She'd done this only a couple of times to Dal and was in unfamiliar territory with this far more experienced man, but she did her best to lave over his length and draw him to the back of her throat. His hands clenched gently in her hair.

She wanted to please him. She wanted so much to make his iron-hard control snap. *She* wanted to have power over *him* for just a little while. Taking him as far back into her mouth as possible, she drew on him and used her tongue to tease him.

He groaned and moved his pelvis forward and then halted, as though he tried very hard not push himself down her throat. "Yes, Lilane. Your mouth is so sweet, so soft. You're driving me crazy."

Her pussy was swollen and throbbing with the knowledge of how much she could please him with her lips, teeth and tongue. Just pleasuring him this way alone had her near the brink of climax. She moaned around his cock, and then brought his length past her tonsils and down her throat. His body tensed as she worked it in and out.

He shouted as he came. She swallowed his ejaculate down greedily, wanting even more from him.

Hands gripped her shoulders, and then lifted her out of the water. He laid her face down on the soft grass. Their breath came in fast pants.

He slipped his hand under her, resting his forearm on her pelvis and lifting up so her buttocks were elevated. She felt completely exposed and vulnerable to him in this position...*again*, and she liked it.

He drew a finger from the small of her back to her anus and circled it. She closed her eyes at the riot of sensation that ripped through her body.

"You deserve a reward for that fine suckling, Lilane," he murmured. He coated her nether hole with her juices and she felt the press of his finger against it. "Has a man ever loved you here?"

She shook her head.

He slid his fingertip within her and she gasped. The sensation was strange, yet very erotic.

"Are you all right, Lilane? Remember that you can say no and I'll stop."

Her chest was heaving from her intense arousal. Goddess help her, she didn't want him to stop. "I remember."

"You have such a beautiful body I want to explore every single inch of it." His voice sounded awed and full of emotion. The way someone might speak of an exceptional sunrise. He slid his finger in a little further. From beneath, he massaged her clit with skillful fingers, wringing a moan from her. "Do you like that, Lilane?"

"Y...yes."

"Good. That's for later." He withdrew his hands from her sex and flipped her over. He kissed her long and deep as he played with her breasts, then moved down and slipped two fingers into her slick, hungry passage. He worked her slow at first, then faster and faster, until she keened.

Lilane's hips came off the ground as she came apart on the hardest, longest climax of her life. Spasms of pleasure racked her body and she moaned out her satisfaction brokenly.

The orgasm left her weak, boneless. He brushed a gentle kiss across her forehead. "My beauty," he whispered.

Rue carried her back to camp and laid her on the bedding. He smoothed the hair away from her forehead. She was ready for sleep now...*again.*

She snuggled into the blankets and looked up at him with drowsy eyes. "If you're on an important mission from Marken, why do you dally here with me?"

He fished an apple out from his pack and offered it to her. She shook her head. She needed answers, not food. "There are troops passing to the south of us, Lilane. It is true I have a schedule to keep, but I must stay here until they pass by. This area is swarming with Sudhraian and Nordanese soldiers alike, so I rest here until tomorrow morning and leave then."

"What will you do with me on the morrow?"

He bit into his apple and smiled a slow, lazy, confident smile. "Ah, you go where I go, my sweet, little Lilane. You're mine. Do I need to remind you of that?"

"We're going to Sudhra?" She tried to keep the edge of fear from her voice and failed.

"Yes, but you have my word that you'll be safe with me, Lilane. No one will touch you in a way you don't desire. If they do, they'll answer to the edge of my sword." Steel threaded his voice. She believed him.

Her eyelids drooped and she yawned. "You perplex me, Rue. Why do I feel safe enough to sleep in your presence when I haven't slept a wink in days on end?"

"Maybe because you know I won't hurt you or let another harm you. You're safe with me. You're a captive, yes, at least for a little while, but you're safe. Sleep."

* * * * *

A sound jarred Rue from his sleep. He opened his eyes and stared up into the smattering of bright stars above him. Lilane whimpered and he turned his head to look at her. Her beautiful face was contorted in anguish. She whimpered again, louder this time. Firelight flickered over her hair as she tossed her head in her sleep.

Rue rolled up onto his feet, closed the distance separating them, and knelt beside her.

"No," she whispered, then louder, "No!"

She'd drowsed on and off all day long, and Rue had allowed her it since they didn't have anything to do but wait anyway. She appeared to need sleep and food, two things that he'd been sure she received.

She seemed tough, but beneath that façade was a vulnerable woman wracked by grief and sorrow. She tugged on more than simply the strings of his lust, but also on strings of his heart. Lilane stirred emotion in him that he'd long thought vanquished by the sight of a broken, female body and the knowledge of his failure to prevent it.

She threw her head from side-to-side, her face contorted by her nightmare and Rue could stand it no longer. He drew her carefully into his arms in an attempt to wake her gently.

* * * * *

Lilane woke with a start and gulped in air. Warm, strong arms held her close. Her breath came fast and her heart pounded hard in her chest. Strands of hair clung to her damp forehead.

"It's all right," a deep voice soothed. "You were trapped in a nightmare."

Rue.

She stiffened, but she was loath to move. His touch felt good to her, especially now. Yes, she did feel safe in his arms. That was ridiculous since he was her captor, but true nonetheless.

"You sounded like someone was trying to kill you. What were you dreaming?" he asked.

All at once her nightmare crashed into her mind. *Her cottage burned and smoke clouded her vision and choked her. People ran, lost children wailed. Soldiers raided their way through the village, cutting the men down, raping the women. She held her sword in hand, searching desperately for her mother and father. She spotted Dal across the village square, a Sudhraian solider running him through....blood coursing....*

She flinched in Rue's arms, tears stinging her eyes. She pressed herself against him, searching out his warmth, because despite the hot summer night, she'd gone deathly cold. "Goddess," she swore under her breath.

His arms tightened around her. "I'm sorry I asked," he murmured. "Are you all right?"

She just needed to be touched and held. If it was Rue that did the touching and holding, that was more than fine. She only shivered in response to his question.

"I'll get you a blanket." He tried to pull away from her.

She cursed her bonds that she couldn't grab onto him. "No!" she cried. He stilled and looked at her as though she'd grown an extra head. She looked away, blushing. "I mean I prefer human warmth, body warmth." She glanced up at him. "If you don't mind."

He didn't hesitate. He pulled her close and up against him. Knowing he couldn't see her face, she closed her eyes and sighed. He stroked her hair, and she laid her head against his chest, listening to the steady beat of his heart. She snuggled against his bare chest and laid a kiss there.

Rue went very, very still.

She wanted so badly to feel the length of him within her. Would there be any harm in seducing him just a little, just for tonight? She stretched against him, rubbing her breasts against his chest and moving her hips against his. Pleasurable shivers ran the length of her body.

His body tensed. "What are you doing?" he growled. "Do you want me to take you?"

His breath stirred the fine hair around her face and his face was shadowed, lit only by pale moonlight. Still, she saw that his blue eyes had darkened and that his full lips were parted.

"I need the comfort now of something real, something hard and long stroking into me to give pleasure and drive away the pain." She laid her mouth to his chest, reveling in the smooth muscle that pulsed beneath her lips. "Yes, Rue. Please."

Her hand went to the waistband of his trews and tugged. The coarse line of hair running from his stomach to his cock brushed her knuckles. She shivered against the loss of his body heat for only the few moments it took for him to shift and remove the garment.

He parted her thighs with his knee and positioned himself between her thighs. Chest-to-chest, stomach-to-stomach and hip-to-hip, he stayed that way, looking down at her with a dark expression and an aroused gaze. He moved to press the head of his cock against her passage, and then hovered there above her, unmoving.

She moved her hips and moaned. She was wet and she was ready. What was he waiting for? "Don't tease me, Rue. Not now. Please. Chase away the demons of this night. Will you?"

He pushed the head of his cock within her and she gasped at the breadth of him. His cock stretched the muscles of her pussy further than they'd ever gone. He eased out, drawing out her moisture and sliding back in a little further. He did this several times, using her natural lubricant. He pressed until he was halfway in.

She threw her head back into the bedding in pleasure and he kissed along the length of her throat.

"Lilane, you're so tight," he said, shuddering against her. "Am I hurting you?"

She bit her lip. "A little, but it's good. You are making me forget, Rue. I need to forget the nightmare. I need you to drive it away. She jangled her manacles. Please, I want to touch you. Let me. I promise not to run away."

He hesitated, and then covered the manacles with one large hand. With a couple twists and turns in some secret combination, he released her hands. She sighed.

"If you try and escape, I *will* catch you," he threatened darkly. "I'm warning you now."

"I promised I wouldn't run."

She laid her hands to his chest and ran them over his muscles, touching his long scar and the bandage covering his more recent wound, in awe at the exquisite feel of him. She could not think of it long, however, because he chose that moment to surge into her, touching her very womb.

She cried out at the combination of pleasure and pain, and a climax ripped through her instantaneously. Her fingernails bit into his arms as she tossed her head back and forth and moaned. The muscles of her vagina pulsed and contracted around his thick shaft.

His arms shook as he held himself motionless, as though allowing his cock to absorb the tremors of her orgasm. While pleasurable spasms still racked her body, he began shafting her slow and easy. His eyes glittered in the moonlight, concerned and full of lust and affection for her. It was the last that held her gaze to his.

She took advantage of her freed hands and touched him everywhere she could, running them over his shoulders and back, and cupping his fine, rounded buttocks as he plunged himself in and out of her.

He stared into her eyes and she held his gaze until the dark heaviness of it, the intenseness of it became too much to bear. She averted her eyes and arched her throat. "Faster, harder, please, Rue. You're killing me with this slow pace."

He obliged and his strokes became progressively harder and faster until he pushed her over the edge once more. She splintered beneath him and pulled him along with her. His seed bathed her womb and she sighed with contentment as he collapsed next to her, drawing her against him and laying kisses along every inch of her exposed skin within reach of the crane of his neck.

Lilane savored the sweet aftermath of her climaxes and the slight ache of her pussy where the breadth and length of his cock had breached her. She missed him inside her even now, she realized with a start.

What a strange notion.

She shifted onto her side, away from him, suddenly upset by that idea and stared into the star-lightened darkness leading up to the thick blackness of the surrounding forest. The clouds from the earlier rain had passed and the full moon and bright stars lit the clearing they were camped in.

"Can you not sleep?" Rue asked.

"No. I'm weary, but my mind is too active now for sleep."

Rue stood, went to his saddlebag and extracted a bottle that made a sloshing sound when he carried it back to her.

Lilane sat up and watched him in curiosity.

He uncorked the bottle with a pop and offered it her. "The finest Sudhraian sweet juice flourentimes can buy."

Lilane raised an eyebrow. In other words, very potent liquor. "I've never drunk anything but watered down wine and Nordanese ale, dark lord. I fear such an exotic brew might prove my complete undoing and you may undo me even further, then."

"Would that be so bad?" His lips quirked in a sexy little smile. "Most women enjoy being completely undone by the right man."

"Yes, but I am not one of them."

He brought the bottle to his lips and drank deep. He closed his eyes and groaned. She watched his throat work as he swallowed. The liquid sloshed enticingly as he lowered it. "Suit yourself, but it will aid you in sleeping."

If that were true, maybe it would stave off more nightmares. Relenting, she shrugged and reached for the bottle. The brew was rich and smooth and passed her tonsils easily. The night was summer-warmed, but the liquor warmed her further. She passed the bottle back to Rue and sighed contentedly.

"So how do you know where the troops are?" she asked, watching him take another swig.

He handed the bottle back to her. "I hear and smell and see for great distances, a skill bequeathed to me by my heritage. They are there, passing to our south, but will move on soon, I suspect."

Lilane took another pull on the bottle and grew lightheaded. She put a hand to her temple. The liquor *was* strong. "We'll beat Sudhra, you know. Regardless of your secret errand for Marken."

Rue shrugged. "I don't know. The countries are evenly matched, though Nordan has the great advantage of being underestimated. I saw first hand how well the Nordanese are trained. Sudhra believes all the Nordanese men do is lie around with numerous women, rolling over to fuck one of them occasionally. That is far from the truth. Nordan has well trained warriors to back them."

Lilane took another pull from the bottle and furrowed her brow as her entire body began to tingle. "Idiots," she muttered. "The Nordanese are simply not afraid of their sexuality. That doesn't mean we are weak."

Rue extricated the bottle from her hand and set it to the side. "*You* are definitely not weak."

Lilane stuck her chin out. "I've trained all my life to fight with a sword, a dagger, or without any weapons at all."

"No weapons at all? Just those delicate hands?"

Her voice hardened. "They're not delicate when they're fisted and connecting with flesh."

Rue stood up. "All right. If you're so strong, show me."

"What do you mean?"

"I mean, get up and punch me. Give me your best hit."

She went silent for a moment before speaking. "But I'll hurt you."

Rue simply laughed.

Lilane stood, annoyance rippling through her. She staggered and caught herself on a nearby tree. She hadn't realized how much the sweet juice had affected her until she'd stood. She gripped the tree trunk and glared at him through the hair that had fallen into her face. "You're so sure of your skills."

"I'm not trying to be arrogant, Lilane. It's a simple, undeniable fact that most men are larger and stronger than women. I simply want to see if it's true that you can defend yourself adequately against someone of the opposite sex. Most women in Sudhra cannot."

Lilane straightened. "I'm not Sudhraian, and I can defend myself just fine against either sex."

He cocked his head to the side. "Then put your fists where those claims are and show me."

She went at him without warning, her fist clenched. Her swing went wide as the sweet juice controlled her limbs. Lilane staggered to the side, stumbled, and nearly fell. She bent over and braced her hands on her knees and let a loud laugh escape her.

Rue echoed her laughter. Combined, it ricocheted off the leaves of the trees, and eased the tension. He walked toward her to help her stand. "Perhaps we should do this when you haven't drunk so much sweet juice."

She stood and he faced her before him. He widened her stance, situated her arms in fighting position and closed her hands into fists. The fact that they were both completely nude was not lost on her, but for some reason it was all right. In some strange, twisted part of herself, being completely exposed to this man didn't bother her a bit.

He stood in front of her, bending a bit to make their heights more even. "All right, go ahead. Swing at me."

"Are you sure?"

He nodded. "Completely.

She screwed up her face. "Absolutely sure?"

Rue sighed and straightened. "Woman, you are not strong enough to—"

Lilane swung fast and hard and her punch landed true this time—right in the jaw. Taken by surprise, Rue staggered back against a tree trunk. She watched as he rubbed his mouth with his hand. He looked at his fingers and shook his head in seemingly surprise. Had she blooded him? She waited with her breath caught in her throat, wondering at his reaction.

A loud, booming laugh filled the air. The genuine sound of his mirth warmed her to her toes. "All right. I guess you gave me what I asked for." He winced. "You have a quite a punch in that delicate hand."

She cradled her sore fist. She'd pay for it, too. The impact would leave a bruise.

Dark blood seeped down Rue's stomach from the wound she'd made the night before. Suddenly ashamed at how hard she'd let loose on his jaw, and walked to him. "I made you bleed." She glanced at his bottom lip, where a thin line of blood trickled. She sucked in a surprised breath. "In two places."

He took her chin in his hand tipped her face up to his. "I have a feeling you'll be able to do that most easily," he murmured.

She glanced away from the look in his eyes and the double entendre. "I'm sorry."

"Don't be. I'm happy to know you can defend yourself, Lilane. It gives me ease."

"Why?" She cocked her head to the side. "Why do you care?"

He shrugged and worked his jaw back and forth gingerly. "Not sure, actually. Still working on the answer to that one."

She regarded him, biting her lower lip. Finally she said, "Come, let me treat those wounds for you. I'm feeling a little guilty, though goddess knows why."

Rue sat down on the bedding beneath the canopy and Lilane gathered the small tube of ointment that lay nearby. She settled down beside him and wiped the blood away from his abdomen and his lip with a scrap of towel and squeezed some of the ointment onto her index finger.

She looked up from her work to find Rue's gaze intent on her. "What's the matter?" she asked. "Why are you staring at me?"

"Do I need a reason?"

She looked down at his stomach nervously and smeared the ointment on the length of his wound. The gash wasn't deep enough to cause any serious harm, but he'd definitely have a second scar to match the first that ran the length of his chest from shoulder to hip.

When she was finished, she laid the ointment to the side and Rue drew her into his arms. "Sleep now," he said.

She nestled down against his chest and closed her eyes. Again, intense weariness—a catharsis of the last month of her life—took over and darkness sought her.

* * * * *

She woke not much later, as the light began cracking the blackness of the sky. Rue's bare limbs were wound around hers. His chest rose and fell against her back in the easy rhythm of sleep.

Biting her lower lip, she eyed Rue's sword, sheathed in its scabbard and braced against a nearby tree. Her smaller, lighter blade lay against it. She wiggled her free hands in contemplation.

She'd promised she wouldn't escape, but would she ever have such a perfect opportunity to free herself again?

The thought of staying here with him had fear arching through her, but not because she feared he'd hurt her physically. No, this man did strange things to her and they didn't all concern her body. The look as they'd loved each other earlier had been too close to true affection for her tastes. If she stayed she felt sure she'd return that look at some point in the very near future. She could not afford such entanglements, such emotional bonds. It hurt too badly when they were broken.

What if she truly did start to care for this man and what if he were killed? What if she had to witness his death as she'd watched Dal be murdered? What if she had to find him dead, as she'd found her parents dead?

No, far better to be on her own, without any such emotional ties. No possibility of repeating the depth of grief she'd experienced so recently.

With care, she extracted herself from him and stood. With one long, lingering look at him laying there with his tousled blond hair and his broad arm flung out to the side in his sleep, she made her way to her sword, picking up her shirt and trews that lay over a tree branch as she went.

She slipped into the early darkness of morning as she picked her way quietly into the trees. She'd almost stolen her horse, but thought the noise of it would wake him. Instead she'd steal away on foot and hope for a nearby village.

She hadn't gone far when Rue's furious yells echoed through the forest, practically shaking the leaves of the trees above her. At the enraged sound, Lilane didn't hesitate, she ran. Dodging trees and leaping over bushes and fallen branches she fled. Pine needles and other sharp objects stabbed her bare feet, branches slapped and scratched her bare skin, but she had no time to entertain the pain.

A crashing sound in the woods behind her signaled Rue's arrival. He seemed to fly toward her he came so quickly. She remembered his wings and risked a glance behind her. No wings. Only a very angry looking, and very naked, Rue bearing down hard on her.

He pushed her roughly to the ground and her sword and clothes went flying. Her sword was only just in front of her and her fingertips gouged the ground, straining to reach its grip.

Rue grasped her wrists and held them down. "I trusted your word," he said close to her ear.

She struggled to breathe under both his weight and the sensation of his hard, naked body against hers. "I'm a captive, Rue. You must expect I'll break it to escape."

He nuzzled her ear. "I judged from your body's reaction to me that you would not try. I did not expect you to *want* to escape."

She laughed, short and bitter. "You're so goddess-bedamned arrogant." But even now fissures of pleasure were crumbling her resolve. The man performed powerful magic on her she didn't understand. "Well, at least it's nice to know I can surprise you."

"There are Sudhraian soldiers out there, woman," he growled angrily. "What do you think they'd do with a beautiful, barefoot Nordanese woman? Do you have a death wish?"

She grimaced. "No. I have a sword."

"That would mean nothing, you little fool." He parted her thighs with his knee and settled himself between them, pressing his chest against her back. She gasped as he bit her on her throat, not hard enough to break the skin. Still, it was a blatant symbol of his dominance over her.

"Mine," he growled in her ear. "You're mine. I staked a claim over your body and made it so."

"Not yours, Rue," she yelled. "My body is my own. *Mine*. I choose whom I give it to and when."

"Yes," he purred, nipping at her earlobe. "But you choose me. You *want* to be mine. Even now, your body readies itself for my attention."

She closed her eyes in defeat. Moisture coursed out of her sex and coated her tender folds. Her clit pulsed to life at the shift of his skin against hers, at his warm breath on her ear and throat, at his silky, slightly angry, and very aroused voice purring over her.

He brought her wrists together over her head and held them in one of his broad hands. The other he slipped down to her anus and circled it, drawing a low moan from her throat. With a pace slow enough to make her insane, he coated her anus with the moisture from her pussy.

"I'm going to show you just how much you are mine," he threatened. He slipped a finger in her nether hole and she moved, gasping. His hold tightened on her wrists and she stilled. He slipped another within her. "I'm going to take you here." He thrust his fingers in and out of her and her clit throbbed, plumping with excitement.

"You like that don't you?" he asked.

She bit her lip and said nothing.

"Tell me. Tell me you like it, Lilane."

She nodded her head, her cheeks flaming. The unnaturalness of the act, the sheer forbidden quality of it—may the Goddess help her—aroused her. "I want more, Rue," she breathed. "More."

He removed his fingers, released her wrists and pulled her hips up so she was on all fours. He set his cock to her nether entrance. "Do you want this?"

"Yes, yes, I want that."

He pushed the head of his shaft very slowly into her and she sucked in a breath. Her fingers curled into the grass beneath her. "I want this, too, Lilane," he groaned. "Are you all right? Can you take more?"

She nodded her head. It hurt, burned, but the pleasure that came with the sensation drowned out the discomfort.

He pushed into her inch-by-inch, slowly, carefully, and she dilated to take him. When the entire length of him was within her, he pulled out and thrust back in.

Lilane tossed her head and keened her pleasure.

Gently he pushed her head down to the grass, so her rear was completely exposed, offered totally to him. "So hot, so tight, so sweet," Rue groaned. He shafted her slow, driving her insane.

Her climax built as he worked in and out of her. Her anal muscles fought to hold him as he slipped in and out of her faster now. He slipped both hands down to her sex. Two fingers slipped into her pussy and her hips bucked at the incredible sensation of his pistoning cock within her rear and his fingers within her vagina. He added to the mix a seductive massage of her clit and she was gone.

She broke apart beneath him crying out his name as powerful climatic waves shook her. She clawed the ground, unable to retain any kind of dignity at the force of the sexual spell he wove over her.

Behind her Rue broke as well. He called out her name as his own climax wracked his body.

He came down over her, freeing himself from her and pulling her close. "You're mine, Lilane, mine," he crooned over and over.

Exhausted, defeated, sated, and pleasured like she'd never been pleasured, she relaxed against him. "Yours," she conceded.

Chapter Four

Rue lifted Lilane onto his horse. He'd manacled her wrists again since he didn't trust her not to try and escape. This close to Sudhra it would be very dangerous for her to be alone and unprotected, especially now.

He'd taken to the air yesterday to scout the area while she slept. The Sudhraian troops were moving out, as he'd thought they would, but lone soldiers and mercenaries still roamed the area. It made travel dangerous for him, even more dangerous with Lilane with him. So he'd dressed her strategically this morning. He'd play a slaver, she his slave.

He'd prefer not to have to engage the ruse, however. He could fight a few men intent on taking Lilane for their own—but not an army. He hoped it wouldn't come down to that because he'd only let her be taken over his cold, dead body.

He wasn't dead now, however, and he definitely wasn't cold. His gaze roved over her hungrily. The thin linen shift he'd dressed her in showed her hard ruby-red nipples thrusting up toward the material and the outline of her eager little breasts. The shift came to her mid thigh the way she sat on the horse, and he...and his cock...were rigidly aware she wore no undergarment beneath it. When shifted the right way, he glimpsed the full, pouting lips of her bare, silky smooth pussy. He couldn't get his fill of her, and that alone made what he suspected about Lilane even more perplexing.

He mounted behind her and took up the reins, leading her horse behind them. "How's your sweet little behind this morning?" he whispered in her ear.

She shifted on the blanket he'd laid on the horse's back to cushion her. "Sore," she groused.

"Was it worth it?"

She grunted. "I wouldn't tell you if it had been."

He smiled as he eased the horse onto the road that led straight into Sudhra. He'd plaited her long, thick hair that morning and had taken great pleasure in the act. Her silky locks had slipped through his fingers as he'd twisted and turned the sections to create the lovely weave she now wore down her back.

Rue loved women. He always had. He worshipped them, really, which was one of the things his countrymen had never understood about him. He'd taken an easy hand with his students in Sudhra, lavished them with careful attention and gentleness. He did not often think back on that time now. It was a dark spot of blood on his past. A part of his life he'd love to erase.

"What did you do in Sudhra?" asked Lilane. "I mean, before you began aiding the Nordanese?"

Her question jerked him from the reverie he'd slipped into. *Great Anot!* Could she read his mind? "Uh, I was a sort of teacher."

"Really? What did you teach?"

He could answer her without *really* answering her. Tell the truth without telling *all* of the truth. "I taught swordplay, hand-to-hand combat, and other things."

She nodded. "That makes sense. You're wickedly skillful with a blade."

"I am a leader of my people, the Aviat. In Sudhra they live secretly, blending in as normal inhabitants. I learned to use the skills bequeathed to me naturally as Aviat to my best advantage. I went very high in the Supreme Priest's Court." The Supreme Priest was ruler of all Sudhra. All other petty priests answered to him.

Lilane shivered delicately. "Really? The Supreme Priest's Court? I...think I don't want to hear this."

He rubbed her upper arms with the palms of his hands. "Lilane, my allegiance lies elsewhere now. Do you understand? Lord Marken is one of the most powerful leaders in Nordan and he has offered my people protection and sanctuary, a place where they can live out of the shadows and not fear the hunters who decimated our population for our wings. This is something Sudhra, because of its culture, can never offer us. This means much to me, very much. Marken has my unquestioning loyalty because of this. In any case, I broke with the philosophies of Sudhra long ago, if I was ever truly aligned with them."

"Do you promise?" she asked in a small voice.

"Yes. I would like to see Sudhra beaten by Nordan. My country grows arrogant and careless. Sudhra's leaders believe that because Nordan worships a female deity that they are weak. They are wrong and they will pay for that presumption. They are paying even now—"

She twisted around in the saddle to look at him. "What news do you have?" she asked excitedly.

"There is a band of Aviat scouts, working for the Lords of Nordan. They report that Nordan has made great gains in pushing the Sudhraians back toward the border, but have not managed to cross into Sudhra yet. Many lives have been lost so far."

Lilane turned back to face ahead. "Many more will be lost before this is through."

"Aye." He sighed.

"What brought you to Nordan in the first place?"

He shrugged. "A woman. Someone I thought to be one of ours, an Aviat. We are rare. To find a full-blooded Aviat is like finding a rare jewel."

"Ah. It is the woman Raven you speak of. Talyn, the Captain of Lord Marken's Guard has claimed her for his monogamous mate. The lorddom was astir with that news when I was there."

"Yes, she's the one." Rue had thought to make Raven his woman, but it had turned out well in the end. Raven had a far stronger bond to Talyn than to himself. "I went looking for one full-blood and found two instead." Talyn had turned out to be pureblooded Aviat and he'd sired at least one half-Aviat in Marken's Lorddom, maybe more.

"I saw them fly together once, Talyn and Raven, when they were in my village. It was an incredible sight. One I will never forget." Lilane's voice had taken on a quality of awe. "They jumped off a cliff and I thought for certain they would plunge to their deaths. Then their wings emerged and they soared over us." She sighed.

"And what of you, Lilane? What did you do before Gadstone Village was attacked?"

"Me? I was making wedding preparations."

Rue was instantly sorry he'd asked.

"But, as I said, Dal and I weren't a love match, not a *romantic* love match anyway," she continued. "At least not on my part. He'd been my best friend from childhood and defended me from the slavers that would make runs over the Sudhraian-Nordanese border from time to time. He taught me how to fight and protect myself. When he was grown, he became the village blacksmith and made me the sword I fight with now. But he never made my pulse race or my heart pound not like...." she trailed off.

A twinge of jealousy of the man she spoke of speared his stomach. "Like who, Lilane?" he pressed.

She shook her head. "No one. I misspoke."

His lips twisted. "Right. So did Dal take your maidenhead?"

"What a question!"

"Well?"

"Yes, he took it, tenderly, kindly. He was very gentle for such a bear of a man."

"Not like me."

"Definitely not like you, Rue. He was a great gentle, cuddly bear. You are a lean wolf who snaps if you don't do his bidding."

Rue leaned forward and nuzzled her ear. "But you like it when I snap sometimes."

She shivered. "Maybe. Dal loved me very much, though I could not return anything but the love of friendship for him. Bears can love deeply. Wolves...I think not. I think they stalk and go in for the kill only. They ravage their prey."

"Untrue and unfair. Wolves mate for life."

She twisted around to look at him again, her head cocked to the side and a playful smile around her lips. "So, have *you* ever loved, dark lord?"

She didn't know how close she hit home by calling him *dark lord*. Her comment gave him pause. He hesitated before answering and she shifted forward again. "I did love, long ago. But it is not something I care to discuss because the story ends tragically." Steel threaded his words. He had not meant to sound so harsh. But Sania was not a topic open for discussion. The wounds were closed now. No sense in reopening them.

"I understand the pain in your voice because it mirrors my own," she replied softly. "We won't talk of it then."

He forced levity into his voice. "So, do you desire love?"

"No," she answered quickly. "Not love. It hurts too badly when it's taken away. I want your cock, Rue. Only that."

His arms tightened around her at the raw emotion in her voice. "Perhaps together we can find a way to salve each other's wounds, Lilane. I want to remove those manacles." *And chase the shadows from your eyes,* he finished in his mind.

She sighed. "I cannot run now anyway, Rue. We are over the border and in Sudhra. I leave your protection and it is death or slavery for me."

"I would like to know you stayed with me because you wanted to, not out of fear. However, if it is fear that keeps you by my side, I will accept it."

He worked the manacles to release them. Just as soon as they were off, five mounted Sudhraian soldiers, dressed in Sudhraian red and gold, picked their way out of the woods to their left, stopped and regarded them.

Rue stilled, watching them. Lilane reached over his thigh to touch her sword in its sheath that he'd attached to the saddle. "Easy, Lilane," he murmured. "We don't know what they want yet."

"It better not be me," she murmured back.

One of them, a heavy-set dark-haired man, and probably their highest-ranking officer, approached astride his horse. "Halt, traveler. State your name and your business in Sudhra."

"My name is Rue d'Ange, formerly of the Supreme Priestdom, but more recently of Kappan."

"*The* Rue d'Ange?"

Rue nodded.

"I have heard of you. You're recently estranged from the Supreme, are you not? A mercenary now, I heard."

"I am. My blade is for sale to the highest bidder, and so is my information. I have such information I'm carrying from Nordan. I mean to travel to the Supreme and present it in the hopes I may once again attain my place in his court."

Lilane stiffened at his words. Rue wanted to tell her it was only a ruse, but that would have to wait.

The soldier turned his gaze on Lilane and it flared with sexual interest. "Who is she?"

"She is a new slave. I am training her."

A smile curved the man's lips. "What a hardship *that* must be. I bet she's a spitfire between the sheets. Look how she meets my eyes with such boldness and enmity."

Lilane cursed under her breath and turned her head immediately, averting her eyes, as a proper Sudhraian woman should.

"She's Nordanese and in need of much training yet, and punishment." He cupped one of her breasts and rubbed the nipple back and forth through the fabric until he heard her sharp intake of air and the nipple hardened to a solid point.

He slipped his other hand down and lifted the edge of the shift so the soldiers could see her shaved pussy. He slipped a finger into her passage and slowly thrust in and out.

Lilane squirmed and let out a low, angry sound, but moisture from her arousal soaked his hand all the same.

The soldiers all moved closer, their hungry gazes eating her up from the tips of her bare feet to the top of her head.

"Punishment," he purred near Lilane's ear, "must be swift and memorable," he said loud enough for the soldiers to hear. "The slave must know her master possesses her body completely and totally, and commands her pleasure at his own. Whenever, wherever, and in front of whomever, he chooses."

He added a finger to the first and used his thumb to brush over her clit. She grasped his thighs and bore down. He could tell she was fighting a moan. "Let it go, love," he whispered. "Let the soldiers have their show and be left with no doubt you are my slave."

"Damn you, Rue," she grit out.

He twisted his fingers within her to rub at the bundle of nerve endings deep within her. He knew well that would drive her over the edge.

She moaned, long and low, and he smiled.

"She is magnificent," said one of the soldiers. His eyes glazed over in lust. "I want her."

Rue knew well the chance he took by dangling such a luscious prize in front of them. However, it was more important he and Lilane keep up the pretense of slave trainer and student.

In addition, the commander of these men knew him, and therefore knew enough not to cross him.

Anyway, it excited him to bring Lilane to orgasm in front of these men. His cock was hard yet again from feeling her under his fingers and shift and sigh against him as she fought the climax that swiftly overtook her body.

He massaged her clit with his free hand, and kept up the incessant thrusting of his fingers within her. "Come for me, Lilane," he commanded harshly. "Let it go."

She tensed and then cried out. The muscles of her passage pulsed around his fingers and her hips bucked. The air filled with the sweet perfume of her release.

Before Lilane had even come down from her climatic high, a solider reached out and touched her bare thigh. "Let us have a taste, Master R—"

Rue had his sword drawn and at the man's throat before he could finish his sentence. "Remove your hand from my property," he ordered in a steely voice.

The man carefully removed his hand from Lilane's leg.

"She's *mine*," Rue stated unequivocally. "And not ready for another's touch," he added hastily.

The commander reined his horse around to stand beside the interloper. "Back off. There are camp whores you can ease yourself within. Leave Sword Master Rue's woman alone." He glanced at Rue and grinned. "Anyway, don't you know who he is, Falk? He'd take your head off in a fair fight any day, soldier."

Falk nodded shakily. "My apologies, Master Rue."

Rue removed his blade from the bastard's throat. "Accepted. We will be on our way now."

"Of course, Sword Master d'Ange," said the commander, reining his horse away from Rue's. "Happy journey to the Supreme Priestdom."

Rue sheathed his sword and urged his mount past the soldiers. "Long live Sudhra!" he called as he continued down the road.

"Long live Sudhra!" came the answering cry of the soldiers behind him.

As soon as they were out of sight of the soldiers, Lilane slid from the back of his horse, baring her perfectly curved ass prettily as she did it, and turned to face him. "You bastard," she cried.

Rue sighed and dismounted, letting the horses graze in the grasses near them. "Lilane—"

"No, *Sword Master*, I don't want to hear it. You just humiliated me in front of those men!"

He smiled, but it only seemed to enrage her further. Her fists clenched at her sides. "Lilane, you were writhing and mewling in pleasure under my hands. You hardly seemed humiliated."

"Oh!" she stepped forward and brought her palm toward his face. He could've stopped her, but he chose to take the slap instead. The flat of her hand stung his cheek. "Don't you understand? That's the problem. My body is no longer my own. It's yours to command now. I become excited by the mere brush of your finger against me."

He touched his cheek gingerly and winced. She had a hell of slap in that slim arm, same as her punch. "You stalked and tried to kill me, Lilane. To pay for that transgression, you've submitted to me." He stared at her for two full heartbeats before finishing to accentuate his next point. "And you *enjoy* that submission, that much is clear. I'm sorry if your desires scare you."

She looked down and away. "They do scare me."

"I know. It's all right. You'll get over it."

She looked back at him and the sight of her eyes glistening with tears twisted his heart. "They called you Sword Master," she said by way of query—maybe to change the subject that seemed uncomfortable to her.

"Aye. I was Sword Master to the Supreme Priest for a time." He'd had another title before that one, but he didn't want her to know it yet. She'd find out soon enough, anyway.

She smiled faintly. "No wonder I couldn't best you blade-to-blade."

"You're good at swordplay, Lilane, and I don't mean good for a woman. You're good, period."

"I had a lot of practice."

"What I said back there to the soldiers, about selling information to the Supreme. That was a ruse."

She nodded. "I understand."

"Then you trust me?"

"Do I have a choice at this point?"

"Good." Rue looked around the clearing. He could see no one in the area. He could not hear or smell anyone, either. Deeming it safe. He took off his shirt and laid it across the horse's back.

"What are you doing?"

He shushed Lilane, closed his eyes and concentrated on the scars that ran along both his shoulder blades. His wings ripped through sinew and flesh and unfurled. He winced. It hurt every single time he did it, though he was accustomed to the pain.

He opened his eyes to her wide, surprised ones. Her mouth was a pink 'O'. "Let's fly a bit. I want to scout ahead so we don't run into any more soldiers for a while."

"Falcon w…wings," she stammered.

"Yes." They were huge, stretching out to either side of him.

"Can I…uh…can I touch them?"

He nodded and watched as she circled his back, running her fingers through his feathers and exploring the place in his shoulder blades were they jutted from his body.

"Dear Goddess," she breathed. "They're incredible."

She came around to his front and he snagged her by her waist, pulling her close. "Gorgeous," she sighed, as she stared into his eyes. She tipped her head forward tentatively, brushing her lips against his.

Rue shuddered with pleasure. She kissed him now because she chose to, without any prompting on his part. She teased his lips again with hers and he wound a hand around her nape and pressed his mouth to hers. She opened her lips for him and he slipped his tongue inside, allowing it to dance against hers. She melted against him, sighing.

He pulled away and turned her so her back was pressed to his chest, then wrapped both arms firmly around her and shot up into the air with strong flaps of his wings.

Lilane made several exclamations of surprise and then laughed. The leaves at the top of a nearby tree brushed her feet. "This is wonderful!" she cried.

"I promise I won't drop you," he whispered in her ear, laying a quick kiss on it.

She laughed again, a little nervously. "Good."

Rue swooped and soared through the air as much as he dared in broad daylight. He admitted to himself he might have been showing off a little for Lilane, but to hear her laugh lightened his heart.

He set her down near the horses. While in the air, he hadn't spotted anyone and had deemed the rest of the journey safe.

Rue lifted Lilane back onto his horse and furled his wings. "Once we reach the Supreme Priestdom, I want you to stay close to me, and remember, *always* play the submissive slave. And *never* meet a man's gaze directly. We'll get in and get out as quickly as I'm able and I'll have you back in Nordan as soon as possible."

"Are we close?" she asked. Fear put a quaver in her voice.

He nodded. "We'll be there before nightfall. I saw the Priestdom from the air.

Her brow furrowed. "I saw nothing—"

"I'm Aviat, remember? I can see great distances and I have night vision." He mounted behind her.

"What will happen once we're there?"

Rue reined the horse onto the road and kicked him into a trot. He wondered the same thing himself. Would he be welcomed after the debacle with Sania? God's Blood, he'd hoped to never have to face these people again.

"I don't know, Lilane. I don't know."

Chapter Five

As the fortress rose in the distance, Lilane pressed herself back into Rue's chest.

"Easy, Lilane," he soothed. "I won't let anyone hurt you. Just remember what I said about staying close to me."

The horse's hooves clattered on the drawbridge and a soldier stepped out from the guardhouse, crossing his staff in front of Rue's mount.

"I am Rue d'Ange, here to request an audience with the Supreme."

The guard squinted then smiled. "Master d'Ange," he greeted with pleasure in his voice. He removed his staff. "Of course you are granted entrance."

Rue guided his horse past the man and into the outer bailey. "Well, that was easy enough," he said under his breath.

He dismounted and handed the reins of his horse over to a stable hand. Then he lifted her from the back of the horse and gathered the packs. Lilane glanced around at the Sudhraians milling around the outer bailey and fought the panic rising in her throat. She was surrounded by her enemies and feeling more than a little vulnerable.

"Rue?" A male voice bellowed from behind them. Lilane turned to watch a tall, well-muscled man with short dark hair and brown eyes walk to them. A smile lit up his handsome face. "Rue d'Ange! I thought to never see the likes of you around this Priestdom again.

Rue turned, a smile spreading across his mouth. "Jad! So nice to see a friendly face."

They slapped each other on the back in the way of men and Jad turned his attention to her. "Rue, are you training again? I thought you left that when Sania asked you to. I never would think to see you with a new slave student." I guess it's in your blood, though, eh?"

Training? Slave student? In his blood? Lilane's confused gaze flipped between Rue and Jad as she fought for understanding. It sounded as if....

"There is no reason to keep myself from training new sex slaves now that Sania is gone," answered Rue.

Lilane felt all the blood drain from her face. He wasn't a slaver; *he was a trainer.* A Goddess-bedamned Sudhraian slave trainer.

Rue indicated her with a shrug of his shoulder. "And this one is special, Jad. She's the first I've taken in many years."

Jad's light blue eyes narrowed on her. "She's pale."

Rue regarded her, his brow furrowing. "Not normally."

Jad frowned. "And she's bold. Look how she meets my eyes."

Good Goddess! Lilane quickly looked down. Why couldn't she ever remember that part?

Rue went silent for several long moments before speaking. "Actually, I'm beginning to think she simply likes the punishment," he said wryly.

She shot him a look of scorn from the corner of her eye.

Jad laughed. "You were always so soft on them. They never wanted to leave your training, Rue. I suppose you're still like that. Spare the rod and spoil the slave, eh?"

"You're the same way, Jad, and don't pretend differently," answered Rue, laughing.

Jad sobered. "Well, they should have pleasure when they can get it, because it's an evil world out there." A trace of sorrow tinged his words.

"She's the only one I'm taking on, Jad. Don't think to give me any others while I'm here. She's the only one," he repeated.

"All right, Rue. Whatever you say. She'll have to be examined by me, of course."

"Fine. I expect to follow proper protocol, though I would like to participate. Let us settle into our chambers and I'll bring her to the room. Say, twenty minutes?"

"Sounds fine. Why are you here, anyway? I thought after Sania—"

"We can talk later, Jad."

"Fine." Jad snapped his fingers and a boy ran over. "Show former Sword Master Rue and his woman to guest chambers, please."

"Right away," answered the boy.

The boy led them to opulently furnished rooms. A large four-poster bed dominated the center of the chamber. Thick blue damask curtains fell around it. A table and chairs stood on one side of the room and a large bathing tub on the other. Set into the wall opposite the bed was a large fireplace.

The boy turned and left them. Questions churned in Lilane's mind as she watched Rue bolt the door behind him. He turned on his heel and walked toward her.

"Slave *trainer*?" she yelled.

He held his hands up. "Before you say another word, let me explain."

She crossed her hands over her chest. It galled her to no end that she was letting the very sort of man she'd fought against her entire life—that she hated with all she was—bring her such sexual pleasures as Rue had. "Go ahead."

"I told you before I was raised in this culture—Aviat first, Sudhraian second."

"And Sudhraian traitor third?" she poked in a sweet voice.

He winced as if she'd slapped him. "Aye," he whispered. "If being a traitor will help my people, then yes. No one ever said I was a hero. And could you keep your voice down?"

"*Do* continue," she whispered back furiously.

"I was drawn into slave training early, before I'd weighed out the magnitude of it. I ceased later on, and began instructing men in swordplay and other kinds of combat, because I realized how wrong slave training was, and also" --he pushed a hand through his hair— "also because a woman I loved, Sania, asked me to stop."

"So that makes it all right?"

He shook his head. "No, of course not. But what's done is done. The past can't be changed. If it's of any merit, I ensured the women I trained enjoyed it. I've never forced a woman into any act she didn't desire."

Lilane's lips curled. "I can well imagine. Sounds familiar, in fact. You seduced them."

"You probably met Sienne, Lord Marken's monogamous mate?"

She nodded.

"She was a Sudhraian sex slave kept by a cruel man named Cyrus. Cyrus was a typical slaver and occasional trainer. He didn't care if the woman enjoyed his treatment. Sienne never even had an orgasm before she arrived in Nordan last winter. Jad and I are both atypical. The slaves he trains and I trained knew kindness and pleasure."

"Until you sent them out there." She threw an arm wide toward the window.

His face grew gray, near haggard looking. Lilane saw then how that truth had weighed on him. "You're right. That's exactly true. I think of that every day."

"Did you lie to me? Are you training me like a slave because you intend to leave me here?" she asked in a small voice.

He closed the distance between them and caught her up in his arms. "No, you're coming back with me. Do you understand?"

She nodded.

He sighed heavily. "I'll set you free once we get back to Nordan. Your debt to me I'll consider paid and we can part ways."

She nodded again, trying push down the curious knot of conflicted emotion that rose within her at his words.

Rue undid her plait and ran his fingers through her hair. She closed her eyes, remembering how he'd twisted the strands into the elaborate braid that morning. He'd done it with careful patience and deep care—almost as though he loved her. He rubbed his fingers over her scalp, massaging until she wanted to purr.

"You deserve a far better man than me, Lilane," he said. "You need to find an honorable man like your Dal." His voice hardened. "But until then, until we get back to Nordan, you're mine, mine in every way. Do you agree to my terms?"

She shivered at the dark promise of his words and part of her thrilled at the possession in his voice. "I agree," she murmured.

His fingers threaded through the hair at the nape of her neck and he tipped her head back, taking her mouth in a hard, satisfying, near bruising kiss. He set his forehead to hers. "Now you go to Jad's hands. He knows how to touch a woman—"

"He's going to touch me?"

"Intimately. As the Master Trainer of this Priestdom, it is his right."

She stiffened.

"If you let yourself go, you'll enjoy it, Lilane." He stepped away from her and walked to the door. "Come with me now. If we are to convince this Priestdom I am the old Rue d'Ange, we must follow the procedure for bringing a new slave within walls. It will be painless, Lilane. It should be very pleasurable, actually. You, as Nordanese, should not have your mind closed to the possibilities."

She hesitated and then walked toward him. He led her out of the room and to another. It was decorated much like their chamber, though the bed in the center of the room was larger than normal.

She glanced back at Rue who stood behind her.

He placed his hands on her shoulders and braced her back against his chest. "It's all right, love," he murmured. "I'm not going anywhere."

He slipped his hands down her upper arms, over her stomach and down to the edge of her shift. He pulled it up and over her head, leaving her completely bare to Jad's gaze.

Jad stood in the center of the room. Intense light shone in his blue eyes as he assessed her from head to toe. Very little kept her from turning and running the other direction, although she couldn't help but notice the tightness of her sex. A part of her was very excited by the notion of two men at once, which was the direction this appeared to be headed.

Rue's strong heat warmed her. He cupped her breasts in his hands and flicked his thumbs over her nipples. She could feel his erection pressing into the small of her back. He slipped his hands back down over her stomach and grazed his fingertips over her clean-shaven mound. Moisture flooded her sex.

Jad made a low sound in his throat and walked toward her. "She's magnificent, Rue. Absolutely beautiful." He cupped her chin in his hand and tipped her face to his. She kept her eyes carefully averted this time. "You can look me."

She raised her gaze to his.

"What's your name, puss?" he asked.

"Lilane."

He slipped his hands down to cup her breasts and she sucked in a breath. "Does my touch scare you, Lilane?"

She shook her head. "N—no" she stammered.

Jad smiled. "I think you're lying." He raised a dark brow. "I will have to show you there is nothing to fear."

Rue rubbed her back, as though trying to calm and relax her. He dipped down and cupped her buttocks as Jad feathered her collarbones with his fingertips, and then tipped her chin up, forcing her gaze to meet his. "Don't worry, Lilane. We will not hurt you. He laid a large hand over her breast, covering it over completely. "On the contrary. That is not what we're here to do."

"What is the purpose of this?" she asked in a small voice.

"It's my right as Master Trainer of this Priestdom to sample every slave that enters," answered Jad. He rubbed her nipple until it hardened. "It is a very old tradition and the gravest of insults to keep a new slave from the Master Trainer. Rue has told me he wants to participate and so he will take part in this also."

Rue pushed her hair to the side and laid a kiss to her neck. Lilane shivered.

Then, suddenly, she was in the air, cradled in Rue's arms. He walked over and laid her on the bed. The silk quilt shifted, soft against her skin, as she turned to watch Jad and Rue disrobe.

Jad had a fine body, sculpted and well built, but it was only Rue she had eyes for. She wiggled on the bed in anticipation as she watched him walk toward her. How enamored she'd become of him in such a short time.

Rue slid onto the bed beside her, slipped a hand to the nape of her nape and rubbed with strong fingers. She sighed as the tension left her body in a whoosh.

His mouth came down on her hers and she closed her eyes, allowing him to part her lips and stroke his tongue into her mouth. He pulled her against him and her breasts brushed the rough hair of his chest. Her body felt heavy with desire. It practically hummed through her.

A hand stroked her inner thigh and moved up toward her sex. She started, knowing it was Jad that touched her.

Rue pulled away and searched her eyes. "Relax," he murmured. "I know you're aroused. Just allow yourself to be."

Rue held her gaze as he dropped his head to taste the skin of her stomach. Lust and something dangerously close to love shone there so intense it made her lose her breath. He kissed her abdomen, running his tongue to her pussy, where he teased her clit. She let out a sharp hiss of breath and her hips bucked.

Jad spread her labial lips. Rue rose and rubbed his finger through her folds. "You see. She's perfectly healthy," stated Rue.

Dark light in Jad's eyes flared. "I do see," he replied. He slipped a finger into her, then another and pumped her with them. Rue caressed her clit and, as usual with his touch, she could not fight the desire that rose within her.

"She's wet," Jad growled. "You taught her to take pleasure from sex."

"I always do," answered Rue. "That's my way, as it is yours. You know that." He flicked her clit as Jad worked her with his fingers. She let out a small, frustrated sound.

"Come on, love, let it loose. It's okay if you like this," Rue soothed.

Goddess help her, she did. She closed her eyes and let her head fall back. Her pussy gripped Jad's fingers. A finger found her nether hole, stroked around it and then slipped inside. She let a low moan and tossed her head from side-to-side.

"Rue and I will take you together," purred Jad. "We've done that often with slaves in the past."

Those dark words poured over her, lighting a fire in her lower belly. Her climax built slow and intense. It wouldn't be long before she exploded.

A second finger was added to her nether passage and the fingers pistoned in and out of her, driving her crazy. Her moans filled the room and her back arched, thrusting her breasts into the air, her nipples hard and demanding attention.

Rue's head came down to her breast as he played over her clit with his devilishly skillful finger. "We won't hurt you, Lilane," he murmured. "You say stop, and I'll stop him." His voice lowered. "Unless you want to be fucked senseless by two men. Unless you want both those pretty, tight little orifices filled with hard cock." He groaned. "I confess I want to hear the moans you'll give us when you're filled by two men."

Rue laved her nipple with the flat of his tongue and then nipped at her. The little bit of pain combined with the incredible amount of pleasure tilted her over the edge. She screamed as she came, her vaginal muscles clenching and releasing as she poured out her hot juice over Jad's hand.

"Oh, yes," Jad murmured.

Strong arms gathered her up and she opened her eyes to see Rue, his light blue eyes dark with lust. He lay down on the bed, positioning her above him. Her passage, now slick with moisture, rubbed the head of his cock. She pushed her hips down, trying to slip him within her.

His hands went to her hips and he guided her movements until his cock slid within. "Yes," she breathed as his length and width filled her. She closed her eyes and pressed down, pushing him within to the hilt. He groaned, a deep, reverberating sound.

Jad covered her back. His warm flesh teased her sensitive body. He touched her buttocks and a thrill of speculation coursed through her.

Jad pressed a finger into her anus, then two, widening her. All the while, Rue moved beneath her, thrusting his cock in and out of her so slowly she thought she'd explode. Her clit was swollen and sensitive. Her body felt as though it would explode from all the sensation.

"All right, puss?" Jad rasped in her ear. "Does it hurt?"

She shook her head. It did hurt, actually, but the slight pain was actually arousing. It made the pleasure so much more pronounced.

Jad's cock pressed at her nether hole, circled it, and then entered. She gasped as his full, broad length filled her. He wasn't as large as Rue, but Goddess, he was close.

She moaned as the men started to shaft her slowly...so very, very slowly, both attuned to the other's pace. Rue still held her gaze, watching the play of emotion and pleasure across her face.

Rue shifted his hips so the tip of his cock paid special attention to the spot within her that felt so very good when it was rubbed.

"So sweet, so tight," groaned Jad. "Good god, she's perfect, Rue."

He stared into her eyes as he answered. "I know," he drawled out. Strong affection flavored his tone. "And she's mine," he whispered. "All mine."

Their pace quickened. They shafted her hard and fast now, driving her toward another climax that would shatter her world.

Lilane dropped her head down on a moan, feathering her hair over Rue's shoulder. Rue put his mouth to her ear. "You're so hot and wet, Lilane. You're making me come. I'm so close. I just need to hear you peak. Come for me, love. Yell out your climax."

Her climax ripped through her and she did yell out. Rue groaned as he released a hot jet of come into her. Jad did likewise, coming on a hoarse shout.

Jad pulled out from her and staggered away, but Rue held onto her, basking in the aftermath.

Jad pulled on his trews. "When can I tell the men they can have her?"

Rue raised his head and brushed his lips along her cheek as he went. "Never."

Jad went still. "What do you mean?"

"I claim her as my own."

"That's highly irregular, Rue, and very, very unlike you. I've never known you to become attached to a slave."

"There's a first time for everything."

Jad chuckled and walked to the door. "Fine, she's yours, then." He cast her a long look, winked and smiled at her. "Lucky bastard."

Chapter Six

Rue rounded the corner at the far end of the corridor and came face-to-face with a vision from his past. He went very still, watching the woman's ruby red lips part in a smile and one of her perfectly sculpted dark brown brows rise over an equally perfect dark brown eye. "Rue," she said smoothly.

He locked his jaw as he attempted to reconcile the face that tipped to his, her coifed, silky chestnut hair in an elaborate twist on the top of her head. The crown of her head reached his shoulder, just as Sania's had.

"Anaisse," he acknowledged in a tight rush.

"Were you expecting another?" she asked with a smile in her voice.

He cleared his throat of sudden emotion, of the guilt clogging it. "You look much as your sister, Supreme Lady Anaisse." Belatedly, he bowed deeply out of respect for her title. Unlike other women of the realm, the few daughters of the ruling families were given the utmost respect and could meet the eyes of Sudhraian men.

She touched his sleeve and he straightened. Tears glistened in her eyes. "You were once to be my brother-in-law, Rue d'Ange. I require no such formalities from you." She looped her arm through his and compelled him forward. "Walk with me now and tell why you've come back here. Jad tells me you've been here for nearly a week. I never thought to see you again, but am happy I was wrong."

"I am awaiting audience with your father concerning a delicate matter."

The silk of her dark blue skirts shifted over her legs and the tiny bells sewn into her girdle made music with every step she took. "Must be important to draw you back here."

"It is. How are your sisters, Anaisse?"

She laughed. "I see you don't want to share your secrets with me, Rue. That was a very nice turn of conversation. They are mostly married off now. As the second youngest after Sania, I am the only one remaining. Gallia went to the king of Laren'tar, Dara to the Exalted Ambassador of Sorance, and Fatia to the High Priest of Port Kendle to the far south. Father has managed to secure political alliances to practically all of Sudhra's neighboring countries through us. All of them except Nordan."

"The Nordan nobles don't marry like we do, Anaisse." Rue's mind drifted to Lilane and Dal. "Well, the peasants marry upon occasion, but the nobles—"

"Participate in nonstop debauched orgies and allow their women to take any man they please, whenever they please," she interrupted. "All in the name of the freedom of procreation."

Rue smiled. "I wasn't going to put it quite like that, but you've got the right of it. They don't call it *marriage*, either. They *take monogamous mates*. It's a practice near unheard of there."

"I heard Lord Marken of Nordan took a mate recently, a Sudhraian sex slave, no less. I also heard Talyn, his Captain of the Guard did as well. The captain took some strange creature to monogamous mate, a woman with wings."

Rue quirked his lips. "Aye, I heard the same."

Anaisse sighed. "If only a simple union between our two countries could stop this war. But those pagans to the north would never agree to a peaceful solution," she said angrily. "Never mind a holy union between man and woman."

Rue halted their progress down the hall and turned her to face him. "The Sudhraians started this war, not the Nordanese, Anaisse. Although, from the news I hear, the Nordanese might just be the ones who will *finish* it."

Fear and anger flashed in the depths of her eyes. "Marken's woman killed Lord Cyrus, Rue, a respectable Sudhraian nobleman. She was the catalyst. A silly little sex slave with a dagger."

He fought not to tighten the grip he had on her upper arms and spoke swiftly and without thought. "Sienne killed Cyrus after he raped, beat, and scarred her repeatedly, and then threatened not only the man she loved, but her foster family as well. She was well within her rights to kill him."

Anaisse went silent and studied him. He released her arms under her careful perusal and stepped away from her lest passersby believe he molested her. Anaisse smiled, showing white, even teeth. "You've changed, Rue."

He pushed a hand through his hair. "What do you mean?"

"You've spent far too much time in yon pagan country to the north, I think."

"Ridiculous."

Anaisse took a step toward him and Rue took a step back before he realized he'd done it.

"I even heard you brought one back with you and that you keep her in your room all of the time and make love to incessantly," she said. "Jad says her cries of passion, mingled with your own, can be heard at any given time of night or day when passing by your door."

"She is only my slave. I am training her."

Her brow arched. "Hmmm...your heart has always been easily attachable, Rue. Jad tells me you will allow no other to touch her, nor take on any other slaves while you're here. I wonder if a slave is *only* what she is."

Damned intuitive woman might be the death of him. He forced cold steel into his voice. "Lady Anaisse, I am a businessman who has chosen to take on a woman to train to sex slavery. That is all that lies between this Nordanese woman and myself. If I should take extra pleasure in this particular woman's body such is my right as a man, and is no one else's concern."

Her dark eyes sparkled. "I would like to meet her."

"Uh."

"I will have my maids sent to her with a new gown suitable for a banquet. What is her coloring? How large is she?"

"My lady, please—"

"Tell me, Rue," she commanded sweetly.

"She's blonde with green eyes, fair of skin and is about your size," he replied in defeat.

Anaisse's pretty mouth spread in a wide smile. "It may be a week or so before I can arrange a dinner. I want to ensure my father can attend." She winked at him conspiratorially. "It may be the only way you get an audience with him."

She turned and flounced down the corridor in her silk and brocade gown, casting a sly backward glance at him over her shoulder.

* * * * *

Rue lay on the bed with Lilane beside him. He fingered a tendril of her hair, reveling in the silky texture of it, and then wrapped it around his finger and pulled gently, bringing her face closer to his. She smiled, her eyes lighting with rare and fleeting joy, and kissed him.

She tried to pull away, and he tugged on the lock. "You're not going anywhere, my lady," he teased, smiling.

She laughed and relaxed against him. The sound of her laughter warmed his heart. It was a sound he could get used to. "I don't want to go anywhere," she sighed, laying her head on his chest.

He released her hair, content to have her resting against him, and smoothed the sheet over her shoulder. "Really, Lilane?"

She didn't answer.

Two weeks had passed since they'd arrived at the Supreme's Priestdom. Still he waited on the Supreme's pleasure for an audience. Rue knew well that he was making him wait because of Sania, because of the grief he and the Supreme shared over her. As soon as they saw each other, they'd mirror it and it would hurt again, as it had before.

Perhaps Anaisse would come through on her dinner invitation.

Lilane shifted and moved to straddle him. Her bare pussy brushed his cock, causing it to stir. Her breasts thrust out proudly, and it stirred even more. She stared down at him with an intense gaze. "Who is Sania?" she asked.

Rue stilled. It had been as though she'd read his mind again. He traced a pattern on her bare arm. "Lilane, before I answer that question, I want to ask you one. How much do you know of your heritage, your bloodline?"

Her brow furrowed. "Why?"

"Humor me, pet."

"Well, I know who my maternal and paternal great grandparents are."

He rubbed his palm over her flesh, massaging absently. She shivered in pleasure under his hand. "Where did they come from?"

"My paternal great grandparents were always in Gadstone Village. My great maternal grandfather as well. But you must realize they are not all blood relations, Rue. Because of the Goddess's curse, bloodlines dry up and adoptions are made. However, I know my blood runs true through the maternal line. My maternal great grandmother came from the north of Nordan. I know not where."

"Hmmm. Do you think perhaps the Northern Forests?"

She shrugged, wiggling against his hardening cock as he made larger circles with his palms, brushing one elongated nipple with his fingertips as he moved. "I don't know," she said breathlessly. "Why?"

He swallowed hard. "I have an insatiable hunger for you, love. I cannot seem to get enough of your body—of you—to satisfy me. That is indicative of something. Something I've wondered about since first I looked into your pretty green eyes." His lips quirked. "You know, on that day you tried to kill me."

She licked her lips, her gaze flicking down to his chest before rising to meet his eyes once more. "I can't get enough of you either."

"I near fucked you unconscious after our encounter with Jad." Seeing Jad's desire of her, and Lilane's excitement that day in the inspection chamber had driven Rue crazy. He'd dragged her back to their room, parted her silky thighs and hadn't pulled his cock from her warm body very often since.

She smiled. "You're given me more climaxes than I ever thought my body capable of. But you've also successfully changed the subject. *Who is Sania?*"

He raised a brow. "Do I detect a note of jealousy?"

She ran her finger over his nipple, and arousal jolted through him. "Never," she replied softly. "It is not my place."

She raised her eyes to his and smiled, though it didn't reach her eyes. "I'm simply paying off a debt, remember? I'll be gone when the first brush of the sweet Nordanese wind bathes my cheek once more."

His hands tightened around her waist, as though to keep her with him. He deliberately relaxed his grasp. This was turning into something far more than debt repayment to him.

Rue cleared his throat before speaking. "She was the Supreme's daughter, one of five. No matter what the Nordanese may say about how the Sudhraians treat their women, they love their daughters and the Supreme is no different. He nearly had a fit when Sania declared her love for me, since back then I was the Master Trainer of this Priestdom. She was chaste, demure — the way the Sudhraians keep their family women. She asked me to give up training, since in Sudhra sex slaves are condoned, but not publicly acknowledged by the ruling powers."

"Were you to marry her?"

"After I became the Supreme's Sword Master and garnered a reputation for myself, he deemed me worthy enough to take his youngest daughter to wife, yes. At that time, he didn't need to secure any political alliances, and he figured if he did, his other daughters would do. So, we were to marry. He cared about her happiness."

"What happened to her?"

Rue sighed, unwilling to relive these memories, but feeling Lilane was entitled to an explanation. "There is a group of slavers here in Sudhra called the *Ganotte*."

"The *Ganotte*? I know this name. They came once to my village."

Rue nodded. "This group makes an almost religious practice of capturing and enslaving women. They have much anger toward Ariane, the Goddess of Nordan, and therefore against the women who embody her. They feared that because the Supreme gave his daughter to marriage for her happiness and love, and not to gain political alliance, that he was growing soft. They kidnapped Sania one night to intimidate the Supreme. I don't think they meant to kill her," he finished quietly.

"They killed the daughter of the Supreme of Sudhra?"

"I tracked them and went in to free Sania with some of the best warriors this country has to offer, but it was too late. One of them had been far too *enthusiastic* in his treatment of Sania and he'd killed her."

"I'm so sorry, Rue."

"Oh, I got my revenge. I truly was a *dark lord* that eve. I shed the life's blood of every *Ganotte* in that camp that night and relished it, bathed in it. But it never brought Sania back. He traced the older scar across his chest. "This is from that night." He traced the newer gash that was almost healed now. "This one is from the night I met you."

Lilane reached out and ran her fingertip behind his, tracing the thin mottled white scar tissue of the old one and the reddish and puckered mark of the new one.

"The Supreme blamed me for the debacle," Rue continued. "He divested me of my title. But I was ready to leave this place anyway. I went to Kappan Priestdom and instructed men in swordplay there. I never trained another slave."

Images of Sania's violated, broken body crashed through his mind's eye. When he'd finally located their camp, she'd still been warm to his touch, though lifeless. Rue swallowed hard.

Lilane laid her head on his chest and he let his fingers trail through her hair, which lay in a wide swath of golden sunlight across his arm and the mattress. She laid there for a long while, and Rue closed his eyes, letting the healing essence of her seep into his skin, into his heart.

He detested the thought of giving her up...*ever*. But he was not the man for her—too jaded, too twisted, not honorable enough. Not by a long shot. No, he was not good enough for the likes of Lady Lilane of Nordan, just as he hadn't been good enough, strong enough, or fast enough for Sania.

"You mean you never trained another slave until me," she said finally.

"Ah, yes, but you're not my slave, love, you're my obsession. Anyway, submission is far different from slavery."

She raised her head and regarded him with sleepy, half-lidded eyes. Her thick hair fell over one shoulder and shadowed her face. "Speaking of submission." She smiled and chased away all the phantoms that had been clinging to his psyche. "I've a mind to make you taste a bit of what you dish out."

He cocked a brow. "Do you?"

"I want to tie *you* up for a change. *I* want control over *your* body for once." Her voice lowered seductively. "I want to hear your helpless moans as I ply my sexual talents on your body. Turnabout, after all, is fair play." Rue's cock hardened at her words and the look in her eyes.

"Stay here," she commanded. She lifted off him and walked across the room, grabbing the lengths of rope recently employed to restrain her limbs from the bedside table.

He watched her bare ass twitch as she walked and couldn't resist rising from the bed and pulling her against him by her waist so his cock nestled between her perfectly rounded cheeks. "Come back here, love," he growled in her ear.

She laughed and turned in his arms, one hand holding onto the rope as she bussed his lips with hers. "You don't follow orders very well, dark lord. I think you may be in need of punishment." She pushed him back onto the bed and he tumbled willingly.

"Punish me then," he said in mock surrender.

* * * * *

With excited, shaking hands, Lilane tied Rue spread eagle to the bed. One strong jerk of his arm and he'd probably break the ropes. All the same, Lilane thought as she stepped back and looked her fill, it was a satisfying sight to see him bound and at her mercy. His eyes had followed her as she moved, catching at her breasts, hips, and ass. She'd done her best to torment him by brushing against him as she worked at securing his wrists and ankles and had been reward by his thick shaft standing up at full attention.

She walked toward him with a small smile on her lips and her head cocked to the side. "It's arousing to see you bound and waiting for me to take you," she murmured, echoing the words he'd once spoken to her. Knowing that this magnificent male was under her power now was a heady thing. That knowledge alone made her pussy pulse with desire.

Climbing onto the mattress, she straddled one of his powerful thighs, brushing her sex against it deliberately. She lowered her mouth to his cock, pulled the foreskin the rest of the way down and blew on it experimentally.

"You're going to torture me, aren't you?" he asked.

"Mmmm…that's definitely in my plans, yes." She ran the flat of her tongue from the top of his shaft to the base and then up the other side.

"Sweet, sacred Anot," swore Rue under his breath.

She poked her tongue into the slit on the head of his cock and let her tongue dance around the delicate, sensitive underside before sinking him into the hot, wet recesses of her mouth. Rue let out a long, low groan as she suckled on him with strong pulls of her mouth from the base of him to the tip. His cock slipped down her throat and she closed her eyes, her pussy going damp with the knowledge that she was pleasing him.

His hips bucked and Lilane felt sure it was in an attempt to gain some control, any control. "Release me," he said. "I want to feel you."

She pulled her mouth from his shaft. "Oh, I can manage that without releasing you." Lilane moved up his body to straddle his pelvis, making sure her sex pressed against the length of his cock. "Can you feel me now, dark lord Rue?" she teased.

He strained against his bonds, a movement that flexed his biceps and chest muscles in a way that sent a jolt of arousal down to further slicken her already wet pussy. "You're going to kill me, woman."

She pulled her lips into a mock moue and leaned forward to dangle her breasts just in front of his face. "Not enough? Want more?" She cupped a breast and made to feed it to him. He strained to take her nipple into his mouth and she took it away at the last moment.

He gaze grew dark, the way she liked it best. "You're going to pay for this you know, love," he threatened sweetly.

She pretended not to hear him. Instead, she leaned back and cupped both her breasts in her hands, drawing her elongated nipples out with her index and thumbs as she moved her hips sensuously over his cock, gently grinding her pussy against the side of the thick length. It rubbed against her clit and the sensation had Lilane closing her eyes, letting out a soft moan.

"Lilane, let me free," he pleaded.

She ignored him. Her eyes popped open and she climbed off him, feigning a yawn. "You know, I do believe I'm going sit down over here and take a bit of a rest." She pulled a book at random from the shelves flanking the table and chair adjacent from the bed, sat down, opened it and settled in for a leisurely read.

"Lilane," came Rue's tightly controlled voice, "your book is upside down, love."

She laughed and snapped it closed.

"Why don't you come back over here and let me free," he purred seductively. "I want to be between your sweet thighs. I want my hands free to slide down your perfect ass as I take you hard and fast, to massage your breasts and tweak your nipples. I want to be able to rub that pretty little clit of yours until you break apart in climax beneath me."

Lilane set the book aside, got up and sauntered back over to him. His cock looked painfully hard. She straddled him and without warning, sank him straight into her pussy, sliding him home. "Yes," she breathed, tipping her head back. "That's it. That's what I wanted."

Rue answered with a ragged groan of relief.

She felt the best when joined with him. Somehow, when his cock was thrust inside her pussy, she felt whole.

Lilane moved over him, impaling herself on his length, lifting up and impaling herself again. All traces of teasing left them both as she set into the serious task of fucking him. She leaned back and caught the bonds at his ankles, freeing them. Then, still moving on his cock, she reached forward and released his wrists.

He grasped her waist and he held her midair and thrust his hips up, driving his cock in and out of her. Then, before she could finish her moan, he flipped her. He grabbed her buttocks as he promised he would and with a savage groan, began to shaft her hard and fast as he held her there.

She reached up and grasped his shoulders, her fingers digging in at the delicious onslaught. Her climax built inexorably. He shifted the angle of his entry so it rubbed against her pleasure point deep within and Lilane exploded in orgasm beneath him. She cried out, pressing her head back into the mattress.

Rue came down on her exposed throat and bit her where her shoulder met her neck. That small pain accentuated the pleasure rocketing through her body and mind. He groaned deeply against her as he came, shooting a hot stream within her.

Rue slipped his hands up to the small of her back and wrapped around her, holding her pressed against him. She felt the rapid thud of his heart against her breast. They were both out of breath and slick with the perspiration of their exertion. He laid a lingering, sweet kiss to her skin.

Contentment filled Lilane more completely in that moment than she'd ever known in her life. She rubbed her cheek against his shoulder and closed her eyes.

A knock sounded on the door, startling her and pulling her from her reverie. Rue pulled away from her and laid a blanket her nude body, then pulled on a pair of trews and opened the door.

Two finely attired maids stood in the doorway with stunned looks on both their faces. One held a delicate light green silk overdress over one arm. The other held all the proper accoutrements that should accompany such a fine garment, and also a bag containing what looked to be cosmetics and objects for properly coiffing a woman's hair. Suddenly self-conscious, Lilane pulled the blanket around her more securely.

The first maid averted her eyes from Rue, staring intently at the floor. Her cheeks blushed crimson. "B—by the order of Supreme Lady Anaisse, we've been sent to ready the woman Lilane for banquet. The lady said to tell you that her father, the honorable Supreme Priest of Sudhra, shall also be dining this eve and looks forward to conversing with you."

The maids stepped to the side and a line of servants bearing pails of steaming water entered the room and poured them into the bathtub.

"Lord Rue," said the other maid, her eyes also carefully averted. "Lady Anaisse has instructed us to treat the Nordanese peasant Lilane as a high born Sudhraian lady and thus we must prepare her as such, since there are no such things as sex slaves in Sudhra."

Rue sighed. "Ever keeping our dirty little secrets, aren't we?"

"Forgive me, but I don't know what you're talking about, Lord Rue. If you please, your clothing and bath are both waiting in Lord Jad's chambers. He has generously allowed you use of them until this evening." She motioned at the door. "If you please, my lord."

Rue looked at Lilane and hesitated, looking pensive. He rubbed his hand down over his mouth and chin. "All right," he said slowly. "I'll see you at the banquet, then." He bowed sweepingly. "*Lady* Lilane." He winked at her and backed out the door.

An hour later saw Lilane scrubbed, toweled dry, lotioned, scented, and stuffed into more layers of silk and satin than she'd ever seen. Delicate, tantalizing and very sexy undergarments made from white lace cupped her breasts and sex. Silky, thin stockings grasped her legs from the tip of her toes to the top of her thighs and were adhered to the bottom of what one maid had called a *bustier* by thin white leather straps and tiny silver clasps. The bustier pushed her breasts up so that they peeked above the top of her gown, making them appear much larger than they actually were. They looked fair ready to tumble out at any moment. Fine kid slippers sheathed her feet.

The gown itself had an underdress of thin silk, a shade of green so light it was nearly white. The overdress was of a darker shade of green, a color that nearly matched her eyes, and under the skirt was a wide flounce that billowed the skirt out and made her waist appear absolutely nonexistent.

After her bath, her maid had instantly rolled small rags and cylinders into the lengths of her wet hair and adhered them to her scalp using long pins. That alone had taken forever. Then they'd applied kohl around her eyes and a smudged a light substance across her eyelids that seemed to make her eyes stand out. They'd rubbed a light pink powder into her cheekbones so skillfully it looked like a natural blush and rubbed a subtle red cream across her lips.

"Raise your arms," commanded one of the maids. Lilane raised them, and she slipped a heavy girdle around her waist. It was also made of silk and satin, the same very light green of her underdress and it tinkled with tiny bells and even tinier dark green crystals.

The maid pulled on the strings in the back…hard. All the breath left Lilane in a whoosh as her lungs and ribcage compressed. "Dear Goddess," she gasped.

"Ah, yes. You are Nordanese, are you not?" asked the second maid in a clipped, cold tone.

"Yes," squeaked Lilane.

"I know they do not have this sort of dress for their women there. I hear of something called *flaxcloth* the women wear there. It is nearly the same as going naked, is it not?"

"The noblewomen wear that. I am a peasant and have never worn such."

"The Nordanese are pagan barbarians," chided the first maid. She yanked strings at the small of Lilane's back, pulling them even tighter and drawing an agonized hiss from Lilane. "This will make your waist look thin, tiny."

Lilane glanced in the full-length mirror across from her. She hadn't had much waist to begin with, now it looked as though Rue could practically encircle it with one of his large hand. *What was the point?*

"Do the Sudhraians often torment their women with such contraptions?" Lilane asked, biting her lower lip and hoping she wouldn't pass out.

"It is pleasing to the men to see a woman with such a small waist and such large breasts," snapped the first maid.

"But it's an illusion," countered Lilane.

"Our way is best, Lady Lilane," said the second maid. Lilane bit back a saucy retort.

The first maid finished the torture of her ribcage and began pulling out all the pins and unraveling the twisted material and tiny cylinders from her hair. Her locks fell in a shiny mass, now dry after the hours all the other preparations had taken, to her waist in a series of small ringlets and twists. The second maid primped and arranged her hair a bit and led Lilane to the mirror.

"You're incredibly beautiful, my lady. Lord Rue will trip over his tongue when he sees you."

* * * * *

Rue stared at his wine goblet and inserted a finger into the tight collar of his finely woven linen shirt and attempted to loosen it. He'd grown accustomed to not having to wear such formal attire in his time away from the court of the Supreme. Jad talked and laughed with the some men he did not recognize across the long table at which they sat. Anaisse had been able to procure him a place at the head of the table, where the Supreme would sit, and for that, he was eternally grateful.

The doors on the far end of the silver and gold decorated banquet room opened and the women entered. He searched for Lilane in the feminine throng, realizing how much he'd missed her presence in the hours she'd been away from him.

The sea of women dispersed, taking their seats and greeting their men and still there was no sign of Lilane. Rue stood, concerned something had happened to her.

He lost his breath as she entered the room. She hadn't seen him and her gaze darted anxiously around the chamber, searching for him.

"Who is *that*?" asked a man near him. "She's exquisite."

Rue's gaze met hers across the chamber and locked. Her eyes lit up and she smiled.

And Rue fell headlong and undeniably in love.

Chapter Seven

It had nothing to do with the finery she wore or the emeralds glittering at her throat, wrists and ears. It was in her eyes; sure as he'd seen the first night they'd met and battled. That night she'd nearly wounded his heart by the tip of her blade, now she had the power to injure him even worse because he loved her and if lost her now….

"My lord Rue," she said smoothly as she approached.

He bowed. "My lady Lilane." He pulled out the chair beside her and ushered her onto it. "You look stunning this evening. That gown does amazing things to your eyes."

"What? You say nothing about my waist?" She laid a hand to her stomach and winced as though in discomfort.

He glanced down at the bell and crystal encrusted girdle. His brow furrowed. "Uh, your waist is lovely as ever. You're as lovely as ever."

She smiled. "Ah. Thank you."

Rue glanced around at the men at the table and noted they near slavered when gazing upon Lilane. It was enough to make him want to stand and lead her back to his chamber.

Lady Anaisse sank into the chair one down from her father's right hand, aided by a tall man with sand colored hair, who sat down in the chair between the Supreme and Anaisse. Rue sat across from the man and Lilane sat across from Anaisse. Now they awaited the Supreme's presence before the food would be served.

Anaisse glanced between Rue and Lilane, a smile flirting with her well-formed lips.

"Lady Lilane, this is Supreme Lady Anaisse," Rue made their introduction.

"I have been wanting to meet you, Lilane," said Anaisse. "But Rue is very covetous of you and has not allowed you to roam the keep."

Lilane glanced sidelong at Rue, seeming unsure of what she should say. He saw clearly she was unclear with her place in all of this. She, after all, had been born in a small village, and had no knowledge of the ways of the highborn, especially the Sudhraian highborn "Well, I do as Rue bids me, my lady. It is my place to obey."

Rue stifled a smile. She played her role of slave well.

"You are Nordanese," said the man with the sand-colored hair. "I can hear the accent."

"This is Lord Vant," Anaisse explained. "He is the current Sword Master of this Priestdom."

"Yes, my lord Vant," answered Lilane. "I am Nordanese." A touch of pride entered her tone with those words.

Vant leaned forward. The skin around his blue eyes crinkled with sudden interest. "How must it feel, Nordanese *slave*, to be under the thumb, and cock, of a Sudhraian man?"

Rue didn't like the venom in Vant's voice at all. Anaisse laid her hand on Vant's arm. "Lilane is our guest, Vant. We will not antagonize her further." Steel girded her seemingly smooth tone.

Vant leaned back in his chair.

"Anyway," continued Anaisse with a smile. "We all know, even if it is not said aloud very often, that most our children come from slave women. These days, when our females conceive but rarely, it is the slaves who populate our land simply because they spend so much time on their backs. Truthfully, they are breeding stock here in Sudhra. I, myself, come from a slave and was adopted by my father when but an infant."

"My mother birthed me herself." Lilane replied. Pain that likely only Rue recognized flavored her words.

Anaisse smiled. "How rare and special! You are very lucky to have known your birthparent."

Lilane's eyes flashed dangerously. "I knew them both," she said low, angrily. "I knew them up until the time Sudhra decided to wage war on my people and they were run through by marauding soldiers."

Lilane glanced at all within hearing distance. "What mind fever has taken all of you?" Her voice rose. "To kill us off when it's so very difficult to make more?"

"Lilane," Rue said in a warning voice. He snaked a hand under the table and tightened it on her thigh. Inwardly, he urged her to heed her words. The errand he would hopefully complete this eve could very secure her country's dominance in the war. It was worth a small sacrifice of pride.

Vant laughed short and hard. "Seems your *slave* is need of more training, my Lord Rue."

Indeed. "Oh, don't fear. She will be roundly punished for her unruly tongue."

Vant leaned toward Lilane. "What do you mean by kill *us* off? You speak of the slaughter of *your* people, not ours. Why should we care if pagan barbarians are difficult to make?" He sneered at her. "We should kill them all down to the last babe."

Lilane's hand clenched on Rue's under the table. "Do you not know your own country's history? The Nordanese and the Sudhraians *are* one people, split only by religious ideology and cultural differences. When you kill us off, you kill yourselves. Especially since the Sudhraians steal women for slavery from beyond their borders on a regular basis. We are mixed thoroughly." She tipped her chin at Anaisse. "Even she could have had a Nordanese mother."

"Enough!" came the roar of a bass voice.

Everyone stilled. Rue looked over to see the Supreme standing at the head of the table, dressed in ermine robes. Long white hair trailed down his back in a queue secured at his nape. Bright blue eyes flashed from a face much older than Rue remembered it. He had a feeling it was more than mere age that caused the lines to crease his face.

The Supreme gave them all a lingering, hard stare—the stare of a patriarch reprimanding his children. He swept his robes beneath him and sat down with the aid of an attendant.

The Supreme sighed heavily before speaking. "It is true the Nordanese and the Sudhraians were a single people once, worshiping the Goddess Ariane and the God Anot in tandem. But the Goddess cursed us when we didn't comply with her notion of how we should treat our women. *They*, the pagan Nordanese followed Ariane in some misled attempt to regain her favor. We forsook her and followed Anot. So, we are *not* one people any longer, girl."

"That is untrue," said Lilane calmly.

Anaisse gasped.

The Supreme raised a hand to quiet the shocked murmur that ran through all those within earshot. "This woman is Nordanese, and a captive, and therefore under a great deal of ill ease. We will allow her opinions to stand, though we do not share them."

He looked pointedly at Lilane, who did not meet his gaze. "The Nordanese," The Supreme said with a heavy look in his eyes, "are spilling quite enough blood on their own at the moment, young woman. There are no heroes in this war. There is only death and heartbreak."

"The Sudhraians attacked first," stated Lilane quietly.

"Silence!" commanded the Supreme. "I have allowed your opinions to stand thus far, but my patience grows thin." He inspected the table, which the servants were adorning with bowls of rice and vegetables and plates of steaming meat. "Now, let's eat."

"Will you allow the insolent Nordanese to remain, Supreme?" drawled out Vant with a lazily confident look at Lilane.

"Yes." He squinted at Lilane. "It is Anaisse's wish that she dine with us." He finished as though that was all that mattered.

Since the Supreme had not acknowledged him yet, Rue set about filling his plate as the others did. To steady his nerves after Lilane's display, and his own uneasiness with the situation, he took a long, deep drink of wine.

"It is odd," the Supreme said at last, "to have my old Sword Master upon my left and my new one upon my right." The Supreme took a bite of meat and chewed it slowly, his eyes shrewdly observing Rue. "Why have you come back here, Lord Rue?"

Rue set his wine glass down, weighing his words out in his throat before freeing them. "I would only return for a very important reason. I think you, Supreme, understand this. I have spent many long months in Nordan where I resided in Marken's Lorddom. As you know, Lord Marken is one of the most powerful leaders of that country, equaled perhaps only by Lord Gregor."

Anaisse choked on her wine.

Vant took the goblet from her and placed a hand to her back. "Are you all right, my lady?"

She coughed and put a bejeweled hand to her chest. "I'm fine. I'm sorry to interrupt. Please go on, Lord Rue."

"Lord Gregor and Lord Marken are in command of the Nordanese troops. They two alone direct their movements and design Nordan's war strategies." Rue took a leisurely sip of wine and replaced the goblet. He looked calmly, confidently at the Supreme. "And I spent much time with Marken. I convinced him I'd left Sudhra for good and wanted to aid Nordan. I gained his trust and his information. Need I say more?"

The Supreme set down his fork and grunted as though mulling Rue's words. "It is intriguing enough for me to grant you a private audience."

"Very good, Supreme. I don't think you'll be sorry."

"I had better *not* be, Lord Rue," stated the Supreme as he speared a chunk of meat on his plate.

* * * * *

Rue pressed his hand to the small of Lilane's back and led her down the corridors toward their chamber. He moved quickly, wishing a safe sanctuary after the subtly barbed conversation they endured all through the banquet. "Did I mention you look spectacular this evening?"

"Four times, actually. Although I fail to see what's so spectacular with such an elaborate illusion as this." She made a sweeping gesture over her skirt. She fingered her girdle and winced. "And it's painful. It's like some subtle instrument of torture designed by men."

She lowered her head. "I apologize about my behavior this evening, Rue."

He shrugged. "I don't believe they'll think much of it. A new, untrained slave, which is what they believe you to be, can be unruly. That, coupled with the fact that they also believe you to be a Nordanese captive, makes your behavior somewhat plausible."

"It was too much to have to sit there and listen to that Sudhraian rhetoric. Anyway, I really *am* a Nordanese captive, Rue. Remember the manacles? Remember the rope?"

His cock hardened at the mere mention of it. His voice lowered. "Yes, love, I remember."

He spotted an alcove set into the wall and pulled her into it. She gasped as he pressed her against him, gripping her upper arms. He rubbed his lips over hers with agonizing slowness. "I remember all too well." He ground his pelvis against her so she could feel exactly *how* he remembered it.

Lilane shuddered against him in a way that signaled her arousal. "I am truly lost, because the memory of it excites me, too."

Footsteps sounded on the stone corridor beyond the alcove and Rue watched two nobles pass. They cast a long, curious look at Rue. "Come, love, let's get back. This is not a Nordanese keep. If it were, I'd take you right here and now." He pulled her from the alcove and got them quickly to their room.

Rue shut the door and Lilane fell against the wall, clawing at her girdle. "I'll die if this doesn't come off *now!*"

Rue pushed her gently against the wall, stilling her movement. He drew his hands to the small of her back. "I'll die if it doesn't come off right now, too," he murmured, catching one her earlobes and drawing it into the recesses of his mouth. "Let's get rid of these highly offensive articles of clothing, shall we?"

With deft, practiced fingers, he unlaced her girdle and dropped it. It made a tinkling sound when it hit the wooden floor.

"Oh, sweet goddess." Lilane's chest expanded as she took a long draught of air.

Rue wasted no time in peeling her over and underdress from her, leaving her clad in her stockings, tiny white lace bustier and equally tiny white lace panties. He stood back and looked his fill. "Sweet god," he breathed.

She set a hand on her hip and raised a brow. Her long hair hung loose and untamed around her. "You got all these complicated pieces of clothing off me easily, dark lord. Have you had much practice undressing noblewomen?" There was a teasing lilt to her voice.

Closing the distance between them in several footsteps, he twined an arm around her waist. He simply needed to touch her. "You're the only one I want to undress from now on, and I don't care what you wear, the dress of a noblewoman, peasant, or slave."

She looked up at him with uncertainty in her eyes. "What do you mean, Rue?"

"I only want you."

She pushed away from him and crossed to the bed, curling her hand around one of the posts. She kept her back to him and he couldn't see her face. "But I will leave you once we're in back in Nordan. What will you do then?" she asked quietly.

Rue stiffened. He'd been a fool to assume she'd share his love. Emotion swept through him. His heart was bared now and she could hurt him so easily with only words. No, he couldn't live without her now.

He crossed to her and pressed his chest to her back. She sighed almost imperceptibly. He brushed her heavy hair away from her neck and laid a tender kiss there. "Maybe I won't have to do anything. I have a little time to convince that you really don't want to leave me."

She turned toward him. "I want no secrets between us. I *will* want to leave, Rue." Uncertainty sparkled in the depths of her green eyes. He seized on it and used it to salve the bruised part of his heart.

She looked down and away.

"We will see," Rue answered. He tipped her chin up to get another glimpse of that uncertainty shimmering somewhere in the depths of her thoughts. She parted her lips as she looked up at him and lowered his mouth to take them in a soft kiss. No demands, no expectations. He merely needed to feel her mouth on his.

She returned his kiss with enthusiasm; rubbing her lips firmly over his and parting her lips to allow him to brand the inside of her mouth with his tongue.

She brought her hands up and smoothed them over his shoulders, then threaded her fingers as best she could through the short strands of the hair at his nape. His fingers strayed to the clasps at both side of her panties and undid them. The two small noises were like promises echoing through the room. Her lacy white panties dropped away, leaving her sex bare and vulnerable to his touch.

Lilane reached between them, undid the buttons of his trews, and pushed his pants down enough to free his shaft. "I need to feel you inside me," she murmured as she stroked his hardening length.

She pushed him back a step and his calves hit the mattress. He sat down at her urging and she straddled him, guiding his cock into her pussy and sheathing him in her to the base of him. Their sighs of pleasures mingled.

Rue pushed her hair behind her shoulders, baring the lovely arch of her throat. He kissed her collarbone as she gently, slowly, began to ride him. "You see, my love, how much better we feel when joined? You and I are meant to be as one…in all ways, physically, spiritually, and mentally."

"Shh…." She kissed his lips. "Just feel me now."

Rue felt her.

Lilane rode him for a long time, drawing out their climax. Rue's hands strayed over the silk stocking sheathing her long legs, and her lace bustier. He pulled her breasts out from the small cups that held them and ran his tongue over her nipples.

Finally, after Lilane had found her pleasure, he found his, and shouted her name when he came.

* * * * *

"Supreme." Rue bowed and entered the Supreme's private chambers.

He hadn't been in these rooms since the night Sania had died. He'd been injured, both inside and out, and had bled all over the Supreme's expensive imported carpets. Being here again made the memory fresh.

Rue looked down, concentrating on the new carpets that covered the floor—a rich design of royal blue, pale pinks and light yellows—and tried to control his emotions, regarding sharp memories of Sania's death, Lilane, and not least the fact that if all went well, he'd betray the man who sat before him now.

"Something interesting down there, Lord Rue?" asked the Supreme.

Rue looked up. The Supreme sat in a polished wood chair, elaborately carved with prancing horses. "Forgive me." He cleared his throat. "It's a fetching pattern."

"Apparently," answered the Supreme. "Why don't you come to your point, Lord Rue. I have just received ill news from our front and I have much to do."

Rue stepped forward and a servant ushered him into a chair. "Sudhra is on the defensive," Rue stated. He suspected strongly that was the case.

The Supreme nodded. "Yes. They've pushed us back past our borders and are currently in the process of trying to take Madsine Priestdom. We need to draw up new strategic plans." The Supreme's face grew suddenly gray. "We never thought we'd end up defending our own priestdoms from them."

"You underestimated them. You poked a sleeping dog with a stick and now they're biting." Rue nodded slightly. "You realize this is to the death. The Nordanese know well they cannot simply push you back beyond your borders. They'll try and take the country now. You've given them no choice."

Arrogance overtook the older man's features. "We will turn the tide, Lord Rue. There is no possible way those pagans will take mighty Sudhra down."

Rue saw the future in the Supreme's words. Sudhra would fall because of the country's shortsighted pride. What Rue attempted to do for his people in betraying the Sudhraians would hasten that fall. But if he chose to cease his treacherous errand now, Sudhra would *still* likely fall.

A weight lifted from Rue's shoulders.

"Please, come to your point, Lord Rue," the Supreme said exhaustedly.

"All right. I have detailed information regarding Nordan's military strategy. I know how they will move through the country, which priestdoms they will attack and in what order. With my aid, you can anticipate their moves."

The Supreme sat forward, a smile overtaking his mouth. "Then let's talk."

Chapter Eight

Lilane kicked the blanket away and sighed. The nights had grown progressively hotter over the season, as though building for a climax. In the month that had passed since Rue's first meeting with the Supreme, she'd embroidered at least twenty shirts and learned to weave intricate patterns in rugs and blankets under the patient tutelage of Lady Anaisse.

Because of Rue's insistence Lilane not be given to other men as an ordinary sex slave, she had not been treated as one. Instead, the daughter of the Supreme had bid Lilane spend her days in the lady's solar, learning all the things Sudhraian ladies learned.

Lilane had detested every single moment of it, but had endured it all with a smile. The only way she could've borne the last month in the Supreme's Priestdom was because she knew well that Rue was working hard to bring about an end to the war with Nordan as the victor.

It was costing her a lot, however, and not just in hits to her Nordanese pride and her bloody, needle-pricked fingers. Rue was gone constantly from her, always at the side of the Supreme.

And she missed his presence greatly.

Lilane rolled over and buried her head into her pillow. The beat of her heart was amplified in her ears and she felt Rue's presence at her back, hot and arousing. He'd come back to the chamber late that evening, as he had for many evenings, after the conclusions of late meetings with the Supreme and his advisors. Rue had successfully earned the ruler's trust.

She'd heard the Nordanese had breached the Sudhraian border and caused the retreat of their aggressor enemies to the south. They made their way ever south, to the Supreme Priestdom. It was the winning piece, the one they had to capture, in this game of bloodshed and strategy. The last news she'd heard placed them north of the Supreme Priestdom, stalled out in deadlocked battle with the Sudhraians.

Lilane stood and looked down at Rue. In the wan light cast from the open window and silver starshine streaming within, she saw his chest rise and fall with the breath of slumber.

She feigned sleep when he'd come in that evening and he'd watched her as she watched him now. Carefully, so as not to wake her, he'd brushed the hair away from her brow and from where it lay heavy against her collarbone. It had been a gesture full of love and it had made her eyes grow wet with tears beneath her closed eyelids.

Damn him. She loved him back.

She stalked to the open window and stood before it, letting the slight breeze blowing in bathe her warm skin. Her very sleeping gown clung to her flesh. She closed her eyes and sniffed the air. The slightest tang of dying leaves wafted on the wind — the trademark scent of cool, fresh autumn when everything grew ready for a long-needed rest. Hopefully the dogs of war would also be ready to lie down and sleep.

Lilane opened her eyes and stared hard at the star-strewn sky above. By autumn hopefully she'd be gone from Rue. She couldn't stay with him. The man was far, far too dangerous. Too easily able to wound her so badly she'd never recover.

Warm hands clasped her shoulders and startled her. Lips brushed her neck and laid a kiss. "I'm sorry," he murmured.

Lilane's throat clogged up. "It...it's all right," she answered.

"Can't you sleep?"

She shook her head.

"Nightmares again?"

"No. It's hot." She laughed, short and nervously. "It's too hot to sleep."

"The air feels heavy and slightly violent. Now it is the time for late summer storms. I think we are in for a bad one."

"It will cool things down, maybe even be a harbinger of autumn."

"Perhaps." He laid a kiss to her shoulder and her body stirred. She closed her eyes and sighed. "I will be leaving in the morning," he said against her skin.

Her eyes popped open. "Where?"

"I have what I needed from the Supreme. It took me a month to obtain it but I have it now. I've got to get it to Marken."

"What is the information?"

He turned her toward him. "I thought when I first began discussing the war with the Supreme that Sudhra was destined to be defeated because of their arrogant overconfidence and underestimation of Nordan. To some extent, I still believe that. However, Nordan is set up right now for a sly trap instituted by Sudhraian forces. If I don't warn Marken and Gregor of the ruse Sudhra intends, those troops may very well fall, and the course of this war will turn in Sudhra's favor."

Lilane shivered. If Sudhra won the war, they would rape Nordan, culling Nordanese spices, silks and women. They would crush the worship of the goddess and punish those who would not renounce her. "We don't want that."

Rue turned and walked across the room, pushing a hand through his hair in frustration. "My people grow restless. After centuries of having to pretend not to be Aviat, of having to hide their true selves, they are restless and highly impatient now that this new opportunity has presented itself. They yearn for freedom and the only place they can have that is in Nordan."

He turned to her. "I must do this thing, Lilane. I must leave this morning."

"Won't the Supreme miss you?"

"He believes I travel out to take a look at the troops."

"How long will you be gone?" She tried to ask in a way that made it seemed as though she didn't care, but the sadness bled through her voice anyway.

"I don't know, love, but I'll return as quickly as I'm able. I'll miss you, too."

She turned toward the window so he couldn't see her eyes. "It's not that I'll miss you," she said with faux coolness. "I simply wish to know how soon we'll be traveling back to Nordan."

He went silent and she felt twinge of guilt.

"Where *are* your people, Rue?" she asked to break the sudden, uncomfortable silence.

"All around us, Lilane. But you'd never know any one of them from a non-Aviat." He came to stand beside her at the window. The pink and orange hues of dawn were just beginning to break over the horizon. "I should leave. Get this over with. It weighs on me."

Sorrow passed through her. She *would* miss him, no matter the act she put on. She didn't say anything as he turned and dressed, all the while explaining to her that he'd ride out on horseback. When he was far enough from the Priestdom, he'd leave the horse with an Aviat peasant he knew and take to wing.

Strong hands braced her shoulders as he kissed her. "I'll be back soon," he said, then turned and walked out the door.

From the window, she watched him ride out of the courtyard, down the drawbridge and across the grassy plain that spread before the castle. She stared out at the horizon long after he'd disappeared, all the while examining her heart.

What she found there frightened her.

Chapter Nine

"Lilane."

Lilane turned and saw Anaisse trying to catch up to her.

"My lady Anaisse," Lilane said, curtsying.

"Cook has made gingerbread. It's hot yet, fresh from the oven. Would you like to come with me to have a bit?" asked Anaisse. She flashed a smile that would probably bring the stoutest man to his knees.

Lilane had been pleased to see the gifts of fine Sudhraian gowns Rue had presented her with several weeks back, however next to Anaisse's silver and gold shimmering finery she felt like the peasant she was.

But...Lilane mused, *she* wasn't the one burdened with the dreaded girdle.

"Certainly, my lady Anaisse. I'd be honored."

The kitchens were warm—too warm for a day as hot as it was. So they gathered a chunk of gingerbread and headed out to the gardens. Summer flowers bloomed all over the lush, enclosed area and bees, heavy with nectar, hovered just above the cobblestone paths.

Heavy, angry looking clouds were rolling in from the north. It had stormed on and off for several days, though this one looked far worse than they'd had thus far. Thunder boomed distantly.

Lilane wondered where Rue was right now. He'd been gone three days and she expected him back at any time. Hopefully, he wasn't traveling through the approaching storm.

Lilane bit into the gingerbread and the sweet taste of it spread over her tongue. "May I ask why you choose to be kind to me," she asked after she'd swallowed. "After I behaved the way I did at the dinner? Why should you associate with me at all, knowing I am what I am—a sex slave? And a Nordanese besides."

Anaisse shrugged a delicate shoulder. "Rue is a special person to me. I'm sure you know the story of my sister by now."

"Yes, my lady. It's a tragic one."

"Especially for Rue, who loved her, fought to save her and failed."

They came to a stone bench and sat down. "He did everything he could to save my sister and was devastated when he could not," said Anaisse. "He didn't forgive himself for that failure for a long time, too long. Perhaps he never really has. I suppose I want to see him find a love again. Whether it is with a highborn lady or a sex slave taken from Nordan matters not to me. I believe he's found that with you."

Suddenly the gingerbread did not taste as good. "What makes you believe he loves me?"

Anaisse popped the rest of her gingerbread into her mouth and chewed thoughtfully. Finally she said, "It's in his eyes when he looks at you. It's the same way he once looked at Sania. His face is stoic, but his gaze" --Anaisse shivered—"I can only dream a man would ever look at me that way."

Lilane set the rest of her gingerbread on the edge of the bench. "You're well-born, monied and beautiful. You have many such gazes in your future, I'm sure, Lady Anaisse."

She shook her head. "No. I'm destined to marry the man my father believes would make the best political alliance. I have no part in the choice. Likely my husband will be old and frail and probably cruel." She laughed. "Hardly the type to look upon me with true love in his eyes. Not the way Rue looks at you."

"Lord Rue does not truly love me, my lady. I believe you mistake lust for love."

She shook her head vigorously. "I mistake nothing." She looked at Lilane and narrowed her eyes. Keen intelligence glimmered in their beautiful dark brown depths. "You're afraid of Rue's love, aren't you?"

Lilane looked away, suddenly finding the red poppies blooming on the opposite side of the path extremely intriguing. "Afraid?"

"Why ever should you shy from the tender regard of a man such as Rue? Is it because you're beneath him? Do you think yourself unworthy?"

Lilane took a deep breath. "It's not that." She turned to Anaisse. "I have known much loss in my life, Anaisse. It hurts to lose those you love. You know this."

It seemed completely absurd to be revealing this to a Sudhraian, her enemy, but Lilane could not seem to stop the flow of her words. "To love someone and then lose them is to reach the pinnacle of grief. I recently reached that pinnacle three times over. I would like to avoid it happening again, that's all."

Anaisse smiled. "But, Lilane, you can't live your life in fear of loss. You must take the loves and joys you find today and not think about the tomorrows."

Lilane stood. She couldn't sit here and discuss this with her. She was a Sudhraian. Her people were the ones who'd brought the loss to her in the first place. "Thank you for the gingerbread, my lady."

"Lilane, you don't have to go."

Lilane bowed. "I leave you in the shining light of Anot, my lady." She smiled weakly. "I'm fatigued and would like to lay down for a nap. Please excuse me."

She didn't wait for a response, but turned and started down the path leading back to the castle. The sky above them had darkened and a blot of lightning shot through the clouds.

"Lilane," called Anaisse. "Please remember that to push Rue away because you're afraid is the same thing as losing him. You'll still be grief-stricken in the end."

Lilane closed her ears to her words and picked up her skirts, hurrying back into the castle.

She took the stairs leading to her chambers two at a time, as though she still wore her comfortable men's trews instead of heavy skirts. She turned a corner at the top and came nose to chest with a powerfully built man. She looked up into the face of Lord Vant.

Could her afternoon get any worse?

His well-formed lips twisted in a cruel smile. "The little Nordanese sex slave. Where is your trainer? Hmmm? Oh. He's away, isn't he?"

Lilane took a step back, but he grabbed her by the upper arms, his fingers digging into her flesh painfully.

"What good luck," he said. A sneer crossed his handsome face.

Before Lilane could even draw a breath, he began dragging her down the hall. "Let's see what Lord Rue has taught you, shall we? We'll put that pretty mouth to a use better suited to it than sass."

Lilane struggled against him, forcing him to stop and throw her over his shoulder. "You pig" she yelled. "You filthy Sudhraian pig. Let me go!" From her lofty perch, she glanced around anxiously, looking for aid. A couple strolled leisurely down the hallway, but they pretended as though she was invisible.

Goddess-bedamned strange country.

Vant caressed her buttocks. "With such fire, you'll likely make an excellent fuck. I can't wait to sink my cock into you. I hope you struggle. That always excites me."

Lilane kicked as hard as she could, landing a solid blow to his solar plexus. He grunted and tried to hold her legs down, but she was a wild thing. She wiggled and fought. He lost hold on her and she slid down the length of him.

Walking forward, he pinned her between the wall and himself, which was like being pressed against a boulder. "You better calm down right now, girl. I'll make you pay for this in my bed. With every struggle, you owe more."

"Bastard!" She lunged forward and bit the tender flesh of his ear...hard. Blood flooded her mouth.

He yelled out and released her. As soon as Lilane's feet hit the floor, she ripped one of the decorative swords from the wall and unsheathed it. She whirled on him in battle stance, the edge of the blade angled toward his throat. "I didn't fight against men like you my whole life to be raped by one now," she bit off.

Vant stood there with a hand clapped over his ear and dangerous storm clouds passing over his face. They matched the dark skies outside. In the silence of their standoff, thunder boomed. A heavy, hard rain started outside the window near them.

A bell clanked from the north end of the castle, then from the south. The castle burst into motion. "The Nordanese are here!" cried someone from the corridor. "All arms to the battlements!"

Vant removed his hand. Blood coated it. "You bitch. You just got a reprieve. But know you just made it three times harder for yourself when I finally take you." He stalked off down the hall.

Lilane lowered her sword and fell back against the wall behind her in relief. The castle's inhabitants were coming out of their chambers, hurrying down the corridor past her. *The Nordanese are here!* She dropped the sword with a clatter and ran down the corridor along with the ever-thickening throng.

Pushing her way down the crowded stairs and through the panic in the courtyard, she climbed the stairs to the northern battlements. The rain pounded down on them all now and the wind whipped her skirts around her legs, loosed her hair from her coif and plastered it against her soaked face. She knew well she was not allowed up there. It was restricted to the archers and soldiers as they prepared themselves for the coming siege. But she had to see them. Just had to see....

"Woman! Get down from the battlements!" A large soldier strode toward her with purpose. "Off now, you silly wench. You'll catch your death out here in the rain, if the Nordanese don't give it to you first," he yelled over the fury of the storm.

Ignoring him, she ran to the edge of the battlements. Her fingers spread flat on the stone barrier as her eyes searched the horizon desperately. Yes....*there*.... Strong Nordanese soldiers dotted the skyline, standing proud and stoic against the onslaught from the skies. Some were on horseback, other on foot. All looked ready to take this Priestdom.

Rue had been successful.

Strong arms grabbed her and pulled her back. Even the soldier's rough hands biting into the bruised flesh of her upper arms couldn't wipe the smile from Lilane's mouth.

"Are you a simpleton, woman? Didn't you hear me?" He pushed her hard toward the stairs, causing her to stumble. "Get down from here now. You're underfoot."

She caught herself before she pitched headfirst down the narrow stone stairs, and descended slowly. The wind had grown nothing but worse. Small bits of hail now pelted her skin. The courtyard, what she could see of it through her wet, whipping hair, was emptying out as the panicked people sought shelter within doors.

Nothing, not even the storm, could diminish Lilane's happiness now. The only thing that put a damper on it was the fact that she could not share her excitement with Rue. Rue made everything sweeter, sexier, more pleasurable, she realized with a start—even the smallest, most commonplace thing, like waking up in the morning.

Sorrow stabbed through her. What would she do without him?

Deep in thought, she reached the bottom of the stairs and began to cross the courtyard toward the keep.

"Lilane!"

She turned and saw Jad fighting his way through the storm toward her. "Jad?"

He reached her and laid a strong hand to her forearm. "Lilane, you must come with me now. It's Rue," he pitched his voice over the wind. His face looked grim.

Fear and shock tore her breath away. "What's wrong?"

He shook his head. "You've got to come now. It's an emergency. Come!" He motioned toward a door leading to one of the towers.

"All right," she replied. Dread clenched her stomach. She couldn't stand it if something had happened to Rue.

They hurried toward the tower.

* * * * *

The hooves of Rue's mount pounded over the muddy ground, racing toward the Supreme Priestdom.

He'd traveled back with the Nordanese troops after having advised Marken and Gregor past the series of cleverly placed decoy troops the Sudhraians had been manipulated them toward utilizing a network of disinformation. Rue had been aware of all the true troop placements in Sudhra and had routed the Nordanese through a clear area. It'd taken them an extra day to obtain their intended destination, but, if the Nordanese could take the Supreme Priestdom, it had won them the war.

A few short sentences could fell a whole country, he mused bitterly.

The Nordanese troops were only steps behind. He urged his horse to a faster pace. Now he had to get back to the Priestdom and get Lilane before someone discovered what he'd done. It was far too early, he assured himself. No one could possibly know yet. But even the slimmest chance of Lilane being in danger had him in a near panic.

The castle rose in the distance. Through the driving rain he could make out little. Though he did see archers and soldiers on the battlements, preparing their weaponry for the coming battle.

Dark threat gathered in the very air around him. Violence loomed in the black clouds overhead and conflict pulsed through the very earth.

His horse's hooves clattered up the drawbridge. The portcullis had been secured and the guard on duty brought behind the fortress walls. They recognized him, however, and raised the claw-like portcullis just high enough to admit him. Behind him came the sound of heavy chain and the scraping of a piece of ponderous wood against the earth—the drawbridge being pulled in.

That alone should have put him at ease. Had they known what he'd done, they would've had an archer spear his unprotected heart before he'd even crossed the moat.

Still, a glimmering of unease clutched at him. Perhaps some connection he had to Lilane that went past the ordinary. Usually only an Aviat bonded pair felt such an extrasensory tie, and Lilane was not an Aviat, at least not a full-blooded one. Rue suspected somewhere in her bloodline lurked a pair of wings. Something was wrong; he could feel it, and that reinforced his opinion that he and Lilane truly were a bonded pair.

At the moment he hoped it was not true, and these suspicions he now had were simply fanciful.

He galloped into the courtyard. Villagers, brought in from the surrounding countryside huddled against the inner walls, taking shelter from the coming onslaught as best as they were able. He dismounted, leaving the horse to find its own way to the warm, dry stables, and ran toward the keep.

Within, people hurried down the corridors, in and out of rooms. Panicked looks passed over their faces. Quick commands volleyed from one castle inhabitant to another. The Sudhraians had never expected to have to defend the Supreme Priestdom. The possibility of it had never even entered their minds. The surprise of it all showed clearly. He pounded up the stairs, headed straight for his chamber and, hopefully, Lilane.

He slammed the door open and found the chamber empty. He entered the room and found her nightdress still lying on the bed. Bringing it to his nose, he inhaled the scent of her still clinging to it. Her clothes were still hanging in the opened armoire. At least she hadn't been fool enough to leave the castle on her own. No. She remained within castle walls. He knew that because he could feel it. If she'd been of stronger Aviat blood, he'd be able to pinpoint her exact location within the castle. As it was, her presence was only a whisper.

Rue turned on his heel and left the room. In the corridor, he pressed himself back against the wall to avoid the crush of people hurrying through it. Tiny hands clutched at his arm and he looked to see Ana, a fellow Aviat, looking up at him with frightened, yet hopeful eyes. In the rare times she could spread her wings they were of a sparrow. Her slight stature complemented her Aviat breed.

"Has the time come, Lord Rue? Will the Nordanese take Sudhra and free us, finally?" she asked.

"The war has not been won yet, Ana, but the Sudhraians know well that they are outmatched here. They've sent most of the troops away from this Priestdom, thinking they wouldn't have to defend it. I cannot promise anything, but I would make a guess you'll be flying free very soon."

A smile spread across her mouth as she danced away down the hall. The rapturous figure she struck was much in contrast to the worry around her. It was a striking symbolism. Soon his people, after generations of fear and extermination, would once again be able to be themselves.

He could not rejoice, however. Not now. Not when so many lives would be lost this day—had already been lost to pride and the power of warfare.

Catching glimpses of the windows on the opposite side of the corridor showed that the rain had slowed to a drizzle. The sound of a cannon ripped through the air, women screamed and ran for cover within the corridor.

The siege had begun.

Where was Lilane?

* * * * *

Lilane's sopping gown slapped against her legs and clung to her skin as she climbed the winding tower stairway, following Jad. She shivered uncontrollably. The storm had brought with it a mass of cold air and the temperature had dropped considerably. It seemed to get colder every step she took, or maybe she only imagined it in her worry over Rue.

Outside cannons rolled like thunder, mixing with the shouts of men and the terrified screams of women. The battle had just started. It shook the tower they mounted—the very steps she climbed.

Jad had remained silent. His labored breathing had been audible at first, but now only the sounds from outside filled her ears.

Finally, they reached the top of the tower and Jad pushed it open. Lilane rushed through the doorway and searched the area for some sign of Rue, but found none.

The door behind her slammed shut and Lilane whirled. "What do you mean by bringing me up here? Where is Rue?"

Jad's normally sunny expression darkened.

Her heart crashed to her toes. It had all been a ruse. Jad wanted her up here alone with him, but why?

He took a step toward her and she backed up. "Simple. There are no swords up here, my lady Lilane. Rue has told me of your skill with those, and I take no chances. There is nothing at all up here, in fact, and no one to hear you scream."

"Why would I want to scream, Jad?" she asked carefully. He'd begun to circle her like a wolf circling prey.

"I scented something strange on Rue when he first showed up here after years of avoiding this place. Especially since he had you in tow, a Nordanese woman he claimed was a new slave. But I know Rue, my lady, better than probably anyone, and he has never, *ever* kept a slave exclusively for himself. So I began to suspect maybe you weren't truly meant for slavery at all, maybe you never were, maybe Rue was lying to his old friend, Jad."

"What?" she shouted. "Do you think me aligned with a Sudhraian pig of my own free will?" She spat on his shoe. "I hate you and all you stand for."

He ignored her outburst and continued to circle her. That reaction had her even more nervous than the anger she'd been expecting. His gaze was steady and intent. There was murder in his eyes, and it was no easy death for her that shone in that heavy gaze.

He raised an eyebrow and dangled a key in one hand. "To the door, my lady." He glanced at the door that opened to the only exit from the very, very high tower. He slipped the key down the front of his trews to settle, she assumed, securely in his braies. "You're not leaving this tower alive."

"Why are you doing this? Why does it matter that Rue should care for me?"

He motioned to the battle raging around them. "Rue shows up with a Nordanese woman he seems to care for. He insinuates himself back into the good graces, and confidence, of the Supreme. Rue leaves the Priestdom, and by the time he returns, the Nordanese have inexplicably changed their course. By all accounts that's what they must've done, and bypassed every single clever snare we'd set for them."

He shook his head. "Do you think me simple, my lady? Rue betrayed his homeland to the enemy because he's besotted with a Nordanese witch." He shrugged. "His actions might well take something very dear to me, so I will take a thing dear to him."

Jad had guessed nearly all of it right on. He simply didn't know Rue's true motive.

Jad took a step toward her and she stepped back. Wariness and weariness warred within her body. She was so sick of fighting, of having to defend herself. She glanced around, hoping for a weapon to use, a rock, perhaps, *anything*. Only uneven weather-beaten granite met her gaze, no loose stones that she could see.

He cocked his head to the side. "But, you don't deny it, my pet?"

"I have nothing to do with any of this," she answered honestly. "I am Rue's prisoner. You're about to kill an innocent."

He snorted. "Innocent? I think not, my lady. I remember how you moaned against my body that first day you arrived. Innocent. Hardly."

"So I deserve to die for that?"

"No, Lilane." His voice hardened. "You deserve to die merely because I say you do."

He moved, faster and more agile than she'd believed such a large man could. He nigh pounced on her, grabbed her by her hair and forced her to her knees. Lilane cried out in pain and surprise. With incredible force, he kept her there. She was unable to move her head, unable to move at all—completely unable to fight him.

One meaty hand closed around her throat and squeezed.

Chapter Ten

Rue searched the castle, exploring first the areas she'd most likely be and then the areas that were less likely. Every place he searched and did not find her made his heart grow heavier.

The battle raged hard and the Sudhraian forces fought with all they had. Still, Rue knew it would not be long before the Nordanese overtook the Priestdom. The Supreme, in his misplaced confidence had ordered most the troops gone from the castle, on the strategic errand meant to trap the Nordanese — the plan Rue had foiled. The move had left the Priestdom not guarded with a full force and vulnerable to attack.

Rue's only worry was that word would reach the far-flung Sudhraian forces and they would return, coming up behind the Nordanese. That was not a thought worth considering. The results would be disastrous.

Something tightened around his throat and Rue reached a hand to pull it away. He groped air. Something tightened again, hard, cutting off his air supply.

Lilane.

Was this an empathic reaction to something that was happening to her right now? Rue concentrated on the choking sensation and eased the phantom fingers away from his throat. He couldn't help her this way. He had to remain calm, extricate the tightening around his throat and find her, *now.*

Using the force of his will, he eased the worst of the pressure. He knew that since Lilane was not a full-blooded Aviat, he would not be able to get specific mental imagery of her location within the castle. Instead, he focused on the empathic response and Lilane's fear behind it. Shutting out the noise and tumult surrounding him, he honed into that shared mental link.

The fear she felt flooded through him, threatened to overwhelm him. She believed she was going to die. Rue suppressed the desperation he felt. He had to stay calm. To be anything other than that right now condemned Lilane to death.

It didn't take long to begin to feel all of what Lilane was feeling. He felt a sharp stiff breeze, nearly cold. He heard the sound of the battle, but the sounds were not engulfing and surrounding Lilane wherever she was, they came from…below.

The tower.

Rue ran into the courtyard. He vaguely noted that the Nordanese forces had successfully breached the battlements and were fighting the Sudhraians atop it.

In the tumult and panic, Rue unfurled his wings and drew not one glance. With a powerful flap, he lifted himself into the air. Furious emotion tightened in his stomach like a fist and exploded through him. Whoever was trying to kill Lilane right now wouldn't see the morning light.

* * * * *

Lilane clawed at Jad's hands, but couldn't pull them away. Panic gripped her as her windpipe closed and cold reality slapped her in the face. She was going to die. Her vision blackened and dimmed, and her hands slipped away from Jad's. All she could think of was Rue. Out of all the people in her life, he was the one that made intense emotion tighten around her heart.

Goddess, she didn't want to leave him. They still had so much to share.

Suddenly Jad released her. She fell to her hands and knees gasping and coughing, drawing air into her starved lungs. She bowed her head, forcing herself to stay conscious.

"Lilane, are you all right?"

She looked up and saw Rue landing on the roof of the tower with his wings outspread. Concern and rage hardened his handsome face. Relief and joy flooded through her at the sight of him. She nodded. He snapped his wings shut and stalked toward Jad with single-minded purpose.

Jad stood, apparently stunned at the sight of Rue and his wings. "What manner of creature from the Underworld are you?" he breathed.

Lilane narrowed her eyes. She struggled to her feet and walked toward Jad, propelled by sheer rage and nothing more. "Bastard!" she rasped from her sore throat and brought the fist hard into his jaw. Pain exploded in her hand at the force of her blow.

Taken by surprise Jad stumbled back and would've fallen if Rue hadn't grabbed him by his shirt and slammed him into the wall behind him. Blood dripped from Jad's nose and he gasped for breath in the face of Rue's rage.

Lilane found the ledge running around the edges of the tower and braced herself against it, drawing air into her lungs to calm herself.

"Why, Jad?" Rue bit off angrily, throwing Jad up against the wall with a force that looked as though could've broken bones.

Jad closed his eyes and grimaced. "You betrayed your country, didn't you, Rue? You gained the Supreme's trust, took what you needed from him and used it to gain Nordan an advantage." Jad sounded anguished.

Rue released Jad and pushed away from him. He ran a hand through his hair in gesture that screamed weariness. His shirt was ripped in the back, where his wings had erupted and pushed through the material. Blood had trickled down and soaked it. "I didn't do it for myself, Jad. I did it for my people. The Nordanese will allow them to live free while the Sudhraians never would. I had no choice but to do what I did, and I'm not sorry I did it."

Rue went silent and below them they could hear the battle, mixed with cries of exaltation from the Nordanese.

Relief flooded Lilane. The siege had been exceptionally swift and decisive.

"The Nordanese will not dominate Sudhra as Sudhra would do to Nordan," continued Rue. "This outcome will only be painful for Sudhra because the country's pride will be piqued. Perhaps this may even be the start of a reconciliation between our two nations."

Jad's face contorted into a mask of pain and anger. He stepped forward and drew his sword. "Lying, betraying bastard," he said in a low voice. Impending violence strung like a taut bowstring between the two men.

Rue drew his sword. The length of steel scraped against the scabbard with a ringing hiss.

Jad rushed him and they engaged. Metal against metal, a sound heard often of late, tattered Lilane's heart anew. She knew well, firsthand, just how skilled a swordfighter Rue was. Still, she feared for him.

Rue's blade met Jad's with a satisfying clash, instantly pushing Jad into the defensive. Rue laid a gash right away to Jad's shoulder and his blood welled, staining his white shirt. Determination shone on Jad's features as his swordplay grew more confident. Jad pushed back with vengeance.

Lilane watched Jad look for an opening in Rue's tight offensive strategy. He found it. Lashing out quickly, risking the bite of Rue's blade, Jad aimed for his throat.

Cold fear washed over Lilane. She couldn't scream, couldn't move. Rue darted to the side at the last moment and Jad laid a stroke high on his chest instead. Blood washed out from the cut on Rue's chest.

Lilane gasped. She hoped it was shallow.

"Been practicing, Jad," Rue bit off.

Jad answered by lunging forward, undoubtedly emboldened by his recent success. Rue sidestepped him and Jad went past him. Rue swung around and caught Jad as he turned, taking him by surprise.

It was enough.

That action turned the tide in Rue's favor. Jad stumbled back under the onslaught of Rue's sword. He staggered back, closer and closer to where Lilane stood. She watched in horror and awe, wanting Rue to be victorious, but at the same time not eager to see him have to kill his friend.

As if in slow motion, Jad turned toward Lilane and narrowed his eyes. Blood streamed from the deep gash on his shoulder, staining his white shirt nearly black. Jad hefted his sword and ran at her.

She whirled away, feeling the tip of the blade graze her upper chest. It sliced through her dress and drew blood. White-hot pain flooded her body. She tripped and fell to the ground. Hot blood rushed over her skin and pain blossomed.

The sight of the blood on her seemed to make Rue go insane. Jad turned to Rue and raised his sword, but he never had a chance. Rue lunged toward Jad and ran him through. No hesitation. No mercy. No surrender allowed.

Eyes wide with surprise, Jad slumped to his knees and Rue pulled his sword from his body. Sorrow overtook Rue's expression as Jad collapsed and stilled.

Everything on top of the tower went silent. Below, the sounds of victorious cheers echoed — all in Nordanese.

Rue looked down at her where she still lay sprawled. His chest heaved with exertion. He was wet from the rain and undoubtedly sweat. "He almost killed you," he rasped.

Lilane stood with a hand pressed to her chest. Blood soaked through her rain-saturated dress and seeped between her fingers. She nodded. She wanted to say *'he almost killed you, too,'* but she couldn't get her vocal cords to function.

Rue let his sword fall to the ground where it hit the stone with a clatter. He staggered toward her and crushed her to him, careful of both their wounds.

His hands fisted in her hair and he brushed his lips back and forth over the crown of her head. "I love you. I love you," he whispered over and over.

She encircled his waist and held him against her. The tears came hot and heavy—the first she could remember shedding in a long time. Cathartic grief welled up, scraped from the very depths of her soul. The tears came in a torrent...not for herself, but for her lost family, her lost friend, and the near loss of the man she'd grown to love so very, very much.

Rue held her as the sobs racked her. Together they sank to the stone floor beneath them. The action pained her wound, but it didn't matter. She clung to Rue as though he alone held her life in his hands.

And maybe he did.

He stroked her hair and murmured to her until finally she calmed. She pulled away from him. "I almost lost you."

"But you didn't. I'm not going anywhere, Lilane. I promise."

She sniffled and peeled back the edge of his shirt, exposing the nasty gash high on the left side of his chest. He very gently touched hers, near as high as her collarbone on her left side. "We'll have matching scars," he said.

All Lilane could do was sigh in relief that it was over and they were both still alive. She closed her eyes and leaned her head against his right shoulder, grimacing at the pain of her wound. Her shock was wearing off and the impact of her injury was making itself known.

The sound of fluttering wings filled the air.

Lilane lifted her head to see hundreds of Aviat soaring up over the top of the tower, headed for the sky. A hush fell over the entire Priestdom—all that could be heard was the sound of wings beating the open air. Lilane watched in absolute awe as all kinds of different Aviat soared above them—darting through the air currents and swooping through low-hanging clouds.

"Oh, my Goddess," Lilane murmured.

"Yes," breathed Rue. "Finally."

A small woman with the wings of what Lilane suspected to be sparrow hovered in the air in front of them. "Thank you, Rue," she said with tears shining in eyes. "Thank you so much."

"You and your family be careful making your way to Nordan, Ana."

"We will. See you there!" she exclaimed with a smile and swooped away.

"That reminds me," said Rue.

"What?"

"We should also leave. Time to go back to Nordan. Are you able to travel a short distance with your wound that way? I don't want you here, Lilane. Even though the Nordanese have taken the Priestdom, it's still volatile here."

"Will Anaisse be all right?" Lilane felt concern for the woman. After her own fashion, Lady Anaisse had tried to help her.

"The Nordanese will treat the captives with care, Lilane. You know that. Especially the daughter of the Supreme."

"Yes."

"Ready to fly?"

"Ready to go home," she said in a heartfelt whisper.

A shadow moved in Rue's eyes. She wondered if he thought the same thing she did—what would happen at the Nordanese border? She wasn't sure she knew herself.

She looked away, deep in thought. The pain of her wound had traded itself for another kind of pain.

Rue gathered her into his arms and stood. Blood flowed anew from his wound, but he didn't so much as grimace. Two running steps and a launch off the top of the tower had them in the air and headed north.

Home.

Chapter Eleven

They stopped at small cottage in the forest near the border of Nordan and Sudhra. Rue set Lilane to her feet in the now drying leaves scattered by the storm. The thunderstorm had been a harbinger of autumn by shedding the leaves from the trees prematurely and bringing cold air in behind it.

Lilane shivered and Rue felt regret at having to push her so hard. They were cold, tired, and needed their wounds tended. All the same, it had been necessary they put as much distance between themselves and the Supreme Priestdom as possible.

"I'll gather some wood for a fire and we'll get warm," he said. "I have supplies in the cabin, as long as no one has looted them."

"I'll help you gather wood—"

"No, Lilane. I can do it on my own. You need to take it easy." He guided her to the cottage and unlocked the door. The inside smelled musty from being closed up for so long, but it appeared no one had been inside. A hearth dominated one wall of the one-room building. Two chairs flanked the fireplace. A table stood on the opposite end of the cabin. A double bed dominated the corner opposite the table. Alongside of it stood a cabinet containing some food stores, and what Rue was most interested in at the moment, supplies to treat wounds. He guided her toward the bed and then headed back out to find wood to burn.

He picked up a piece of deadwood and grimaced at the pain it caused him. He stood to find Lilane standing in front of him. Her eyes were deep and somber as she regarded him. "I *want* to help you."

He nodded once and looked away—toward the north and the border of Nordan. Would he be traveling alone on the morrow, after they'd crossed into that land?

They gathered enough deadfall and tinder to start a fire and headed inside. Rue arranged it all and ignited it in the hearth. The crackling embers drove the chill away.

He turned to Lilane, who'd been uncharacteristically quiet, but, then, so had he. "First, we have to treat our wounds." He walked to the cabinet and pulled out what he needed. "Then get some food and water in us." He nodded at the bed. "And get some sleep. We'll feel a lot better after that."

She walked toward him. "Take your shirt off."

He shook his head. "Not a chance. You first. Pull off your gown and sit down on that bed."

She acquiesced with a tired nod of her head and did as he'd requested. He picked up her torn, blood-soaked gown and tossed it on the fire. She made a noise of concern. "I have a fresh clothing here for you," he said.

He walked toward her with a bottle of something in his hand, a sponge and some bandages. Firelight danced over the luscious curves of her nude body, but he couldn't enjoy the sight, not when that gash profaned the beauty of her chest.

"You kept clothing for your former...students?" she asked in a solemn voice.

"No, for my mistresses."

She looked up in surprise. "Whenever did you have time for those?"

He laughed. "A man always has time for those."

She looked down and away.

"That is, until he meets the right woman and doesn't feel a need for others anymore."

She bit her bottom lip and kept her gaze averted. He set his things on the bed, pulled a blanket from the back of a chair and tucked her into it. She snuggled against it gratefully. Rue sat on the bed in front of her and moistened the sponge with some of the antiseptic herbal solution from the bottle. It was a product made especially for sword wounds.

He pushed her heavy hair away from the wound and settled the mass behind one shoulder. Carefully, delicately, he bathed the blood away, starting at the edge of the wound and moving progressively closer in.

He breathed a sigh of relief. "It's not as bad as I'd feared. You will not have to have it stitched closed."

She glanced at his chest. "I'll bet you good flourentimes yours will."

"Maybe so. Let's get you taken care of first."

He cleaned it, disinfected it, and wrapped the bandage around her upper chest. "Does the wound pain you?"

She moved her shoulders a bit, testing her flexibility with the bandage, he assumed. "It's very sore, but it feels better. Thank you."

He helped her don a fresh gown and she stood immediately. It was a very fine, white linen and too large for her. The neckline slipped over one smooth shoulder. He could see the outline of her lush body as she stood in front him, backlit by the firelight. His muscles tensed at the sight. His body always responded quickly to Lilane.

"Let's see to your wound," she said, taking up the antiseptic and a clean sponge.

Rue waited patiently while she fussed over him, in turn wincing at her ministrations and stopping himself from grabbing her around the waist and settling her in his lap.

Finally she stood back and looked at him. Her face had paled. "You need stitches, Rue. The wound goes deep."

He frowned. "Are you all right?"

"I'm...fine. I just want to see this wound closed up. Do you have a needle and thread?"

"In the cabinet with the rest of the supplies. I'll get it."

She pushed gently on his arm when he went to stand. "I'll get it. Stay there."

He watched as she got the supplies she needed and burned the needle with the fiery end of a branch from the fire. With care she stitched the wound up and wrapped a bandage around his chest.

She sat beside him on the bed and drew a shaky breath. Concern flooded him. "I'll make us some dinner, Lilane. Then let's sleep, all right?" He moved to take some of the stored food from the cabinet—dried mixings for a stew, which he combined with fresh water from the spring near the cottage and cooked in the kettle over the fire.

By the time he'd finished, Lilane had wrapped herself up in the quilt on the bed and fallen fast asleep. He brushed a tendril of hair away from her face as he watched the steady rise and fall of her chest.

On the morrow would she leave him after all? Her eyes said she would.

* * * * *

Anaisse stood on the balcony of her chamber, overlooking the gardens. Her sleeping gown moved and shifted with the breeze, brushing her body like a gloved hand. Her long, freed hair moved around her. Below her the flowers shivered delicately. Most had furled their petals for autumn already.

The Nordanese had been far more humane than she'd ever believed they would be, treating those they'd captured with respect and deference. Still, her pride, along with her country's, was badly piqued. Sudhra had set out to conquer and instead been conquered.

Her father and his advisors were under guard. Lord Gregor had told her he planned to talk with them over the next few days in an effort to work some sort of alliance between their peoples. Gregor had said *alliance* with a certain amount of sexual heat in his green eyes. Anaisse swallowed hard, wondering how much of a role she'd have to play in such an arrangement.

Gregor.

She hugged herself and swallowed hard. She'd met him once a few years ago when she'd visited his lorddom with her father. Gregor was a good-looking man in a savage sort of way. He possessed the body of a warrior, strong and honed by strenuous physical activity. His face was somewhere left of handsome, looking as though it'd been hewn from a hunk of granite...but his mouth. Anaisse closed her eyes for a moment, envisioning it. *Anot*, his mouth was beautiful. He had full, nicely shaped lips that smiled very rarely, but when he did, it was breathtaking.

Despite his rare smile, there was an edge of darkness to him, something bordering on the edge of dangerousness.

Anaisse shivered. She hoped her father wouldn't use her as a bargaining chip. Gregor was the kind of man who would chew her up and spit her out. The problem was, she feared she'd enjoy it. The man touched something deep inside her. Some dark place she kept all her desires locked down and away.

Anaisse turned and walked back into her room, closing the double doors of the balcony behind her and drawing the curtains closed. An armed guard stood watch outside her door, making her feel safe in an odd way.

She picked up her lantern and set it on her bedside table. Then she flipped the covers back and crawled into bed. She sighed as the softness of the mattress cushioned her body and the blankets enveloped her.

Anaisse reached over, snuffed the light and closed her eyes. The heavy hands of sleep beckoned and she didn't resist.

A shuffling sound awoke her in the dead of night. Her eyes came open and she sat up, glancing around her chamber. The moonlight bleached the color from the room and cast long, shifting shadows.

"Who's there?" she asked. Nothing. She waited several more moments, but no other sound met her ears. Perhaps she dreamt it. She snuggled back down into her bed.

Another shuffling sound came from somewhere near the door.

Anaisse bolted upright and grabbed for her lantern. "Who's there?" she asked the darkness.

Out of the shadows by the door walked three men. She recognized one of them. "Lord Vant? What are you doing in my chamber in the middle of the night?" She hated the tinny note of fear in her voice.

He said nothing. He only stalked toward her. She tried to slide out the other side of the bed, but he grabbed her arm. He pressed a damp piece of material over her mouth. She struggled and tried to bite him, but he grabbed her nape with strong hands so she couldn't move her head.

A sweet cloying smell emanated from the material. Anaisse held her breath, kicking the blankets off and clawing at his arm. Lord Vant let out a muffled cry of pain and she knew with a measure of satisfaction that she'd drawn blood. Still, he held her.

Finally the need to breathe became paramount. It was either that or pass out. Anaisse drew a deep draught through the saturated material. Her vision almost instantly began to dim. Her body went oddly limp.

"We're here to abduct you, my lady," came Vant's pleased voice.

It was the last thing she heard before darkness took her.

* * * * *

Lilane woke slowly, first feeling her wound, hot and sore in her chest—then feeling Rue's strong, protective arms around her. Morning sunlight slanted in through the windows. Something bubbled in the kettle hanging over the fire, and it filled the small cottage with the aroma of carrots and meat. It was a lovely dream, she decided, so domestic, warm and safe. She snuggled into Rue's arms and enjoyed it. How nice it would be to live here with him. But she knew, all too well, that fairy tale was better to left to naïve children.

She knew that as much as she wanted to stay with Rue forever, she couldn't. Almost losing him the day before had brought that point home to her in a painful way. To stay with Rue meant one day having to watch him die...as she'd watched Dal die.

She closed her eyes as the images assaulted her. She'd reached Dal after he'd crumpled to the ground and the soldier who'd run him through had stridden away. With bloodstained hands, he'd gripped the skirts of her gown, trying to speak and failing. Instead he'd taken his dagger and pressed it into her palm, and then his eyes had gone unseeing—his body heavy and limp.

Her parents she'd found in their cottage. The soldiers had set it aflame and she'd run back in to get them out. Through the choking smoke and falling rafters, she'd seen them prone on the rush-strewn floor. Lilane had run to them both only to find them beyond saving.

With Dal and her family gone, she'd wished for death then. If a soldier had come for her, she would not have raised a finger in her own defense. But the Goddess Ariane had a bitter sense of humor. Of all the days that a Sudhraian would not accost her, it was the one day Lilane would have welcomed it.

Rue shifted beside her and stood. She watched through slitted eyes as he spooned up two bowls of the stew and poured two tall glasses of water. He'd been up earlier, she guessed, preparing their meal.

Her stomach growled loudly and she could feign sleep no longer. She sat up, sniffing at the scent of the food.

"Come and eat, Lilane," said Rue. "You fell asleep last night before the stew was heated."

She stood, walked to him and took the bowl he offered. Together they sat at the table and ate.

"After we eat I'll change your bandage and we'll head out. We're completing our journey to Nordan today."

She looked down and pushed a carrot around her bowl. She'd suddenly lost her appetite. She tried to force herself to tell him she'd be leaving him as soon as they crossed the border, but she couldn't compel her vocal cords into action.

* * * * *

Rue and Lilane passed the border in early afternoon, traveling by air since they had no horses.

Lilane blew a breath of pure relief when her feet touched Nordanese soil. Rue had landed them in the middle of a copse. The forest floor was thick with fallen leaves from the storm that had blown through, but the sky was clear now—bright blue and cloudless. The sight was in direct contrast to her emotions.

She stepped from Rue's embrace with reluctance.

Rue closed his wings and turned to her. "So this is it, Lilane," he said. "Here's where I set you free, though you were free a long time ago, really. You can stay with me." He glanced away, betraying his emotion. "I want you to stay with me."

"I...I cannot, Rue," she said simply. "I'm sorry."

He closed the distance between them so quickly it stole her breath. He took her in his arms and tipped her chin to his face. "Do you really think I'll let you leave me? I love you, Lilane, and you love me. Don't let your fears come between what we could have together. You are my bonded mate. We are meant to be together."

She furrowed her brow. "What?"

"You have Aviat somewhere in your bloodline. It's not much and it's very diluted, but it's there. It's enough to make you and I a bonded Aviat pair, Lilane. It's how I knew you were in danger at the Priestdom. It's how I knew where to look for you."

Confusion swirled through her mind. Could it be true? It would explain her instant attraction to him. She shook her head. If anything, it made the need to leave him more acute. "Rue, that may be true, but it doesn't matter."

"What about this then? Doesn't this matter?" Anger laced his tone. He lowered his head to hers and rubbed his lips slowly…so slowly across hers. Before he'd even kissed her, before he'd parted her lips and slid his tongue in to dance against hers, her body had answered his call. Her sex plumped, readying itself for him. Her nipples hardened and her breathing and heart rate went into double time.

She pushed him away. "No," she said with finality.

"What?"

"It seems like ages ago now, but when we first met you told me to say no if I wanted you stop." She looked away and her voice dropped a notch. "No, Rue."

Silence.

Tears stung Lilane's eyes as she heard him turn and walk away.

She waited until she could hear his footsteps no longer, then sank down and covered her face with her hands. Grief poured out of her, pounded her every bit as harshly as the day she'd lost Dal and her parents. It wasn't supposed to be this way. She was supposed to feel free of the attachments that would cause her heartbreak. She was supposed to feel blessedly numb, not this heart crushing pain that stole her very breath.

Goddess. What had she done?

Anaisse's words came back to her; *you can't live your life in fear of loss. You must take the loves and joys you find today and not think about the tomorrows. To push Rue away because you're afraid is the same thing as losing him. You'll still be grief-stricken in the end.*

Could it be that the grief she tried so hard to avoid was inevitable no matter how close her ties with those she loved? Could it be she would either feel it when Rue died, or she'd feel it now, after they'd been parted? Had she simply traded one kind of pain for another, with the addition of less love and passion in her life?

"Rue," she yelled suddenly.

She scrambled to her feet and ran in the direction he'd gone. She was stupid for ever thinking she could leave him. She had to find him before he'd left. Hopefully he would forgive her. She rounded a large oak not far away and tipped her head up to search the skies.

"Lilane."

Glancing around frantically, she saw him standing not far away. He idly twirled a leaf by the stem.

She ran to him and launched herself into his arms. A torrent of words fell from her lips. "I'm so sorry. I don't know what I was thinking. Please forgive me!"

He held her close and stroked her hair. "I stayed, hoping you'd come to your senses. Otherwise I was going to come back and capture you again. There's no way I'd ever let you leave me."

She closed her eyes and buried her face in his chest, inhaling the rich, masculine scent of him. "I love you, Rue," she murmured.

He sighed. "Those are the words I wanted to hear. I love you too, Lilane."

She stood on her tiptoes and kissed him. He pulled her up against him and kissed her back in a way that left no doubt in her mind that he loved her completely. Desire flared low within her as he parted her lips and branded her tongue with that knowledge. This time she had no reason to tamp it down or deny it, so it spread slowly outward, consuming her.

She broke the kiss, lowered her eyes demurely and stepped away from him.

"I have to have you now, Lilane. Don't deny me," he warned.

Before he could move to take her up again, she raised a hand to stay him.

Catching and holding his gaze, she slid her slippers off. Then slowly, teasingly, she pulled the white linen gown over her head and cast it to the ground, leaving her nude to the caress of the breeze.

He took a step forward with an aroused, impatient growl, and she stopped him with a single look of warning. She raised her hands and undid her long braid, one careful link at a time. His gaze roved over her body hungrily as his shoulders hunched a little and his muscles tensed. "What are you doing, Lilane?"

Her only response was a mischievous smile. She shook her hair out and ran her fingers through it. The ends brushed her waist when she moved or the breeze blew. Her sex was plumped; ready for anything Rue had planned for it. Her nipples were high, rosy and very, very hard. Rue's gaze caressed them.

She cupped her breasts in her hands. "Do you want to touch them?"

His hands clenched. "I want to worship them with not only my hands, but my lips and tongue. I want to suck on them until I bring you to climax by that action alone."

She shivered at the thought. Holding his gaze, she caressed her nipples with her thumbs. "Would you touch them like this?" she asked breathlessly.

He groaned. "Yes."

She pulled on them gently, the action causing her pussy to grow even wetter. "And like this?"

"Yes. Show me how else I would touch you," he rasped. His cock was rock hard and rigid, obviously straining against his pants.

One hand trailed very slowly down her abdomen and ran over the satin skin of her clean-shaven mound. "Do you mean how you'd touch me here?" The pad of her middle finger rubbed over her clit as she slid her hand between her thighs. She bit her lower lip as a shudder ran through her.

"Lay down and bring yourself to climax for me, love," he commanded in a dark voice. Somewhere, somehow the power had shifted from her to him. "Go on," he purred. "Make me crazy."

She laid down in the soft bed the fallen leaves made on the forest floor and spread her legs for him. One hand worked her breasts and the other her pussy as she closed her eyes and imagined it was Rue that touched her now. Her breathing hitched.

"Touch yourself, Lilane. Come for me."

She slid her fingertips over her damp sex, rubbing at her clit that had pulled out of its hood long ago. She slipped two fingers into her pussy and arched her back.

"Yes, that's it," he rasped.

She played with her breast with one hand, rolling the nipple between her fingers, and thrust into her sex with her fingers. Under Rue's hot, aroused gaze, a powerful climax built, tensing her muscles and causing her to arch her neck.

His hot body was over her suddenly, his teeth nipping at the sensitive skin of her throat. "Let it go," he murmured against her skin. "Come for me."

"Rue!" she cried as the orgasm ripped through her. Tremor after pleasurable tremor racked her body.

He was at her sex, gently pulling her hand away. He lapped at her clit, alternating between sucking and gently rasping at it with the very edge of his teeth. It extended her climax, drawing it out until she was chanting his name to the trees around them.

He slipped two broad fingers within her and found that spot way deep within where it felt so good. He rubbed his fingertips over it and over it, catapulting her directly into another orgasm. This one racked her to her very womb and stole her breath. Her fingers locked on his shoulders as she rode it out.

He laid a kiss to her inner thigh after she'd come down from her pleasurable high. "Get on your hands and knees," he commanded.

She turned over and spread her legs wide apart when he nudged at them with his knee. He licked her pussy, drawing a low moan from her and ran his fingers over her sex, playing with her clit and dipping into her vagina. Her clit was sensitive now from being stimulated twice in a row to orgasm, but her body was still unbelievably aroused.

Rue could play her body like it was an instrument—he plunked certain chords and her body made sweet music. It was as simple as that.

He lowered his trews and she felt the head of his cock pushing at her entrance. "Ready, love?"

"Yes." She wanted to feel him in her so badly.

He slid in to the hilt and Lilane cried out. At this angle he had ultimate penetration and the head of his cock brushed over that place within her made so deliciously sensitive from his recent ministration. She fisted a hand and hit the ground. "Oh, yes."

He shafted her slow and easy at first and then faster and faster. With her legs spread apart so wide, she felt completely and utterly at his mercy...and she loved it. He hammered into her, the head of his cock rasping against the walls of her pussy unrelentingly, driving her impossibly toward climax once more.

He slowed and came to halt. She whimpered. Her body was on fire; every nerve ending in her body tingled. "No...I want to see your face when I make you come," he said in a voice rough with arousal.

He had her flipped and impaled in record time and was thrusting into her once more. He slid a hand to her nape and brought his mouth to her throat, careful to keep himself elevated enough not to agitate their wounds. He nibbled on the sensitive skin there, biting once in a while possessively. Every thrust in this position rubbed at her clit.

"I love you, Lilane," he murmured.

Her body tensed to come and he rose up to watch her face. She exploded beneath him, her vaginal muscles tensing and contracting around his cock. He drove deep inside her a last time and came. Hot seed spurted deep within her as he cried out her name.

They lay together, a tangle of limbs, heartbeat and heaving breath. Lilane was sure that to any on-looker they would seem like one animal with no ending and no beginning to a separation. Tears of intense happiness pricked her eyes.

She was finally home.

The Union
Autumn Pleasure

Chapter One

Anaisse breathed in carefully through her nose and exhaled through her mouth in order to remain calm. The hood covering her head didn't allow much airflow and heightened the panic she felt. Staying calm was key. For the sixtieth time since it all began, she reminded herself that fear would do her no good.

Lord Vant, a man she'd known for years and someone she'd always trusted, if not perhaps liked, had abducted her. Anaisse had known Vant since childhood, and he'd been a trusted friend and advisor to her father, the Supreme of Sudhra. Those facts made the present circumstances even more terrifying.

Her abductors had forced her to inhale the fumes of an herbal concoction that had caused her to lose consciousness. When she'd awoken—a day ago? Four days? Ten?—she'd had this hood over her head and had been tied at ankle and wrist. They only removed the sack when she had to eat or use the privy. At those times, she examined her surroundings thoroughly, hoping to find something she could use, anything to help her escape and took note of the exits for the time she did escape.

Anaisse knew she had to try. These men were the Ganotte, a radical religious sect that dealt in female sex slaves and the subjugation of women in general. Nordan, a country to their north, had defeated her country, Sudhra. The Nordanese worshipped the Goddess Ariane, and Sudhra worshipped the God Anot. The goal of the Ganotte was simple, to keep Sudhra from worshipping the Goddess Ariane.

Anaisse wondered how she, a daughter of the Supreme of Sudhra, fit into their objectives. She also wondered how they'd gotten past the Nordanese guards who'd been protecting her. However, they had and now they were in some smelly, old abandoned cottage in the middle of the forest.

The Ganotte. The mere thought of them choked her throat with grief. Years ago they'd raped and beaten her sister, Sania, to death. They hadn't meant to. After all, she'd been their only bargaining chip to use against her father, but it had happened all the same. One of her sister's captors had grown too zealous in his "play" and had killed her. A sob caught in her chest as Anaisse remembered her sister's broken body the night they'd brought her home. Oh, how she'd missed Sania over the years. They hadn't touched Anaisse…yet. Perhaps they'd learned their lesson with her sister.

Or perhaps they just hadn't gotten around to it yet.

She squeezed her eyes shut. *Anot!* She had to get out here before something truly horrid happened.

Time had ceased to be of meaning. She had no idea how long she'd been in the cottage and tended by these horrible men. She hadn't screamed or cried. Pure and perfect terror stole away the indulgent luxury of tears, leaving only a cold, hard metallic tang on her tongue and a silent screaming in her mind.

All she knew was that she needed a bath terribly and that she'd lost a small bit of her sanity.

She squeezed her eyes shut. How had it been for her sister?

The door opened on squeaky hinges. The sound of a guard's shuffling feet met her ears. She heard water being poured into a glass. "Thirsty?" the man growled.

She shook her head. "I have to use the privy."

"Again?"

She nodded.

He grumbled something under his breath, walked over and untied the bonds binding her ankles. She rotated them, trying to work the feeling back into her calves and thighs. The rope they used chafed her skin badly. She felt dried blood crack where it had congealed. Fresh blood trickled down her instep.

Rough hands pulled her to her feet, and she stifled a cry of pain. "Come on then," he snapped. By her upper arm, he pulled her forward.

She'd been in her nightgown when they'd taken her and she felt far too exposed. Her bare feet scraped over the wooden floor of the cottage as her captor dragged her toward the door. When she fell, he paid no heed and continued to yank her along. As she fought to right herself, she stumbled over the hem of her nightgown and heard the material rip. Cold fear flashed through her. All she needed was to inadvertently expose her body to these men. That wouldn't help things at all.

Her captor seemed to take no notice, however. He opened the front door of the cottage and pulled her through. Sharp twigs and rocks cut into the tender flesh of her feet as he led her to the bushes.

He stopped and ripped the hood off. She blinked.

Nighttime.

Dark forest all around lit by the full moon.

The scowling face of a hulking bald man.

He was a new one and was at least three times her weight. Her muscles were weak from a lack of exercise and malnourishment. She had no hope of escape, but she had to try.

"Will you not untie my hands?" She asked every time and every time came the same answer no matter the captor, leaving her to struggle awkwardly as she urinated.

"Nay."

She bowed her head as if in defeat and acted as though she was heading into the bushes. At the same time, she clasped her hands together tightly. She turned, bringing her hands up—*way up*—fast and hard, straight into the giant's nose. A pain so sharp it near brought her to her knees exploded in her hands. He bellowed and covered his face.

Anaisse wasted no time gawking. She whirled and ran, her nightgown billowing out like a beacon in the darkness. Branches caught in her hair and yanked strands from her tender scalp.

They raked over her cheeks until blood trickled into her mouth. The unforgiving forest floor ripped and tore at her feet. She struggled to stay moving and upright without the balance unbound hands would have provided.

"You'll be sorry for that!" her captor bellowed behind her. He was too close...far too close.

Thick fingers wound into her hair and he toppled her to the ground. Her agonized scream of terror and disappointment rent the forest air. She kicked and struggled beneath him. Her nails broke on the hard-packed earth as she gouged it, fighting to free herself from his weight.

Now she screamed.

Now she cried.

It was too much to taste freedom and have it yanked away.

The giant on top of her stilled, then slumped down on her in deadweight, crushing the air from her lungs.

Anaisse also went still, wondering what had happened. Dark, silent forms surrounded her. Their steps crunched the fallen leaves.

A man approached and pushed the giant off her with a booted foot. As he knelt next to her, she wiggled away from him and laid on her side with her bound hands up to ward him off. Her breath came fast and harsh in air that had more than a whisper of the autumn in it.

"Lady Anaisse, it's me, Lord Gregor," he said in Sudhraian.

Gregor. He was a Nordanese. One of the country's most powerful lords, no less. He was an enemy, but a far preferable one to the Ganotte at this point in time.

He leaned into a swath of silver moonlight. It highlighted the savagely masculine lines of his face. His eyes were too shadowed for her to see, but there was concern in his voice. It seemed a shocking admission of feeling from this, the most stoic of men she'd ever met.

She didn't move. She barely breathed. Was it over? Could she hope?

"Are you all right?" He reached for her, gentling her with small, soothing brushes of his fingers on her upper arm. "What did they do to you, my lady?" Steel threaded his voice now.

She opened her mouth to say she was unharmed for the most part, only scared, but an agonized croak issued forth instead.

He drew her carefully into his arms as though he feared she would struggle against him and try to bolt.

The feeling of strong, protective arms around her, the body heat from someone who actually cared if she lived or died, and the rumbling of Gregor's low voice had her relaxing against him, closing her eyes. Perhaps she was safe now.

"Magus!"

Her eyes flew open and she stiffened at the sound of one her captor's voices issuing through the trees from the direction of the cottage. Gregor's body also went on alert.

"Magus, I swear to Anot, you touch that woman and Vant will fillet your dick with a rusty blade!"

"Tol, take Lady Anaisse," Gregor commanded in whispered Nordanese.

Anaisse found herself passed into another pair of comforting strong arms. She stiffened in them as she watched Gregor and his men walk through the woods toward the cottage.

Tol soothed her in Nordanese. "Don't worry. Lord Gregor is about to show those men the sharp end of his sword. I'll wager they're not going to like it very much."

Those were some of the most comforting words she'd heard in a long, long time. She relaxed.

"You're the hope of Sudhra and Nordan, after all. Harming you cannot go unpunished. You're the one who will unite our two countries in peace, hopefully."

She tensed and scowled, wondering what he could mean…

"No one hurts a woman as special to Gregor as you are. You're his intended…ah…*wiff*, after all."

Anaisse stiffened and finally found her voice. "You mean, *wife*."

"Yes, that's it. We have no word in Nordanese with the exact same meaning and my Sudhraian is not good."

"I'm supposed to marry Gregor?" she asked in a low voice. She was going from one distress to another. She'd suspected her father meant to bargain her off to the enemy because of some veiled comments Gregor had made before she'd been abducted. But to hear it like this. For real. For certain… She'd been bartered off to a pagan barbarian.

Sounds of battle met her ears. Sounds of commotion and of agony and death.

Anaisse buried her face in Tol's leather vest. The shock of it all numbed her through. All she could do was concentrate on her breathing—in through her nose, out through her mouth.

"Shhh, my lady. Perhaps this is too much for you after all you've been through."

She didn't answer. Couldn't answer. For the second time she was uncharacteristically speechless.

Tol drew something from his pocket and broke off the end. He held it under her nose. She noted that it was slightly bitter smelling before she realized what it was. Panic consumed her. No! This was the last thing she wanted. Not more loss of control. Not more choices taken from her.

"Inhale, my lady, and dream sweetly. When you awaken this will all be over."

"Bastard…" she breathed angrily at him as thick waves of darkness swallowed her.

* * * * *

Gregor watched Anaisse sleep. The healer said she should awaken soon. The herbal concoction Tol had administered should be wearing off at any time. She'd slept the whole night and the entire day but still darkness marred the delicate skin beneath her eyes.

Gregor had taken advantage of her unconsciousness and traveled at a swift pace. They'd arrived in his lorddom only an hour ago. He'd left the dealings in Sudhra to Lord Marken and the other lords of Nordan for now. For the time being, he had another task to undertake, one no less important to the wellbeing of both Nordan and Sudhra.

Her hair, normally thick and a rich, dark brown, was now tangled and lank. Though the healer had cleaned the worst of the blood from her wrists, ankles and feet much of it still remained, along with painful looking wounds. In places, her skin was still stained pink. Her right hand was bruised beyond belief.

She was clad in only her sleeping shift that was torn in several places, revealing wide swathes of creamy skin. He'd covered her with a blanket to keep her warm.

Anger clouded his vision as his gaze wandered to her face. A bruise marred her cheek where one of her captors had likely backhanded her.

In Nordan there was great punishment for harming a woman. Gregor and his men had meted it out swiftly, decisively and without mercy in the Sudhraian woods. After all, Sudhra now fell under Nordanese law.

Taking that action had only slightly quelled the demons that had roared inside him at the sight of Anaisse cowering in fear from him on the cold, leaf-strewn ground. He'd been attracted to Anaisse since the first time he'd met her. She was so proud, so strong. Seeing her like that had broken a part of him within.

She moved and made a small noise in her throat as she woke up. He ran a hand through his hair, regretting not having had time to bathe. At least he'd washed the blood from himself.

Her dark brown eyes came open and stared into his. She didn't move.

"Are you well?" he asked.

She didn't answer. Instead, she carefully pushed herself up and put a hand to her head and groaned. "Where am I?"

"You're in my lorddom." He cleared his throat. "You're safe now," he added.

"I doubt *that* very much," she muttered under her breath.

"Would you like something? A drink of water, perhaps? You've been out for a while now."

She shot him a sharp look from under her dark lashes. There was a comforting flare of the Anaisse he knew in that icy glance. "That's right. Your man gave me odinroot fumes."

"I know."

"I didn't wish to lose consciousness."

"He believed it was in your best interest to not be aware of the battle. He thought he was protecting you."

"Well, he was wrong. I'm not some weak chit to faint at the sight of blood or the sound of battle."

Aye, that was true enough. Still, Tol had acted well in Gregor's opinion. Sometimes people didn't know what was best for them when they were under great duress. Silence reigned for several long moments. Finally Gregor moved to take her foot in his hand.

"What are you doing?" she asked, alarmed.

"I only wish to examine one particularly bad cut, my lady." In truth he was looking for an excuse—any excuse—to touch her. He examined the deep cut that ran along her heel. It truly did need the healer's close attention. Then he ran his thumb along the gentle arch of her instep. Gooseflesh appeared on her calf and she snatched her small, beaten foot away.

"Inspecting your property already?" she asked.

"What do you mean?"

She raised her chin, her eyes snapping. "I heard I am to be your wife."

"Yes. It was agreed upon as the best course of action while I was in Sudhra. The union has your father's blessings."

"What about mine?" she snapped.

"Your father told me you fully expected him to arrange a match for you. I was told the highborn women of Sudhra never have a say in the men they marry and that you would not balk—"

"Tell me why I should marry you. Tell me why I should not balk."

He sighed. "Lady Anaisse, you are injured, exhausted, and overwrought. You've been through much. You were with those men for an entire week. Perhaps you should bathe, have something to eat and let the healer tend you. She is making herbal pastes for your wounds even now. Get a good night's sleep. Then we can discuss everything at length tomorrow."

She grew pale. "I was there a whole week?"

"Yes, my lady."

"How did you know where I was?"

"We interrogated every person in the Supreme Priestdom suspected to be allied with the Ganotte until we found one that gave us a lead on where they may have taken you."

She fell silent. "Lord Vant was not there when you arrived. He remains free."

"Lord Vant? One of the men called his name into the woods before we attacked them."

"He—he was one of the people that kidnapped me. I've known him since we were young. He was the Sword Master of the Supreme Priestdom."

"Hmmm... I will send word to Lord Marken in the morn to look out for this man."

She nodded. "Yes. That's a good idea." She frowned. "I had the feeling Nordan winning the war had...unbalanced him in his head."

He nodded. "All the more reason to locate the man." He gestured at her hand. "How did your hand become so horribly bruised?"

She glanced down. "I-I hit one of my captors in the nose."

"Ah, that is how you escaped him. I had wondered."

"If you hadn't arrived when you did, I wouldn't have escaped."

He reached out, cupped her cheek in his hand and was happy when she didn't flinch from the intimate gesture. "Who knows, my lady? You're very tenacious. I don't think you're the type to give up easily." And that could work against him, he admitted inwardly.

Her gaze steadied. "I'm not."

Gregor stood. "I will have the servants bring in hot water for a bath and some good, hearty food."

"Thank you." She looked away, cleared her throat, and then looked back at him. "And *thank you*, for rescuing me."

"You half-rescued yourself, my lady. Tomorrow we will talk." He motioned to the door on the side of the chamber. "That door adjoins the chamber I will be sleeping in. Should you ever need me, I am there."

He walked to the door and out of it, casting one last look at the delicate, yet strong woman on the bed before he shut the door.

Gregor walked down the hallway. Yes, he wanted Lady Anaisse of Sudhra, and why he wanted her had nothing to do with political alliances or international relations. But he had a feeling seducing her mind, body, and soul might turn out to be the toughest battle he'd ever waged.

* * * * *

Anaisse combed out her wet hair as she sat before the roaring fire in her chamber and savored the feel of a full belly and a much missed sense of safety. She'd never take the simplicity of safety for granted again. The healer had salved the weals on her wrists and ankles and the cuts and scrapes on her feet. She was now thoroughly washed—twice. She'd felt so defiled she'd needed more than one bath. Aye, she already felt worlds better.

The servants had brought her a long white linen sleeping gown and soft slippers for her bruised and battered feet.

She was perhaps more thankful the servants had all been decently covered than for the clothing. In Nordan open sexual play was commonplace, a part of the cultural fabric of the country. The women here wore a type of material called flaxcloth, which was sheer and left nothing to the imagination. It was designed to entice and lure the men, she supposed.

The chamber they'd given her was richly appointed. A large four-poster bed with dark green canopies dominated the room opposite the hearth. A huge wardrobe made of light-colored wood sat in one corner. A table stood near the hearth with two chairs beside it and a bathtub occupied another corner. Thick rugs scattered the floor. All in all, it reminded her of how a Sudhraian keep might be furnished and made her feel a little more at ease. In fact, if she concentrated, she could almost pretend she was at home.

Except, of course, that her future Nordanese husband's room was right next to hers. She glanced at the door separating her chamber from Gregor's and wondered if he was in there now.

Dropping the comb into her lap, she bit her lip. She'd been drawn to Gregor since the first time she'd visited his lorddom a couple years ago. He was not quite handsome. The strong line of his jaw and the set of his forehead were far too masculine for handsomeness. His eyes were dark and deep—fathomless. Though they never revealed much of what he was thinking. Hard and stoic to a fault was Gregor. His short hair was a deep brown, nearly black. His body was that of a battle-honed warrior. He stood tall and broad-shouldered and hard muscles rippled beneath his clothing when he moved.

His mouth...oh, his mouth was the beauteous Afterworld with its shapely lips, the bottom one slightly fuller than the top. Oh, there was bliss waiting in his kiss, she was sure. She'd fantasized about his mouth before. Fantasized how it would be to kiss him, how it would be to have his mouth on her breast, laving over her nipple with care. How it would be licking over her clit, delving into her passage. She shivered at the thought.

No, she could not deny her attraction to Gregor, but that did not mean she wanted to tie her life inexorably to his until the time one of them died. She feared Gregor was a flame that burned too hot and she would be horribly burned by such a close alliance.

The man had the ability to completely consume her—mind, body and soul.

She sighed. But if his plan was to bind Sudhra and Nordan through marriage, that was a different matter entirely. In that case, she would have no choice but to comply. Though she did not expect such a union to aid the highly damaged relations between the two countries.

Never one to remain passive, she stood. Hesitating only a moment, she limped to the door and knocked. Her mind was awhirl with questions and wonderings. She didn't want to wait until tomorrow morning to discuss all of them with Gregor.

When she heard him call for her to come in, she opened the door and stepped into the fire lit room that was decorated much like hers...and gasped.

Gregor stood before the hearth shirtless. One hand rested on the mantle as he stared down into the fire. There was not a bit of softness anywhere on him. Thick muscle corded his arms, stomach and chest. Low-slung trews made of a soft looking fabric sheathed his powerful thighs. A small amount of dark hair smattered his chest, tapering down to a narrow line that trailed down past the waistband of the trews.

He was even more gorgeous than she'd imagined and the sight of him produced an instant reaction in her body. Her cheeks flushed, her nipples tightened and she grew wet between her thighs.

And she knew she was in trouble.

Chapter Two

Gregor stared at her for a long moment while she fought to get her vocal chords into action. "Are you all right? Do you need the healer?" He walked toward her.

She shook her head. "No, I'm fine. I'm sore and my feet hurt but it's nothing that some time won't heal."

He stood in front of her. "I think you are mistaken, my lady. The wounds you bear within are deep, I'm sure. You were treated as undervalued and inhuman. Those pains will be long in healing."

She snorted in laughter. She couldn't help it. "My lord, do you not think Sudhraian women are not accustomed to being undervalued? Even the highborn women, like myself, who are treated infinitely better than the lowborn ones, grow up *under*valued. Things are not the same in Sudhra as they are in Nordan."

"I know. But I assume this was the first time you'd been trussed up like a pig for slaughter and left to languish on the floor of a dirty cottage." He sounded angry all of a sudden. "Not to mention handled by men who did goddess knows what to you."

She shook her head. "They never raped me. They never even touched me but to drag me around. I think they knew better than to use me that way after they inadvertently k—" she swallowed hard "—killed my sister."

He stood looking at her for several heartbeats, then hummed as though in thought. "Come, let me massage your back."

"W-what?"

"You said you are sore. Let me ease the pain in your muscles."

She scowled. "I came here to talk to you about—"

"The union. I know."

"Yes, so I don't think—"

He moved so fast she had no time to back away, and swept her up into his arms. "You limped over to my room on injured feet because you're so impatient you cannot wait until tomorrow to settle things between us."

She tried to focus on what he was saying. She really did. But the proximity of all that hard male muscle against her drove away most cognitive function. "Uh—what did you say?"

He chuckled and set her on his bed. "You fascinate me. You're proud and strong, yet fragile and feminine all at the same time. Roll over on your stomach now and allow me to massage your back."

She gaped at him for a moment in shock, and then frowned. "No."

"I won't do anything you don't want me to do. You have my word."

She gaped again. He wouldn't do anything she didn't *want* him to do?

"We can talk about the union as I work your muscles," he said.

She shook her head. "I'd rather talk without you touching me."

"I won't talk *unless* I'm touching you."

She sighed. "Oh, fine!" It wasn't like she couldn't resist him.

She rolled over on her stomach. The dark blue covering on his bed was soft and cool against her flushed cheek. He set his hands to her shoulders and began to rub with strong yet gentle pressure. He seemed to know exactly how to loosen up her knotted muscles. She stifled a groan of pleasure. Concentrate on business, she chided herself.

"You and my father expect this match to ease the tension between Nordan and Sudhra, I suppose." Her voice sounded breathy. She cleared her throat and concentrated on hardening it. "It will not work."

He moved down and massaged her upper back. Her nipples peaked under the pressure of his hands on her flesh. Warmth spread out from where he touched her, enveloping her body in comforting pleasure. Arousal tingled in dark, secret places that had never known such sensation. She'd feared he'd have this power over her. It was frightening, yet at the same time she'd thought she'd die if it ceased.

"We believe it will aid the relations. Symbolically, as you and I join, so will Sudhra and Nordan. Nordan is making a great sacrifice in this, as are you," he said.

"I understand that. You are also making a great personal sacrifice," she said softly. "I know well it is not within the boundaries of your culture to link your life with another's in this way."

He moved to her lower back and this time she couldn't stop the sigh of pleasure that escaped her. She felt so warm, so relaxed. So incredibly safe. Suddenly, she realized that not only did she owe her life to this man; she *trusted* her life to this man's hands. His fingers brushed her buttocks and a frisson of pleasure shot through her.

"It's not so much of a hardship, my lady," he said. His voice sounded rougher than it had before.

She stifled a snort of laughter. He lied and flattered to lure her into the arrangement, petted her ego as surely as he petted her body. She sighed in resignation. "I will marry you if you believe it will help our nation's relations. It was what I was born and bred to do, after all. But I will do so only on one condition."

His fingers trailed over her buttocks to her upper thigh. She inhaled sharply and lost her train of thought as he massaged the muscles there until her body felt like butter melting on warm bread. She let out a long sigh.

"What is that?" His already low, gruff voice had dropped impossibly lower. What that a sign of his own arousal?

She fought to regain her reasoning ability. "No—uh—no intimacy between us. The marriage will be but a shell of the true thing, a façade. My people will believe me willingly allied with you and that's all that counts...*ah!*"

He'd nipped her buttock!

She pulled away from him and scrambled to sit up. Shocked, she stared at him. His hair had fallen into his face, his cock strained rigid against his trews and he had a dark, dangerous look in his eyes.

Here was the pagan barbarian she'd expected. Her breath came faster.

"*That* is an unacceptable arrangement," he growled at her.

Scowling, she shook her head. "But why? You will retain your freedom to rut like a stag in mating season with whomever you wish, or *whatever* it is you do here in Nordan." *And I will retain my ability to be my own person and not relinquish my very being to you.*

He crawled toward her on his hands and knees. She tried to scoot away, but he reached out quick as a snake, and grabbed her calf well above her wounds. He pulled her beneath him and her nightgown rode up dangerously high on her thighs. Anaisse was so surprised she didn't even make a noise.

He put his hands on either side of her head and straddled her hips. "I want to *rut* with *you*, Anaisse," he said slowly. "I have wanted you since the first time I saw you. I want to spread your sweet thighs right now and lick and suck on your clit until I feel you shatter in climax beneath me. Then, when you are aroused, relaxed and pliable, I want to free my cock, slide into you and thrust until I feel the muscles of your passage convulse around it during your second peak. I want to hear your cries and moans of ecstasy. I want to taste the inside of your mouth with my tongue and feel your soft breasts beneath my palms."

His gaze flicked down to her pebbled nipples that strained against the thin material of her nightdress. "Tell me you do not also want me. Tell me that if I put my hand between your thighs right now you wouldn't be wet for me."

"I-I'm not," she stammered. "I wouldn't be."

He cocked a dark brow and shifted to her side. She was paralyzed as he placed a gentle hand to the inside of her knee. "That was a challenge issued if I ever heard one, and I don't turn down challenges, my lady."

She jerked at the feel of his hand on her skin and squeezed her eyes shut. Her breath and heart rate sped up.

He dragged his hand up her skin, toward her sex. "With a word, I will cease touching you. That is, if you desire me to stop."

She tried to say stop, but couldn't make the word come out. Her pussy throbbed with heat now, with the desire for his caress, but if she allowed him to do this it would be like losing to him.

Another agonizing inch, and another... His thumb grazed her curls. The heat of his hand radiated out, warming her skin. His fingers made contact, sliding over her swollen, aching vaginal lips. She grit her teeth. It felt so good...

"No!" she forced out.

Gregor gave a feral, frustrated sounding growl and drew his hand back.

Anaisse rolled away from him and got off the bed. She was trembling from head to toe and tingling in her breasts and pussy. *Anot...he* could *consume her.*

One snapping bite and she'd be his.

The words came out in a torrent. "I will agree to this marriage for the sake of my people but only under the condition that you allow me to keep my independence, only if you let me stay my own person. No physical intimacy, Lord Gregor." She turned, wishing she could storm, but all she could do was hobble unsteadily out of the room.

* * * * *

Gregor blocked his opponent's blow and turned to the left, bringing his blunted training blade down solidly on the back of Tol's neck.

Tol gave an enraged howl of defeat and twisted away.

"Never turn your back to your opponent," Gregor chided.

Tol leaned down and braced his hands on his knees. He'd secured his shoulder-length black hair at the nape of his neck, but now it was coming loose. They were both sheened in perspiration and breathing hard. "You don't move like a normal man, Gregor. You're too skilled a warrior." He shook his head. "May I never meet one such as you on the battlefield."

Gregor laughed and wiped his hand across his brow. "And may I always have a warrior such as yourself beside me on the battlefield. You are a fine fighter, Tol. One of my best sparring partners. I would want no other guarding my back in a fight."

Tol straightened. "And you, my friend, are frustrated beyond belief. You are taking all of it out in the sparring ring, aren't you?"

Gregor gave a short laugh. "It is that noticeable? Aye, I'm a little frustrated."

"A little?" Tol walked to the side of the sparring ring and sheathed his sword. He cast him a sidelong look. One Gregor knew well signaled that teasing was sure to follow. "You do have a curious tendency toward monogamy."

"You are one to talk, Tol. It's Melandra you want. That's no secret. If she agreed to monogamy today, you'd fall to her wishes right off and give up all other women."

"Aye, but Melandra does not wish monogamy from me. Therefore, I embrace non-monogamy—" he flashed a smile "— along with every comely woman I can. Your Anaisse also does not ask monogamy of you." Tol shrugged his shoulders at him. "So why do you not take advantage of that and ease your needs with another woman? There are plenty clamoring to warm your bed."

Gregor grabbed his scabbard and slid his training sword home. "I have my reasons," he replied simply.

Tol grunted. "Aye. Well, your *reasons* make you frustrated and even more difficult to best in the sparring ring." He flashed a smile. "Perhaps you should allow her to keep frustrating you so you'll be sharper in future battles."

Gregor grunted. He had no intention of continuing to let Anaisse evade his advances.

"Anaisse is certainly beautiful, though," said Tol.

"Aye."

"You know if she was not your intended that every man in the keep would be after her."

"You included?"

Tol flashed another smile. His blue eyes twinkled. "Oh, aye. Me included."

Gregor slipped his shirt over his head. "She doesn't like you very much, you know."

"Because of the odinroot. I know. I will try and make it up to her."

Gregor gave a short bark of laughter. "Good luck with that, my friend. She is not an easy woman."

Tol shrugged his shirt on. "Ah. But that is why you like her."

"Maybe." Gregor replaced his scabbard on the wall where the other training swords hung and walked toward the door. "Good day, Tol."

"Good day, my lord."

Gregor headed down the corridor, intent on taking a bath. Tol still called him "my lord" once in a while, though they'd been friends since childhood. Tol was now the captain of

Gregor's guard, as well as a good friend. He was in love with a castle woman named Melandra, but in proper Nordanese fashion, Melandra did not want to settle with just one man. It was her prerogative to do so, as it greatly increased her chances of conception to sleep with many men, and she desperately wanted a child. Tol would not admit it out loud, but Gregor knew it hurt him to watch her do it, and retaliated by taking many women to his bed.

He turned into the corridor leading to his chamber and glimpsed a flash of white skirt disappearing around the far end of the long hallway. How he knew it was Anaisse, he could not say. He only knew that he felt her like he'd never felt another person in his life—as though she ran through his bloodstream. As though she were a part of his very being.

He did not understand why that should be. Perhaps it was only fancifulness on his part. Nevertheless, he quickened his pace and overtook her.

She turned toward him. "My lord," she greeted him flatly, as though bored. It was feigned. Intense sexual interest blazed in her eyes, giving her away. Aye she wanted him. She was simply too stubborn to give into it. She was too afraid.

A long gold gown made of shimmering fabric swathed her finely curved body. A Sudhraian-style girdle encircled her waist, pressing her luscious cleavage up to overflowing. Small tinkling crystals and tiny bells hung from it. Her upswept hair was secured within a filigreed golden net. Her bruises were still visible, but fading.

"Where are you rushing off to?" he asked. He allowed his gaze to consume her hungrily from head to toe. The sexual promise in his eyes could leave her with no doubt of his intentions. He was rewarded with a quickening of her breath and an answering flare of heat in her eyes.

She looked away. "Just outside to take a little air." Her gaze snapped to his. "Why am I even answering you? It is none of your concern where I'm going."

She tried to push past him but he reached out and caught her gently, yet firmly, by the upper arm. "Do not make those kinds of accusations, my lady," he warned. "I have no intention of dictating your destination. I was curious, only."

She glanced down at his hand on her arm as if offended and shook it off. "Well, now that your curiosity has been satisfied, I will—"

He took a step toward her, pressing her up against the wall behind her before she could flee. He spread both palms flat against the wall on either side of her head, trapping her. His gaze swept her up and down, finally settling on her face. Her lips were parted and her eyes wide.

"I-I thought you agreed to no intimate contact, Lord Gregor."

"I agreed to nothing, Anaisse. And this is hardly intimate contact."

She swallowed hard and looked up at him. Sexual heat flared hot and hard in her eyes. He glanced down and saw that her nipples were hard and straining against the thin fabric of her dress that jutted above the tight girdle.

He wanted nothing better than to tease her unmercifully until she begged him to take her. He wanted to ease her skirts up and plunge his cock into her tight slit—take her right up against the wall.

He slipped his hand to her waist and fought the urge to lower his mouth to hers. Her breathing hitched. He could practically feel the waves of want rolling off her and how hard she fought it keep it all tamped down.

"You have a place inside you where you keep all your desires locked away. It will be so beautiful when you finally decide to open that door. You will be so wild and free."

She took a ragged breath. "Please," she murmured low. "Please, I beg some time to heal, my lord."

Perhaps he was pushing her too hard. Taking advantage of her without realizing it. He clenched his jaw in frustration. "Of course I will. But remember that you *will* be mine." He pushed away from the wall and backed up. "A part of you already is."

She drew a breath and cast him one long look. "Believe me, I know all too well you possess the key to unlock the door you speak of," she said. She turned and walked away.

Chapter Three

Gregor strode into the great hall where the servants were placing the last of the autumn blooms for the joining ceremony...the *marriage*. He'd given Anaisse more than enough time to recuperate from her ordeal and heal, almost a whole moon cycle. She hadn't acquainted herself with the castle and his people's culture much at all, instead spending most of that time in the sanctuary of her chamber.

Undoubtedly trying to avoid him.

Tonight, however, her avoidance strategies wouldn't work. For tonight, they were to be married.

The castle teemed with Nordanese and Sudhraian alike. Tension was rife. The Sudhraian had not taken their defeat well, no matter that it had been Sudhra that had started the war to begin with. Sudhra that had endeavored first to conquer Nordan.

The Nordanese lords had conferred early on and decided that a conquered and occupied country was a country seething and gurgling with unrest and opposition. Better to try and ally them. Better to try and make Sudhra and Nordan one nation as they had been so very long ago.

Haeffen, Lord Marken's primary counsel, mystic, learned scholar and historian had wondered aloud if they might break the curse of infertility hanging over the two lands by joining them. The Goddess Ariane may be pleased by such an arrangement.

God to Goddess. Male to female. In perfect balance. In perfect equality.

The lords of Nordan had decided upon that as their path of choice and so here Gregor was, readying himself to join with the highest born woman in Sudhra. His god to her goddess. Even as their countries symbolized the opposite—Nordan the goddess and Sudhra the god—joined by both the violence of drawn blood on embattled blades and by his marriage to Anaisse.

Balance. Perfect and complete.

He only hoped the goddess would think so. He only hoped that she didn't ignore the doings and intentions of her children.

He frightened Anaisse. He knew this well, could see it in her eyes. She said she'd marry him—*under the condition that you allow me to keep my independence, only if you let me stay my own person*. Undoubtedly she'd seen many women in Sudhra fall completely under the thrall of their men, so of course she sought to avoid the same situation for herself. But Nordan was not Sudhra, and she didn't understand that it was possible for a man and woman to give themselves completely to each other and for both to be enhanced by the union instead of diminished.

Gregor meant to show her.

Although he had very little experience with such things himself. After all, there had not been a *marriage* on the ground that was now Nordan since Nordan and Sudhra had been one country known as Ecasia.

He swallowed hard. And monogamy. That was something his people didn't engage in very often at all. Gregor hadn't touched a woman since Anaisse had been promised to him, and he'd grown highly frustrated. He'd never, ever gone this long without sex.

Though he wanted monogamy. He desired a sole union with a woman, a partner. Someone to love and care for as she loved and cared for him. It was an attractive idea to him, though an unpopular one with most of the Nordanese.

"We are finished, my lord," said a servant, jerking him from his thoughts.

Gregor glanced around the chamber. Full, late *gartina* blooms of gold and white scattered the floor. Long strings of autumn *falanvine* with their small silver flowers, hung along the walls and draped over the areas on the side of the chamber where the guests would stand to observe the ceremony. A dais had been set up at the far end of the room where a priest from Sudhra would aid Gregor and Anaisse in their slightly altered vows, and an anchorite of the goddess would observe.

One last look around and Gregor nodded. *Great goddess*, were his palms sweating? He drew a deep breath to steady himself. "All right. Allow the guests in."

The guests filtered in and took their places. He greeted them all, Sudhraian and Nordanese alike. They were all dressed in finery. Some of the Nordanese women had chosen gowns of flaxcloth, revealing their beautiful bodies, and that was fine. They would not alter their traditions this eve beyond the marriage itself. Nordan had compromised enough. Sudhra had to also compromise.

The musicians entered and took up their harps and flutes. At Gregor's nod, they began to play.

Gregor fidgeted as he watched the doorway. All eyes were on him.

Then she appeared and Gregor's heart thrust up into his throat. She was beyond beautiful. Her thick, softly curling brown hair hung long and silky over her shoulders. She wore a slight bit of cosmetics, enough to make her dark brown eyes deeper and larger, her cheeks to appear just the slightest bit flushed and her lips seem even more full and luscious than they already were.

Her gown was of a dark green with a white underdress. In Sudhraian style, she wore a girdle encrusted with small sparkling white crystals around her waist. As usual, the girdle thrust her full breasts up to overflowing. Her cleavage looked perfect for scattering kisses on. He wondered briefly what her undergarments looked like and his cock hardened in response.

In order to remedy the evidence of his arousal, he thought of mundane things like the crowd watching them, hearing the grievances of his people in court, and training his horse. He breathed a sigh of relief as his erection eased.

She walked toward him. A smile was plastered on her mouth that didn't reach her eyes. It was obviously a pose for the crowd.

One day he vowed to make her smile reach her eyes when she looked at him. One day he vowed he'd make her laugh.

She curtsied. "My lord." Her voice quavered.

He bowed. "My lady. You are too beautiful for words."

She blushed a little. "Thank you."

He took her arm and they walked toward the dais.

* * * * *

Anaisse faltered through the ceremony, missing her lines and stuttering. She couldn't believe she was actually marrying Gregor. The one man she'd met in her life that had the capacity to truly enslave her.

It didn't help that he looked wonderful today. She'd lost her breath when she'd first seen him. A fine linen shirt encased his gorgeous chest. Thin leather strings laced up the front, leaving a large enough gap that she could see smooth flesh. A black leather vest covered his shirt and matching black leather trews sheathed his legs. Black boots completed his outfit.

He looked good enough to eat, she thought, biting her lower lip.

"...Before the God Anot and the Goddess Ariane, before these witnesses, I proclaim you joined. Lord Gregor, please seal the union with a kiss."

She frowned and glanced at the priest. "Uh—pardon me? I think you're mistaken." There weren't *kisses* in the marriage ceremony.

Gregor twined an arm around her waist and pulled her to him. He cupped her chin at the same time and forced her gaze to his. "I made a slight change," he murmured. He brushed her lips with his fingertips as though memorizing every line. Stunned, Anaisse could only stare up at him. Then his head dipped and those lips she'd fantasized about for so long covered hers.

She was totally unprepared for the passion the kiss ignited within her. Her eyelids fluttered closed as she lost herself to it. The kiss was savage and sweet at the same time. His hand twined at the nape of her neck and compelled her head to tilt a little. At the same time, he teased her closed lips with the tip of his tongue, flicking until she opened to him.

Then he growled low in his throat and slanted his mouth demandingly over hers, brushing his tongue into her mouth. He took his time exploring it in that wild yet tender way. Frissons of lust rocked through her body until she couldn't even think.

She grasped his forearms, and then slid her hands up until they twined in his hair. *Great Anot*, she could kiss him all evening...

Someone cleared his throat. "My lord."

The sound of a murmuring crowd entered her consciousness.

"*My lord.*" Louder this time.

Gregor growled again and broke the kiss. His eyes held her droopy, dazed gazef for a notable heartbeat. The look in his eyes seemed to say, *the gauntlet has been thrown down and I will win.*

Anaisse blinked twice and sobered fast.

Gregor pulled her back up on her feet. She'd ended up completely supported by him at some point.

The priest frowned at them. "Are you finished?" he asked in a low accusatory whisper.

Gregor gave an uncharacteristic smirk. "I haven't even begun," he answered.

Chapter Four

Beside him, Anaisse shifted in her seat. Gregor knew well she was responding to the visual stimulus around them. The celebratory feast had gone well. Good food and better wine had been served. Now the Nordanese, high on the spirit of the event, had fallen to each other's mouths and hands.

In his culture, it was normal to conclude a celebration with sex. His people believed it signified the eternal hope for new life. They believed it was the ultimate act of sharing bliss. This was not considered a shameful thing, and in many cases not a private thing, either. The result was open sex play.

Some of the Sudhraians had left the room. The more intrepid ones had stayed. A very few had actually begun to engage in lovemaking themselves.

Anaisse squirmed again and sighed. "How much longer do we have to stay here?"

Gregor smiled inwardly. "Well, we should follow Sudhraian protocol, Anaisse, and stay until the end of the feast."

She indicated a man and woman in the corner of the room. His hand was under the woman's skirt and his arm moved as he played with the woman's sex. Her legs were spread and her head was thrown back. A look of ecstasy played over the delicate features of her face and she ground her pussy down on the man's hand. "*That* is not Sudhraian protocol," Anaisse sniffed.

"No. *That* is Nordanese protocol. Your new people, remember?" Sometimes he thought she needed to be put over his knee and given a good spanking. His cock twitched at the thought. Her cheeks would redden so nicely under his hand and her pussy would swell and grow damp. It'd be so easy to part her legs as she lay across his lap and tease her.

Gregor watch her eyes roam the chamber and settle on a particularly rowdy couple. A man had lowered his partner face-first over the table, dragged her skirts up to her waist and spread her legs wide. He was shafting her slowly from behind and the woman was clawing at the table.

A flush made its way into Anaisse's pretty cheeks and she shifted again in her seat. Gregor could imagine how damp her gorgeous little pussy was becoming. He imagined her vaginal lips becoming swollen from arousal and her clit distending from its hood and plumping, crying for stimulation.

This time Gregor shifted in his seat.

"Anyway," he added casually. "We're just going back to our joining chamber for the night. Things will be pretty boring there since you've decided you don't want my hands on you."

She looked at him with wide eyes. "Joining chamber? That's a custom that hasn't been kept in Sudhraian tradition in ages."

"I thought the old-fashioned authenticity would please you, Anaisse, and also the visiting guests." He'd had Haeffen scour the old texts for something to use to his advantage and he'd found the old practice of the post-marriage joining chamber. They would be locked in the room together and the door would be guarded until morning. She'd have no way to escape him this night.

"I see." She stared wide-eyed for a few moments. He could see the thoughts turning over in her mind. "Well, we can stay here for a while. I don't want the people to think I'm shunning them."

She feared being alone with him. That much was obvious. Perhaps she didn't trust herself? She wouldn't be able to evade him for long, however. "Of course, Anaisse. I think that's wise."

She fell back to watching the activities in the chamber. It pleased him to know she was aroused by the sight of others enjoying love play. He wondered if the thought of performing in front of others would also excite her.

A woman near them, a Sudhraian no less, knelt before a well-endowed man, taking him deeply into her mouth and laving over the length of him as if in rapture. The man's fingers twined into her hair and Gregor could tell he fought the temptation to move his hips and thrust into her mouth.

Anaisse's eyes were also on the couple. Her fingers went to her cleavage, which was heaving from the increased rate of her breathing, and idly rubbed over the swell of one breast. Gregor let his gaze follow the brush of her fingertips and his mouth went dry.

"Do men—do men like that?" she asked, cocking her head to the side while she studied the couple.

Gregor grinned. "Ah, yes, very much. Seeing a woman's delicate mouth engulf my cock, her tongue playing around it, finding all the sensitive places. It is highly pleasurable."

"Mmmm, really?" She swallowed hard.

"I also enjoy returning the favor."

"W-what do you mean?"

Gregor glanced around the room. "Ah, there, you see?" he said, pointing a woman dressed in gold and a man in a brocade vest. "That's what I mean." The man had lifted his lady onto the table, spread her legs and was feasting on her sex, his head bobbing between her legs.

"I have indescribable bliss when I can pleasure a woman this way. I love feeling her writhe and hearing her moan as I lave her clit with my tongue and lap at her passage."

He heard Anaisse take a sharp breath. "I had no idea such things were possible. I had imagined." She blushed. "I mean, I'd wondered—"

His voice dropped. "Oh, they are certainly possible. That, plus so much more, Anaisse." *And I'd like to show every one of them to you.*

Haeffen, who currently stayed at his lorddom while Marken and Sienne were away in Sudhra, approached. "I believe it is time for you and the Lady Anaisse to adjourn to the joining chamber."

"Already?" Anaisse asked.

"Already," answered Gregor, suppressing a smile. He stood and held out his hand to her. She took it and rose.

Following Haeffen, they walked from the chamber, down the candlelit corridor and to the appointed room. A guard stood outside the door. Gregor opened the door. "After you, my lady."

She hesitated. "But I don't have my nightgown or clothes for the morning."

"All is within, my lady," answered Haeffen. "We have taken care of all your needs."

She hesitated a moment longer, then finally entered.

* * * * *

The door closed behind her with a final sounding click of the lock. Her breasts felt heavy. Her nipples were peaked. Her sex felt swollen with arousal caused by viewing the display in the feasting chamber.

She turned and watched Gregor warily.

Lazily, he kicked off his boots, unbuttoned his vest and pulled it off. His shirt quickly followed. He yawned and stretched, delineating all the muscles in his chest and arms. "I'm exhausted."

"Gregor?"

"Yes?"

"This night we will spend in here is only for show. Isn't that right?"

He walked to her, reached out and touched her cheek. "As I said before, I will never do anything you don't want me to do, Anaisse."

"I-I said no intimacy, Gregor."

"And I said I never agreed to that. I can see you're aroused. Your cheeks are flushed. I can see your nipples poking so invitingly through the thin material of your underdress. Anaisse, you are a woman and it is normal for you to become aroused. I am a man and I can ease the state of intense desire that your body is now in."

She turned her face away and he caught her chin, forcing her to look up at him. "We don't have to make love." he said. "I can pleasure you with my hands and my mouth, as you saw in the feasting room. I have great control. I would refrain from taking you completely. Allow me, Anaisse. It is such a small thing. I would not steal your...how did you put it?— *independence and ability to stay your own person*—by such a small thing."

So said the Ruler of the Underworld, she thought. He'd steal her soul little by little, with innocent kisses and small sexual acts.

She twisted away from him and put distance between them. Her pussy wept in her excitement.

His voice followed her. "I will part your thighs and tease your labia at first to gentle you to my touch. Then I will flick your swollen bud back and forth." His voice grew husky. "Then, when you are crying out for more, I will slide down and impale you with my finger. Work it in and out until your muscles clench and you release yourself in climax. You would like it, Anaisse. I know you would."

Dear Anot...oh, yes, she would. She closed her eyes. She heard him move toward her again, but she seemed rooted in place.

"I know you are a maiden and have never been touched by a man, but have you ever touched yourself, Anaisse, made yourself come?"

She shook her head. "Such acts are forbidden to those Sudhraian women who are not sex slaves."

"Here, they are not." He came close enough so that she could hear his chest rumble when he spoke, could feel his body heat radiate out and warm her. "Climax—it is a sensation rivaled by none. Are you not the least bit curious?"

She said nothing. Of course she was curious and Gregor knew it well.

"Let me show you just once. It will be my wedding gift to you."

So said the Ruler of the Underworld...

He reached out and grasped her shoulders, rubbing them with his large hands. "Put on your nightgown, karisama."

She started in shock. He'd used an ancient Ecasian word meaning little bird as an endearment.

"You have my word, if you allow me to touch you, it will go no farther than my hands on you. I will keep my trews on. You can keep your nightgown on as well." He turned his back. "Go on, I will not look."

She walked to the bed, disrobed and slipped her nightgown over her head. It wasn't flaxcloth. They knew better than to give her that. But the material was still fine, sheer. Small straps secured the gown over her shoulders and the heart-shaped, fitted bodice was dropped, revealing the tops of her breasts. At the waist, the skirt flared out, falling in gentle folds to her ankles. Everything except the sheerness of the fabric was of Sudhraian fashion. She had no doubt it had been designed to Gregor's specifications.

She took her time dressing and folding up her clothing and thought deeply. She'd needed to be honest with herself. If she watched displays like she'd been subjected to in the feasting chamber on a regular basis, there would be no way she'd be able to keep Gregor's hands from her. Not under his masterful onslaught. Not when she was already highly attracted to him.

So the question remained; could she allow Gregor's hands on her while still maintaining an emotional distance? Could she allow him into her body, but not into her heart?

She turned and looked at his back. The firelight licked over his skin the way she wanted to. Her hands itched to touch him. It looked as if she'd have no choice but to try. The lusts within her, the ones she'd suppressed and held back for years, were getting the better of her.

She walked up to him and put her hands to the small of his back. He jerked as though surprised, then stilled. Slowly, she worked her palms over his muscles, reveling in the feeling of him—like silk poured over iron. She fell into her tactile investigation, working her fingers up his spine, vertebrae by vertebrae, and threading her fingers through the soft dark hair at his nape.

A groan rumbled out of him.

Encouraged, she walked around to his front, careful not to meet his eyes. She brushed her fingers over the muscles of his stomach, and twirled them through the line of hair leading down to his sex. Then she moved up and rubbed the pads of her thumbs over his flat nipples. Unable to resist, she leaned forward and swiped her tongue across one.

He drew in a hard breath and his chest muscles flexed in response to her touch.

She glanced up at him in wonder. "I've never touched a man like this before."

"You're doing very well," he said. "You're making me crazy."

Her? Make a man crazy? Surely, not. Women didn't have such power.

He grabbed her wrist and pulled her toward him. With a firm thumb and index finger to her chin, he tipped her head up. "I'm going to kiss you now," he said almost in a tone of warning, as though at any moment she would bolt.

She couldn't bolt. The look on his face and the heat in his eyes held her transfixed.

He twined both hands into her hair and her hands found his sides. He lowered his head to hers and brushed his lips over her mouth, teasing, lightly tasting. She made a small noise in her throat and he took it as an invitation. He slanted his mouth over hers and thrust his tongue within to tangle savagely with hers. This was far from a tender kiss. This was passion. This was power.

And it did curious things to her body.

She pressed up against him, her pussy throbbing and her nipples at full attention as he nipped and licked at her lips, then pressed down and sealed their mouths together, meshing them until they seemed like one.

He pulled away and she rocked unsteadily on her feet. "Come," he said. "I have to touch you." He pulled her toward the huge bed in the center of the room.

She crawled up onto the mattress and he followed. His body heat kept her bare arms warm and the closeness of him made her heart hammer. He moved her so she lay flat on her back and he rested on his side, propped on an elbow, beside her.

He ran the back of his hand down her throat and over her collarbone. He stopped there, brushing his fingertips back and forth and drawing lazy circles on her skin. His gaze dipped to her breasts. "They are hard, straining for my touch. I can see them through the fabric of the nightgown. They look like small, perfect cherries, ready to be sucked on."

He lowered his head and placed a kiss to her collarbones, then dropped down, kissing the swell of one breast, then the other. His breath was hot on her skin. "Can you imagine the tip of my tongue finding all the ridges and valleys of each of your nipples? Can you see my head bent to your breast as I take my fill of each of them?"

She sighed. The images he filled her mind with were potent, arousing.

He moved his mouth back to hers and closed one hand over her breast. Gently, he plumped it, kneading and working it. At the same time his tongue sparred with hers and she thrust back at him in some barely conscious semblance of the primal sexual act.

He dragged his fingertips over the nipple and she started, narrowly missing bumping her teeth with his. She let out a surprised gasp. Her sex was on fire. Her clit throbbed with some strange pressure, building toward a climax. Her body screamed for release.

He traded one breast for the other, playing with the hardened tips of her nipples until she wanted to scream, until she broke the kiss and thrashed her head from side-to-side and clutched the blankets on either side of her with her eyes shut.

"You're so beautiful," Gregor said raggedly. "So responsive."

She felt his tongue on one of her nipples through the fabric of the nightgown, flicking and laving. At the same time, his hand dropped to her stomach, smoothing over the material and petting over her mound. Then he grasped her skirt and dragged it up.

He never stopped the flick and suck of her nipples through the material of her nightgown. She thought she'd go insane with the sensation.

With the back of his hand he urged her thighs apart. The first touch of his fingers to her sex had her hips off the bed. "Shhh," he soothed her. "All is well."

He ran a finger lightly over her labia, stopping to tease her swollen bud, then descended once more to circle the opening of her slick passage. As he circled it around and around, his thumb flicked at her clit, teasing it.

She shook with her arousal and fisted the blankets in her hands even harder. Her breath came in little pants now. She wanted *more*. Her pussy felt so empty.

"Gregor—Gregor, please, I need you within me. Your cock." Her body had taken control of her mind and it demanded satisfaction. All her fine sentiments about not allowing him intimate contact vanished. In that instant, she was a slave to her body's desires. All she wanted was to be filled by him.

"You ask now in the heat of your lust, but if I comply you'll hate me tomorrow."

She shook her head. "I wouldn't."

"No, Anaisse, I told you I would not take you that way this night and I meant it. Believe me, I will make sure your body is happy, but you are not ready yet to take my shaft."

He sucked on her nipple and raked over it lightly with his teeth. "Your nipples are red, hard and wet from my mouth, *karisma*. They look so beautiful through the fabric of your nightdress. How I want to remove this clothing and suck on them unhindered."

Oh, dear, sweet *Anot*. She was on fire. She would explode soon if he didn't do something, anything. Barely aware of her movements, she braced her heels against the mattress and thrust her hips up, pressing her pussy into his hand.

He hummed approvingly. "What do you want, Anaisse? Do you want to come? Do you want this? Penetration?" He pressed his finger just a little way into her passage and rubbed.

"Please," she breathed.

"Should I let you come?"

"Please!" she practically screamed.

He slid a finger within and her muscles clamped over it. It felt indescribably good. She moaned. He worked it in and out, while increasing the pressure and pace of the flicks of his thumb against her bud.

"Let it go," he rasped. "Let go for me, Anaisse."

Pleasure exploded out from her pussy, tingling through her body, overwhelming her. She twisted on the bed under the force of it, crying out. She had no control under the onslaught of the sensation.

Little tremors racked her body still when he brushed his fingers down her sex almost lovingly, removed his hand and pulled her skirt down.

Total disbelief washed through her. It had been devastating, incredible, *wonderful*.

"Sweet *Anot*," she said, stunned.

Gregor lay back on the bed. His cock was hard and pressing against his trews. "You are so beautiful when you come. You're beautiful all the time, but when you let loose you take my breath away."

Her voice hardened as fear gripped her. What was she doing? What spell had she come under? She'd actually *begged* for his cock. She couldn't allow him to seduce her this way. "You mean lose control." She scrambled from the bed.

He caught her upper arm. "No. You aren't going to run away from me." He dragged her back onto the bed and pressed her beneath him. His aroused cock pushed into her leg. "You aroused and tempted me beyond belief just now. I almost lost control to you—"

"You lie. I barely touched you."

A muscle worked in his jaw. "I almost lost control to you because during this encounter, it was you holding most of the power."

"What?"

"I watch you become aroused. I watch your body near orgasm, your muscles tense, and your breathing change. I hear your small cries and moans. You *affect* me with your excitement. You hold me in thrall with it. Both partners in sex have control. Yours is perhaps far more powerful than mine. If you touched me, made me come, you would know what I am saying."

She licked her dry lips and his gaze caught and stayed riveted on her mouth. "Can I do that? Bring you to climax without actually making love?"

He kissed her soundly and gave a little laugh. "What makes you so sure what we do now isn't making love?"

She frowned. "It isn't! You know what I mean. I meant your cock in my pussy."

He stared down at her for several heartbeats. Finally he rolled off her and onto his back on the bed. "All right, Anaisse. You said you've never touched a man before. Touch me. Make me come. I'm yours."

Anaisse let her gaze slide from Gregor's mouth, over his chest to settle on his cock. Her fingers itched to touch him. Her mouth watered to taste him.

Chapter Five

Gregor lay on the bed, looking up at Anaisse. His cock was so hard it almost hurt. Watching her come apart under his mouth and hands had been the most erotic experience of his life, and he'd had many erotic experiences. The thought of her even touching his shaft right now had him close to the edge.

Goddess...he hadn't reacted this way to a woman since he'd been in puberty. It was unsettling. Yes, she held much power over him. She only had to realize it. "Touch me and then you'll see that even as I lose control to you, I will still hold power over you," he finished.

She hesitated, the skirt of her nightgown pooled prettily around her knees on the bed. Then she scooted closer to him and tentatively touched his chest, then ran her hands down him to the buttons of his trews and undid them.

"Take them off," she said. "I want to see all of you."

Gregor pushed his trews down over his hips. Anaisse pulled them all the way off. Her soft intake of breath as she let her gaze rove his body worried him.

"It's beautiful," she breathed. "*You're* beautiful. I had no idea."

Gregor relaxed. "I was concerned that since you've never seen a man unclothed that you wouldn't be pleased."

She reached out and stroked her fingers over his erection. Gregor grit his teeth at the tease. He had to hold himself back and allow her to explore at her leisure.

"I'm beyond pleased," she said with fascination in her voice. Her fingertip followed a large vein down the length of his shaft and she fondled his sac. Then she rubbed her finger over the head. "It's like silk over iron, like the rest of your body."

Her hand—*thank the goddess!*—finally closed around his length. Carefully, she pumped him up and down. He let a soft groan escape his throat. By the blood of the ancients, her hand on him felt good.

She continued her torture, her movements becoming surer. Gregor had to talk himself out of pushing up, pulling her beneath him and sliding into her dark, wet heat. She was not ready for that. No matter how prettily she begged for it.

He was completely unprepared when she leaned down and nipped at his lower stomach with her small white teeth. The woman would be incredible in bed when she finally allowed herself the enjoyment of it, he thought, his eyes coming open.

The motion of her hand ceased as she kissed her way down his stomach to the head of his cock.

"You're going to make me come if you do this, Anaisse. I'm too close to the edge to hold back. Are you sure you're ready?"

"I want to taste you." She didn't give him time to answer, to ask her if she knew what would happen if she made him come. She simply engulfed the head of his cock. It slid into her hot mouth as if it belonged there.

Gregor was lost.

Her simple and unrefined skill made the act all the more arousing. She massaged his sac in one hand and slid her mouth down on his shaft as far as she could. Once in a while she would break away to lick and kiss up and down his length, paying special attention to the portion of his cock she couldn't fit into her mouth. She seemed to concentrate on the signs his body made and his groans of approval, and then returned to the spots she'd been laving when he'd made them.

"I'm coming, love," he rasped. "Sweet—" He broke off as his body started to let loose. He told her to move back, but she didn't heed his warning. Pleasure ripped through him as he exploded in her mouth. To his utter amazement, she swallowed down every last drop of his ejaculate.

As he savored the aftermath, she curled up in the crook of his arm. "I had control over you."

"Yes," he groaned.

"That was power."

"Yes."

"I enjoyed it," she said softly.

He chuckled. "So did I, Anaisse." He rolled her under him and kissed her long and deep, tasting a faint trace of his seed.

Aye, she'd be wild all right.

* * * * *

Gregor shifted on the mattress and felt for his new wife, anticipating the pleasure of pulling Anaisse into his arms...and groped air. He opened his eyes to an empty bed, to an empty room. Her clothing was gone.

He dressed quickly and stepped out into the corridor. The guard was still on duty. "Why did you let Lady Anaisse out of the joining chamber?" he asked.

"It is morning, my lord. You commanded me to keep her in there until daybreak."

Disgusted at himself, Gregor waved his hand. "You're relieved from duty."

"Thank you, my lord."

He checked her chamber first, but she was not there. Then he checked all the places she'd most likely be within the keep and still didn't find her.

Finally, he found her standing in the garden with a pretty blonde woman he'd never seen before. Anaisse's back was to him and the sunlight slanted through the trees and caught in her unbound hair. She wore a gown of light pink today.

He walked up behind her and placed his hands on her waist. Anaisse glanced up at him and then, with the politest of smiles, sidled to the side, out of his reach.

A muscle worked in his jaw. He'd made headway last night, but obviously not enough.

"Gregor, this is Lilane," said Anaisse. "Her monogamous mate is Lord Rue d'Ange. He was formerly the Sword Master of the Supreme Priestdom."

Gregor bowed. "I know of Rue. He did much to aid Nordan during the war. He's in the north, is he not? Helping to settle many of the Aviat?"

Beside him, Anaisse's body tensed. She frowned. "What do you mean Rue helped Nordan during the war?"

Lilane exchanged a look with Gregor. "That is the other reason we came here, Anaisse. Rue needs to talk to you and explain some things. *He* should be the one to tell you, not I."

"Where is Rue now?" asked Gregor.

"In the keep," answered Lilane.

Anaisse frowned. "I will not like what he has to say, will I?"

"Likely not. He will find you before the day is out. Worry not," answered Lilane. "We were not able to make it for the marriage yesterday, but we really wanted to give you both our good wishes." Lilane put a hand to her heart. "We were both sick when we discovered Anaisse had been kidnapped by the Ganotte."

"We're working to uncover the Ganotte's network. I think we'll be able to crush the worst of them," said Gregor.

"Rue will be especially happy to hear that since he lost my sister to them," said Anaisse softly.

Gregor knew Anaisse's sister Sania had been meant to marry Rue before she'd been kidnapped and killed by the Ganotte. He heard the note of pain in Anaisse's voice and wanted to go to her, to touch and comfort her, but he knew that intimate action would frighten her.

"Lord Vant was one of them, Lilane," continued Anaisse. "Remember how he verbally attacked you during the dinner with my father?"

"I remember well. I also remember how he physically attacked me in the hallway on the day of the siege. I barely escaped the bastard." Lilane reached over and took Anaisse's hand. "I'm just pleased to know that you're all right."

"She's very strong," said Gregor.

Lilane glanced at him. "Yes, and Rue says she's very stubborn, too. You have your hands full with Lady Anaisse, I think, Lord Gregor."

"Yes, I believe so," he answered. Lilane didn't know how right she was.

Lilane winked at him. "You may have to put her over your knee once or twice."

"Lilane!" Anaissse exclaimed.

Lilane only laughed in response.

"How long will you and Rue be staying?" asked Anaisse.

"I'm afraid we'll be leaving later today. There are many things that need tending up north."

Anaisse drew Lilane into an embrace. "I hope to see you again before you leave."

"I hope so, too," said Lilane, pulling away. She turned to Gregor. "It was very nice to meet you."

Gregor bowed again. "And you."

With one last squeeze to Anaisse's hand, Lilane walked away.

An awkward silence descended. Anaisse glanced at him. "Well, I have things to see to, so—"

He stalked to her before she could flee. She took several steps back and he followed until her back was up against a tree. He placed his hands on either side of her waist, imprisoning her. "Why are you so afraid of me, Anaisse?"

"What makes you think I'm afraid of you?"

"Because you avoid me and the only way I can get close to you is to lock you in a guarded room, or corner you in the garden or corridor."

"I let you get plenty close to me last night, Gregor."

He suppressed an aroused growl and stared into her eyes. "I remember," he said in a low voice. "I'd really like a repeat of those events."

She swallowed hard. It was the only outward sign of her discomfiture. She gazed up at him coolly. "It was all right, I suppose."

"*All right?*" He raised an eyebrow and tried to minimize the hit to his male ego. "Just all right? You clawed the bedclothes, screamed my name and practically woke the whole keep."

A light flush stole into her cheeks. She looked away. "There's no need to embarrass me."

"*Embarrass* you?" He took her chin and tipped her gaze back up to his. "I told you last night and I'll tell you again now, in or out of bed you are the most magnificent creature I've ever laid eyes on, but when you come—" he didn't suppress his growl this time "—you slay me with your beauty. I want to make you come again and again. If being uncontrollably alluring is embarrassing, then you should flush scarlet, Anaisse."

Her lips parted as she stared up at him wide-eyed.

"I want to do it again. Only, next time I want you naked so I can worship every inch of your body unhindered."

She shivered and dropped her gaze.

"Just think how it would be to crush up against me, Anaisse, skin to skin. Imagine how it would feel to have my mouth on your breasts without the barrier of material."

He noted her breathing picking up and it encouraged him. He went on. "Imagine what it would be like if, instead of my finger, it was my cock sliding into you."

"S-stop it," her voice quavered and her nipples hardened against the material of her underdress, revealing her arousal.

"Come to me tonight. The door will be unlocked. Come anytime you want to feel me against you, or just to hold you close. I'm your husband and yours to command. I will do anything for you."

She looked up at him sharply. "You shouldn't give me such leave. What if you're with another woman and I walk in on you?"

He shook his head. "I haven't taken another woman since I obtained approval from your father for your hand. And I *won't* take another woman, Anaisse, no matter how hard you try to push me away."

He backed away from her while spreading his hands wide. "I'm yours whether you want me or not." He turned and walked into the keep.

* * * * *

Lord Vant watched from the depths of the garden as the two women who'd escaped him talked. He'd once vowed to make the blonde Nordanese woman, Lilane, pay for fighting him when he'd sought to fuck her. He'd been fully within his right to force her to his bed, but the chit had not displayed the submission she should've. The whore had even scarred his ear when she'd escaped him. But she would have to wait. Lady Anaisse had his full and undivided attention now.

He knew well what they intended, the lords of Nordan. They meant to ally Nordan and Sudhra by this marriage. They meant to seduce Sudhra to their bitch goddess.

It simply could not be borne.

Sudhra's way of life was the *right* way of life, the only decent way of life. Nordan could not be allowed to flaunt Sudhraian values and bend his people to their will and religion.

He had to do something, anything, to stop it from happening.

He imagined the warm light of Anot surrounded him. Vant closed his eyes in ecstasy. Yes, Anot *must* favor him and his mission. How could he not? The salvation of his country now lay in his hands and his hands alone. He could not fail his God or his people.

He watched Lilane embrace Anaisse, then turn and walk away. Then he watched Gregor back her up against the tree and the exchange that followed. When Gregor finally walked away, Anaisse looked shaken and pale.

Vant stroked his chin, deep in thought. Was not all well between the pagan Nordanese lord and his new Sudhraian wife?

That could work to his advantage.

He watched Anaisse from the natural alcove formed by the trees and bushes. She looked deceivingly delicate, but he knew well she had a backbone of iron. Proud and fierce was Lady Anaisse of Sudhra. She was a perfect example of a highborn Sudhraian woman. She was a strong link joining the countries.

The strongest link.

He knew the perfect way to rouse and enrage the Sudhraians to rebellion against Nordan. Though deep reluctance at the plan forming in his mind swirled through him.

He'd known Anaisse since they'd been children. He'd respected her as the Supreme's daughter. Had, at one time, even contemplated winning her hand. Strong love still lingered in his heart for her.

Anaisse was a pure Sudhraian woman, but now Nordanese hands sullied her. That alone should be enough to make him do what needed to be done. She needed to be saved. She needed to be put her out of her misery.

But he just didn't know if he could kill her.

Chapter Six

Ice seemed to run through her veins after Rue had finished telling her what he'd done. She forced herself up from where they sat drinking wine at the table in one of the congregating rooms of the keep and paced to the hearth and back.

Finally she stopped in the middle of the room, cocked her head to the side and stared at him. "You mean the entire time you were at the Supreme Priestdom this summer you were gathering information to use to betray Sudhra to Nordan?"

Rue nodded his handsome blond head. "Yes."

She pursed her lips and stared at him before replying. "You mean when I arranged for you to eat at the table of the Supreme, I was unwittingly helping you?"

"I am very sorry for that, if it makes it any better."

Anaisse scowled. "It doesn't."

"I can explain why I did it, Anaisse."

She folded her arms across her chest and sighed. "I know why, Rue. You did it for the Aviat. I saw them all leave the day Nordan defeated Sudhra and quickly learned you were one of them. You did it for them. Isn't that it?"

Rue stood, walked to her and placed his hands to her shoulders. "I am Aviat first, Anaisse. Sudhraian second. It has always been so with me. In Sudhra my people would've been hunted if they'd revealed themselves. We needed a safe place to exist; somewhere we could live free without the danger of someone desiring our wings and killing us for them. I did what I did in order to ensure their safety. Please tell me you understand."

She sighed again and looked up into his blue eyes. She'd always been fond of Rue. "I may not like it, but I *do* understand it. I also understand that Sudhra is not the most hospitable of places. I can't imagine the Aviat were ever happy there."

"No. It was a constant battle to conceal our heritage. And it cut deeply to never be able to spread our wings, so to speak."

"I must confess that I am highly impressed with Nordan's handling of Sudhra. They have treated my father and his advisers with respect and have not raped and pillaged, as Sudhra would surely have done to Nordan. There's a part of me that wishes to see Sudhra and Nordan as one country again." She broke away from his and walked to the roaring fire in the hearth. "Anyway, what's done is done. I suppose it was Anot's will that Sudhra fall."

"Sudhra is not a hospitable place for women either, Anaisse. You're much better off here."

She stared at the flames licking over the wood. "I suppose, though the open sex play is…disturbing. It will take me a while to grow accustomed to it."

"How does it go with Gregor?"

She kept her back to him and didn't answer. *How did it go with Gregor?* The man terrified her. He teased her body to states of being to which she thought she could easily become accustomed. Her body fair hummed whenever he entered a room. He was strong and kind. She grit her teeth. The man invaded her body and soul and threatened her possession of both.

He was a man she could actually come to love.

"Anaisse?" Rue asked from behind her when she didn't answer.

She gave a short, false-sounding laugh. "You ask too soon, Rue. We haven't even been married twenty-four hours yet."

"You don't need twenty-four hours to know you can love a person. I fell in love with Lilane the moment I fought her."

Anaisse turned. "Fought her?"

"It's a long story." He walked to her. "Anaisse, I know I'm not your brother, although I feel like one sometimes. Gregor is a good man. He will care well for you. I know it must be hard for you in this situation. I imagine you're having extra difficulty because of your upbringing. If you ever need someone to talk to, I am here and so is Lilane."

Anaisse lowered her head and went silent.

"Anaisse are you all right?"

She looked up at him. "It's just that I watched what happened to my sisters, Rue. How they were married off to make political alliances to men not of their choosing. They were able to keep a part of themselves in those situations, control, because of the very fact there was no love. The marriages were just for show." Anaisse couldn't seem to stop the flow of words from her mouth. She hadn't realized how much she'd desired someone to confide in. "But with Gregor, it's different. I—I don't know if I can keep my distance." She blew out a sigh of frustration. "Retaining autonomy is an important issue to a highborn Sudhraian woman. We've watched the intense subjugation of the lowborn ones."

"You don't know if you can stay in control and that scares you, doesn't it?"

In mute misery, she nodded.

Rue gave a gentle laugh. "Lilane had some of the same issues with me, Anaisse. I think she might tell you it is sometimes more fun to lose control."

She sighed. She was afraid of that.

* * * * *

I'm yours whether you want me or not... The refrain had beaten at her all day long.

She rose from her bath. Water rivulets coursed down her body as she grabbed the bathing linen hanging over the side of a nearby chair and patted herself dry. Each part of her body she touched, she imagined Gregor hands caressing, his mouth and lips roving over. Her pussy flushed with sudden warmth and her clit plumped.

She stepped out onto the rug covering the hard floor, took her nightdress and donned it. It fell in soft waves all around her, brushing her sensitized flesh and making her shiver.

As Anaisse put her slippers on, she eyed the door to temptation. Her nipples went hard with merely the thought of him. They poked through the thin material of her nightdress. She brushed her fingertips over them and shot of desire went through her, settling in her sex.

She glanced at the door again and shook her head. She was not going to give into her body's lusts. Instead, she went to bed and blew out the candle on the bedside table. Then she settled back into the pillows and let the flickering fire lure her to sleep.

The firelight licked at the strong muscular ridges of Gregor's body as he slid into the bed beside her. Drowsily, she rolled toward him and placed a hand to his chest. His strong arms came around her. He pressed her to him and she came a little more awake, reveling in the feel of her bare skin sliding against his.

His mouth came down over hers, tasting gently at first and then feasting on her. His hands twined in her hair as he rolled her beneath him, pinning her under his strong body.

She writhed and moaned as she sought to touch every part of his body she could. Finally she found his cock and worked him up and down in her hand. Gregor groaned against her mouth and broke away, moving lower to claim a distended nipple. At the same he slipped a hand down her body between her thighs and let his fingers tease her labia and play with her clit.

She moaned and her juices ran down her inner thighs. She had to have his shaft within her. Her body felt empty without Gregor filling her.

She spread her legs, allowing him to settle his hips between them. His cock nudged at her entrance and she spread her legs further and thrust her hips up, urging him to enter her.

Anaisse came awake with a jolt and sat up in bed. Her pussy was drenched and throbbing. Her nipples were so hard they were nearly painful. She slipped a hand down, ran her fingers over her clit and whimpered in need.

She glanced at the door. Firelight bathed it in a red glow.

She clenched her fists on her lap. Damn the man to the Underworld! Why did he affect her this way? She squeezed her eyes shut as images from their night together in the joining chamber assaulted her. Inwardly she warred with herself. Why couldn't she just squelch this attraction she had to him? She pulled together the threads of her willpower and opened her eyes.

No.

She wouldn't just roll over and give into him so easily. Turning on her side, she punched her fists into the pillow several times before settling down and closing her eyes.

She sighed and tossed and turned. Her pussy was swollen like it never had been before. After what seemed like hours, she fell asleep once more.

The firelight licked at the strong muscular ridges of Gregor's body as he slid into the bed beside her. Drowsily, she rolled toward him and placed a hand to his chest. His strong arms came around her He pressed her to him and she came a little more awake, reveling in the feel of her bare skin sliding against his...

She came awake instantly and shot out of bed. "Blessed Anot," she muttered. Anaisse stood in the center of her chamber, hugging herself and staring at the door she knew led to bliss.

Aye, she knew when to admit defeat.

She walked to the door and opened it. The fire in Gregor's chamber was brighter, casting long shadows across the walls and furniture. She approached his bed and lost her breath at the sight of him. He lay with the blankets tangled around his waist. One strong arm was thrown over his head, resting on the pillow. The position outlined his biceps appealingly. She wondered if he was naked from the waist down.

Even sleeping the man held so much power over her.

Suddenly shaken, she turned to go back the way she'd come. He reached out and grabbed her wrist, surprising a small scream from her. He had an intent look on his face. A little like a wolf that knew he'd finally cornered the rabbit.

Indeed, the rabbit had hopped right into his lair.

He released her and flipped the blankets back a little. Still she couldn't see if he was nude from the waist down or not. "Come within, you look chilled."

She hesitated.

"Anaisse, *you* came to *my* chamber, remember? I won't bite." He smiled. "Well, that's not true. I may bite just a little."

Aye, she felt she he'd fair devour her...and she'd like it.

"Come," he repeated. His voice was like warm silk sliding over her skin. "I will never do anything to hurt you. I will never force you to do anything you do not wish. You are safe, protected and cherished by me."

How infinitely nice that sounded. Still, she stood mute and still, fighting a battle of wills within herself and losing.

"Anaisse, come," he said again.

She relented and slid in beside him. "I had a dream of you." Her voice shook a little. He brushed up against her and she inhaled sharply. Oh, aye, he was naked from the waist down.

He wrapped her arms around her and pulled her close. With care, he brushed her hair away from her face and kissed her temple. "I hope it was a good one." His voice was sexy and sleep-roughened.

She sighed and snuggled against him, finally releasing some of her anxiety and enjoying the warm, hard feel of him against her. "It was. Very, in fact. It's why I'm here."

"Ah, one of *those* dreams. I've had many of them about you."

"You have?"

Autumn Pleasures: The Union

"Oh, aye. I told you I wanted you from the first time I saw you. Remember? It was a few years ago. You visited my lorddom with your father."

"I remember. I was also attracted to you."

"I can remember watching the way you carried yourself, with so much pride and dignity. I could tell you were strong and intelligent and I knew you had to be special."

"Special?"

"I realize the highborn daughters of Sudhra are treated better than the rest, but even so, I knew you had to be special to thrive and be so strong after growing up in an environment where women are not valued as anything more than sexual objects, or possessions to be bartered away. You were a flower blooming in a desert. Aye, I was attracted to you right away and for more than your beauty."

"It is strange here in Nordan where the men and women make love everywhere without a care for marriage commitment or even common privacy. You would think that here women would be treated as sexual objects."

"Sex is a pleasurable pastime, a beautiful one that sometimes results in the creation of life. It is a blessing of the Goddess Ariane and the God Anot. We see no reason to hide such a gift away or limit it. And here in Nordan women are treasured and valued by the men, just as men are treasured and valued by women. It is an equal exchange. No one looks down on anyone else for his or her sex."

She sighed. "It is wonderful."

His hand caressed her waist through her nightdress. "Would you like to see how wonderful? I would love to show you."

She didn't answer, but merely grasped her nightdress and wiggled it up with Gregor's help. When it was finally off, she gasped in pleasure at the feel of his naked body against her. She seemed to fit so perfectly against him—like they were two pieces of a puzzle finally placed together.

He cupped her chin and turned her head to his, then brushed his lips over hers. "Let me make love to you, Anaisse."

She nodded. "Yes."

Just like in her dream, he rolled her beneath him. Gregor groaned. "Finally," he murmured right before his mouth consumed hers. Anaisse moaned into his mouth and ran her hands greedily over his body, seeking to touch all the smooth skin she possibly could. Now that she'd given in to him, she couldn't wait to have him touching her.

Gregor kicked the blankets away and broke from her mouth. He dragged his lips and the tip of his tongue down her throat to her collarbone, and then trailed down her breast.

Her heart rate and breathing increased as his tongue flicked over one hardened nipple. With the hand he wasn't using to brace himself, he fondled and caressed the breast not attended to by his mouth, gently pinching and teasing the nipple and awakening every last nerve ending.

Anaisse writhed on the bed beneath him, moving her hips and moaning. Relentlessly, he teased her breast until she thought she'd climax from that stimulation alone.

Then he pulled back and looked down at her. "Part your thighs," he commanded in a soft voice. "I want to taste you."

She spread her legs and watched him slide down her body. His erect cock brushed her leg as he positioned himself at her sex. He laid a line of kisses on her inner thigh, heading straight to the heart of her. The first brush of his tongue against her nearly sent her through the roof. Just the sight of his dark head between her legs was almost enough to slay her. To have his tongue on her was beyond heaven.

He let out a little growl of appreciation. "You're so wet, Anaisse. You taste so sweet." He ran the flat of his tongue up the length of her pussy, making her gasp. He flicked his tongue along her folds and then settled in at her clit, laving and sucking at the tiny bit of aroused flesh. One hand traveled up her leg and played with her labia and circled the entrance to her passage.

He used the tip of his tongue to flick her clit back and forth and up and down. Her climax built steadily, but as soon as she felt she was about to come, Gregor would pull his mouth and hand away from her. He kept her on the edge, teasing her, tormenting her. She whimpered in delicious frustration.

He slipped one finger into her passage and thrust. She let out a long, low moan in response. He added one more finger, stretching her muscles and Anaisse thought she'd die from the exquisite pleasure of it.

"Does this feel good, Anaisse?"

Mute, she could only toss her head back forth on the pillows and nod.

"Your pussy is so beautiful, and so tight. The firelight is just bright enough that I can see it. I love to watch my fingers working in and out of you." His voice lowered. "I am imagining how good it will feel to push my cock into you, how your muscles will hold me like a glove, how they will grip my length as I slide in and out of you."

"Gregor, please."

He kept up the slow glide of his fingers in and out of her and straddled her thigh. She felt his cock brush her again. He was so large, and so hard. She wanted his cock filling her.

He used his other hand to plump a breast and gently pinch a nipple. The slight bit of pain intensified her pleasure and brought her to the edge of orgasm. She gasped and her body tightened.

His hands at both her breast and pussy disappeared. She nearly cried for the loss. "Gregor," she breathed.

"I don't want you to come yet, my love, not yet. You'll come when I say you can." He reached out and tweaked her nipple once more. Her pussy instantly responded. She moaned and writhed on the bed. "Do you like that, Anaisse?"

"Yes," she said breathlessly. "You know I do. Please, come within me, Gregor."

He bent down and took her nipple into his mouth, laving at it and rasping his teeth over it as he positioned himself between her thighs. The head of his cock poked at the entrance of her passage.

Gregor raised his head from her breast and moved her thighs so they draped over his. "Are you ready?"

"Please!"

Slowly, he pushed the head of his shaft into her. Her muscles stretched like they never had before. She gasped and tried to pull away, suddenly convinced this was a bad idea.

He grabbed her waist, stilling her. "It's all right, Anaisse. I'll go slowly. I'll be gentle."

"You're too big. You—"

"Babies come out of this passage," he soothed. "I assure you my cock will fit within." He pushed in a little more.

She felt so exposed to him, so vulnerable with her legs spread wide and his hands bracing her waist. Little by little he impaled her on his shaft. She let out a moan as her muscles stretched further and it became pleasurable.

Anot, it felt so good.

He fed her his cock inch by luscious inch, all the way to her maidenhead. "Are you ready, *karisama*?"

She nodded.

He thrust, impaling her to the base of his shaft. She cried out, but it was more from pleasure than discomfort. She'd never felt so full, so complete, in all her life.

"Are you all right?" he asked through gritted teeth.

"Oh…yes," she breathed in surprise. She gave a little laugh of wonderment.

Bracing his hands against her hips, he pulled out and thrust back in. She whimpered at the pure deliciousness of having his hard, hot cock within her. With a mind-numbing, leisurely pace he shafted her. She gripped his forearms and tried not to go insane. He was taunting her again, teasing her.

"You're so slick and tight," he said. "You fit around my cock so well, Anaisse."

She could feel every inch of his shaft, it seemed, every single vein and ridge as he worked it so slowly in and out of her. She wanted him hard and fast. To feel the power of him that he was keeping so carefully leashed right now. Was he afraid of hurting her? "Let me feel it, Gregor. Don't be gentle. Gentle is killing me."

He began to thrust faster and harder. He reached down between them and rubbed her clit and she shattered. Indescribable pleasure rocketed through her body. She arched her back and cried out under the onslaught. The muscles of her pussy pulsed and contracted around him and it pulled Gregor with her. He groaned and she felt him release himself into her.

She was still savoring the sweet aftermath of her climax when he withdrew his cock. He rolled to her side and held her close, then slipped his hand down to her pussy and stroked her.

"I'm sorry," he murmured in her ear.

"Sorry for what?"

"I climaxed quickly because I haven't been with a woman in long time and also because I've been imagining this night since I first saw you. It is inexcusable I did not give you more pleasure before I allowed my own."

She stifled a laugh. More pleasure? He'd just about killed her with the build-up and eventual explosion of her climax. She opened her mouth to tell him so, but he chose them moment to slip two fingers into her passage, stealing all her words and thought. While he thrust, he teased her clit with his thumb.

He laid a kiss to her throat, and then slowly licked her skin. "Come again for me, *karisama*. I love it when you climax."

She drew a breath and closed her eyes. He could perform such magic over her body. He'd woven a spell over her she was powerless to break. Her clit already responded to his touch. Her heart and breathing and breasts reacted to the feel of his skin next to hers, his voice rumbling through her when he spoke.

He angled his fingers in a different way, so his fingertips rasped over a special place deep within her that was extra sensitive. "Oh, Gregor," she moaned. "Yes, like that."

"You excite me so much. I'm hard for you again." He groaned. "*Goddess*, the things I want to do to your sweet body." He leaned over her and took her nipple into his mouth.

For the second time she cried out under the force of her peak. Waves of it rocked through her and Gregor seemed to draw it out by gently stroking her sensitized clit. As she relaxed into the post-climax languor, he pulled her closer to him and nuzzled her hair. "You completely lost control to me and I lost it to you. Was it so terrible, *karisama*?" he teased.

She snuggled against him and smiled. "I could become used to losing control to you."

"Good, because we've only just started down the road to pleasure. There are many more stops to make, and I'm looking forward to showing you every single one."

Chapter Seven

Gregor awoke to air brushing over his skin and the feel of a woman astride him. He opened his eyes on a guttural groan to see Anaisse moving over him. She presented a tempting picture as she moved on his cock with her hair wild and free, the ends of the tendrils brushing over and curling around her erect, rosy nipples. Her eyes were closed and her sweet lips parted.

Ah, he had suspected she'd be wild and wanton once she let herself go. He was pleased to find it true.

He gripped her by the waist and toppled her onto her back, pinning her to the mattress with his hips. She gave a small surprised scream.

He cocked an eyebrow at her. "Taking advantage of me?"

"When I awoke it was find your cock already semi-hard. I coaxed it the rest of the way." She blushed. "I didn't think you would mind."

He thrust in and out of her slowly, drawing a sigh from her. "I don't."

Gregor made love to her at length, coaxing her to three climaxes before he allowed his own. When he felt sure she was sated, he pulled her close and brushed the hair from her face. They were both breathing hard and a light sheen of perspiration coated them despite the chill in the air of the room.

She turned her face to his. "Have you been with many women, Gregor?"

He smiled. "Are you jealous, *karisama*?"

"No. I'm simply curious."

"I've been with many, too many to count. Such is the way of things here."

"I'm sure you've had many interesting sexual encounters, no?"

He tightened his arms around her. "Of course. This is Nordan."

She traced a pattern lightly on chest. "Like what?"

He blew out a breath. "Well, many things. I've been with several women at once and I've also pleasured one woman with another man on more than one occasion."

He felt her entire body perk up with interest. "Really? How is that possible?"

He suppressed a laugh. Aye, the door to her sexual appetite had been fair flung open. "There is nothing more exciting than seeing a woman's sexual exhilaration at having two cocks at her beck and call. You remember what I told you about a woman's arousal being an aphrodisiac to a man? Well, that is the ultimate."

She paused and sighed. "I'm curious why you would give all that up for a woman you didn't even know, a sexually inexperienced woman, at that. I have made it clear you could have a sham marriage with me, for the sake of appearances to Sudhra. I said I'd play along with such an arrangement, and still you wish to remain monogamous to me. Why?"

He could see why she'd be curious. Most men would jump at the opportunity she'd presented him. He thought how to phrase his response before he answered her. "I'll be honest with you. I've always desired such an arrangement with a woman. Nordanese women, for the most part, do not wish only one man in their lives. It's not practical since lying with many greatly increases their chances of conceiving. When I first met you, there was something that drew me to you. Some small seed of a possibility of *depth* between us."

"You wish for depth?"

He picked up a tendril of her hair and rubbed the silky length between his fingers. "I wish to bond with one woman, for her to know me deeply as I know her. I wish for an exchange of thought and emotional energy that will make us one. I hope to have this with you."

She shifted to her side and laid a palm to his cheek. Her eyes were filled with deep emotion. "I-I will try to give this to you, Gregor, but I won't deny that it frightens me. Your intensity and ability to consume me scares me greatly."

He tipped her chin up and kissed her. "I am not a Sudhraian male. I won't command your total submission to me, make you completely reliant on me and then abuse you." He lowered his voice. "I may command your total submission in bed, but I promise to make sure you enjoy that."

She half-closed her eyes and smiled. "I think I would."

Goddess, a woman had never aroused him as much as Anaisse did. He stared at her flushed face and heavy-lidded eyes. He was afraid that despite her words he had pushed her too hard, too fast. The last thing he wanted to do was frighten her away from Nordanese style sex play.

She stretched and yawned and Gregor relaxed a little. She didn't seem upset, at least. "Tell me of your life, Gregor," she said. "I barely know you save for what you can do to my body."

"My life?"

"Yes. How did you come to be lord here?"

He pulled her to him and kissed her temple. "I was born in the middle of a particularly long period when the castle women were not conceiving. My mother died in childbirth and I nearly died myself since there were no other nursing women to give me sustenance. The monogamous mate of the lord took me as her own. Lyia wished so much to have a child and she was so frightened that I would die, that her body actually began producing milk even though she hadn't given birth."

Anaisse nodded. "I have heard of this happening, but it's very rare."

"Lyia and the lord of the castle, Renan, raised me as their own child. They both died about five years ago. Renan went first and Lyia followed soon after as if from heartbreak."

She ran her fingers over his forearm. "They must have been very much in love. You sound as if you grew up surrounded by love."

"I did. Renan was like a father to me, though he could be a hard man at times. Lyia was always gentle and soft."

"So, that is why you agreed to a marriage. That is why you desire a deeper relationship with a woman? Because you witnessed Renan and Lyia's relationship?"

He tightened his grip around her. "Not just any woman, Anaisse, *you*."

She sighed. "I'm beginning to see that there is no reason to fear this situation. Nay, I'm very fortunate, I think."

"I hope you feel that way years from now. Hopefully, you will look back on our relationship with the same sentiment that Lyia looked back on hers with Renan. I will do everything to ensure that it's so."

Gregor rolled out of the bed and walked to his wardrobe. From it, he pulled a golden flaxcloth gown and laid it on the end of the bed. He looked at her in silent challenge. She would have to embrace Nordanese culture fully at some point.

Anaisse sat up and stared at it. He'd made clear what he wanted. Finally, she nodded. "All right."

He ordered a hipbath scented with *laia* flowers and lovingly bathed her. Then he dried her and slipped the gown over her head.

The gown fell to her ankles and was only partially made of flaxcloth. The sleeves were cut so the material at her wrists was long, falling to about her knees. He'd had it designed so that parts of it masked her breasts, the sweet curve of her buttocks and her mound. There was no sense immersing her in his culture all at once. They could take it step by step.

He undid her hair from the knot on the top of her head that had kept it up and dry for her bath, arranged it around her shoulder and took the headpiece from a nearby table. He set the delicate golden chain piece on her head so it draped over her long hair. A small crystal dangled over her forehead to settle on her third eye.

Gregor stood back and looked at her. The gown was more appealing for the curves and hollows of her body that were merely hinted at and not revealing. His mouth went dry.

"You look beautiful, *karisama*," he murmured.

She stared at him for a long moment, and then walked to him. "Gregor, I will try and suspend my fears." She smiled. "I'm coming to like you very much anyway."

Emotion swelled through him as he looked down at her. "I hope that one day you will come to love me, Anaisse."

As he was coming to love her.

Chapter Eight

"We must tie trade from Nordan and Sudhra together somehow. We must create an economic interdependency."

Anaisse glanced between the Nordanese noble and the Sudhraian merchant he addressed.

The merchant spread thick, meaty hands. "If you sweeten the pot enough, I'm sure most the Sudhraian merchants will choose to trade with Nordan rather than neighboring countries."

Anaisse cleared her throat. "The Sudhraians want Nordanese silk and spice. That's not a secret. That alone is a large inducement for Sudhraian merchants to focus trade here." There were murmurs of agreement throughout the chamber.

That morning, Gregor had herded Anaisse in to participate in meetings concerning policy-making issues concerning Sudhra. Thus far, the council members had listened carefully and with respect when she spoke, and actually weighed her opinions as though she were a man.

In Sudhra she would not have been allowed anywhere near such a meeting. Here she was expected to not only participate but to make decisions. At first she'd stumbled over her words expecting at any time to be reprimanded or sent from the room, but the lords and ladies — aye, there were even other women on the council — had only listened quietly and with interest.

She was still in shock from it.

Now the meeting was winding down from issues concerning Sudhra and some people were leaving the council room. She also rose, as she had no role to play yet in the decisions of local grievances aired before Gregor — complaints from lorddom farmers and the like. As time passed, she would also hear those at his side, however. Gregor they said they'd proceed slowly with the full pressure and weight of her responsibilities.

She took her leave, feeling Gregor's hot gaze on her all the way out the door. What they'd done together the night before had attuned her to him in a way she could hardly believe, let alone understand. Her body was super-sensitized and she was fully aware of all of Gregor's movement, every heated look from his dark eyes.

She closed the door to the council's chamber and walked down the corridor. Another novelty, besides having her opinions and suggestions valued, was the flaxcloth gown she wore. She felt free in it and sexy and aroused. The soft material stroked her thighs, breasts and stomach like the softest bird's wings as she walked and it excited her to know that glimpses of her nude body could be seen when she moved just right. Not having to wear a lung-compressing girdle was nice as well.

She turned the corner at the end of the corridor and entered open walkway running around the open courtyard on the level below. Though she was so deep in thought she barely knew where she was. Gregor's words repeated in her mind, *I hope you will come to love me, Anaisse.*

It was already happening. It was inevitable. How could she not love a man like Gregor? He had awoken something cold and dead within her. He'd caused it to flare to life along with her deepest emotions. He made her feel valued and beautiful, at the same time respected and womanly. They were feelings she'd never before experienced but had always longed for.

On the level below her, warriors practiced swordplay. She rested against one of the stone pillars and set her hands on the railing to watch. For as much the Nordanese made love to each other, they also trained.

Despite the chill autumn air, they were dressed only in training trews and did not wear shirts. One was black-haired and the other blond. They were both good-looking men. She watched their muscles flex as they moved. Although the men weren't nearly as attractive to her as Gregor, the sight of them still kindled a response within her.

She'd awoken that morning deliciously sore from Gregor's lovemaking. Even with the soreness, she'd still become aroused when he'd bathed and dressed her. It seemed he'd woken something within her, something primal and hungry, needy for sexual experimentation and activity. She'd repressed that part of herself for so long. Now it was like a ravenous animal within her that could not be sated.

The blond defeated the dark-haired man by sweeping his legs out from under him and bringing the edge of his blade to the man's chest as though in a killing blow. They exchanged tense sounding words and then laughed. The blond helped his opponent to his feet and they clapped each other on their backs, smiling.

Anaisse turned to leave, but stopped when she glimpsed a red-haired woman in a black hooded cape enter the courtyard from the shadows. She walked toward the men with a seductive sway to her hips, and the men watch her approach, transfixed. All thought of sword training seemed forgotten.

The woman stopped in front of the men and dropped the cape. Underneath it, she was nude. Anaisse raised an eyebrow. Perhaps she was not the only female within viewing range to be fascinated by the men at training.

The men dropped their swords and approached her. Anaisse could not hear what they said, though they spoke to the woman in hushed, loving tones. The dark-haired man drew her into his arms and kissed her while the blond went to her back, swept her long hair to the side and brushed his lips along her shoulder. She laughed at something the dark one said and rubbed herself between the men. Anaisse could practically hear her purr.

What would it be like to be between two male bodies like that? To have two cocks within her grasp? Two men willing and wanting to please her and one of them Gregor? Anaisse's pussy drenched at the mere thought of it.

Autumn Pleasures: The Union

She watched as the woman loosened the ties of the dark one's trews, then turned and did the same with the blond's. The blond kissed her and fondled her breasts as she pulled his trews down to stroke his thickening cock. The dark one slid his hand down her back and over her buttocks to her sex.

Anaisse felt hands encircle her waist and recognized Gregor's touch immediately. He pulled her back against him and laid a kiss to her earlobe. "Does it excite you to watch their play?" he murmured.

She blushed with shame and shook her head. "No. I'm curious, only."

He gave her several swift smacks to her buttocks. She gasped with startled surprise and pleasure as her pussy tingled and grew even wetter.

"Don't lie to me, Anaisse, and don't deny that which arouses you," he growled. "Or I really will put you over my knee."

Her breath was coming fast and hard now. Liquid trickled down her inner thigh. Below them in the courtyard, the threesome had lowered themselves to the carpet of grass. The redhead was on all fours, sucking the cock of the blond and the dark-haired man was licking her pussy from underneath and stoking his own shaft while he pleasured her.

Gregor embraced her and let his fingers flick over her hardened nipples. "I will ask you again," he purred. "Are you excited by watching?"

She swallowed hard and nodded.

"Are you aroused by the thought of two men at once, my *karisama*?"

Anot help her... "Yes," she breathed.

He kissed her throat. "I'm excited by the thought of watching another man pleasure you." His voice was raspy, marking his arousal. "I can imagine the look on your face, the sounds you would make." He groaned. "It could be arranged, Anaisse. Very easily."

Suddenly alarmed, she stiffened in his arms. "I-I'm not sure—" A part of her did want it, yet another part, the Sudhraian part, of her balked at the thought of it.

"No speaking," he commanded. "No objections. Grasp the railing and do not let go."

She curled her fingers around the railing as he'd requested. "But I want to touch you."

"I said no speaking. Watch the play below in the courtyard, love, and keep silent."

The dark one had risen up and was now fucking the red-haired woman with his fingers from behind. He fondled her clit with his free hand.

The blond appeared to be in the throes of ecstasy as she sucked his cock with his head thrown back and his body tense. The muscles of his throat stood out as he reveled in her attentions. The woman let out little moans around his shaft from time to time. Anaisse could see the length of his cock disappear between her lips, reappear, and then disappear once more, over and over.

Behind her, Gregor grasped her hips, pulled her buttocks to his cock, and thrust the hard length between her cheeks. She suppressed a moan, not wanting Gregor to know just how excited she was. Her sex ached for the good, hard fucking she knew he could give her. Gregor ran his hands over her breasts, cradling the weight of them in his hand and gently teasing her nipples. He smoothed his hands down her sides and eased the thin material of her gown up over her hips so she was exposed to anyone who might walk past.

She straightened, suddenly alarmed that just may happen. Gregor delivered another few slaps to her bare buttocks and she gasped and stilled. She closed her eyes. *Sweet Anot*, that had nearly made her come. Her pussy was weeping for him now.

"Do not move, my lady," he said, then brushed his fingers over her aching sex. She gasped. "I know you want this. I *know* you're excited by it. I will not allow you to feel shamed about what we do now. There is no shame in it. Understand?"

He rubbed the flat of his finger over her clit and she moaned. "Yes," she gasped out.

"Good. Now spread your legs to give me better access to your sweet pussy."

She widened her stance and gripped the railing. Gregor played his fingers over her sex. "You're so deliciously wet, so excited," he purred. He slipped a finger within her and pumped.

Below her the threesome had shifted. The red-haired woman was still on all fours, but now she sucked the dark one's cock while the blond pounded into her from behind. His buttocks flexed with every powerful thrust and she could see his shaft sliding in and out of the woman's slit.

"Please, Gregor. Take me," Anaisse moaned.

"You want my cock, sweet one?"

"Yes!"

She heard the blessed sound of fabric sliding over skin and then felt the head of Gregor's large shaft pressing at her from behind. He gathered some of her moisture and circled his finger around her anus as he pushed his cock into her passage. She gasped at the sensation of all the nerve endings around her nether hole being so deliciously stimulated.

Gregor drove hard into her pussy all the way to the hilt and she climaxed instantly at the feeling of him filling her. As the pleasurable spasms racked her body, Gregor slid his finger into her anus and thrust it gently in and out. He moved his cock at the same time so that both her pussy and anus were filled and stimulated. Just as she came down from one orgasm she was catapulted straight into another.

Gregor kept up the play at her anus while he shafted her, telling how beautiful and responsive she was in a low voice. Telling her how much he enjoyed her body and how she made him feel. She could not help the cries and moans he coaxed from her throat as he so skillfully manipulated her.

Gregor finally thrust all the way and went motionless as he let loose within her with a low groan. She felt his hot seed shoot far up within her to her womb. He removed his cock from her pussy and ceased the play at her buttocks only long enough to coat his fingers in more of her moisture then slip not one but two fingers back into her anus. She gasped at the sensation of her muscles being so stretched and tightened her grasp on the railing.

"Imagine my cock here, my sweet. Better yet, imagine a hard cock here and mine here," he purred, circling the entrance to her passage, then pressing two fingers within. Can you do it?" he asked, as he thrust them in and out of her. "Can you see it in your mind. Feel it?"

Yes...she could. She had time to nod once before she broke apart for the third time. She cried out and her knees nearly buckled from the force of it. Gregor rocked her back against him, kissed her head, then turned her toward him. He scattered kisses over her face.

"You're lovely, *karisama*. So perfect and beautiful." His voice seemed to shake with emotion. "Did I push you too hard? Too fast?"

She smiled. "No, Gregor. I am enjoying this exploration."

"That's good, for we've only just begun."

She pulled up his trews and tied them, and then he gathered her up into his arms and carried her back to his chamber.

* * * * *

Tol watched Lady Anaisse settle in one of the chairs by the fire in the common room. He ran a hand through his hair as he considered taking this opportunity to apologize. It was not a good thing to have the Lady of the Lorddom angry with you, he thought. Better to try and smooth things over as quickly as possible.

He drew a breath and approached her. She glanced up. When she caught sight of him, her countenance darkened. "Lady Anaisse," he greeted.

She scowled. "Tol, isn't it?"

"Yes."

He stood awkwardly, with her staring up at him as though she wished he'd go away. Long uncomfortable moments passed. Finally Tol cleared his throat and gestured at the chair adjacent to hers. "May I sit down?"

She shrugged. "You don't have to ask my permission to sit in that chair. I could not stop you even—" she smiled somewhat less than sweetly "—if I should desire."

Hmmm, he thought. Perhaps that was a yes? Tol sank down. He fidgeted a little under her gaze and finally leaned forward. "I just wanted apologize for giving you the odinroot. Gregor tells me you were displeased by my judgment in that situation."

She only stared at him with intense penetration. Idly, she drummed her fingers on the armrest.

Tol shifted in his chair. "I was merely acting in what I believed were your best interests at the time. I thought I was protecting you from the sights and smells of the battle. I thought you'd already had to deal with so much that I didn't wish any more on you."

More silence. A small line creased the skin between her eyes and she cocked her head to the side a little bit. *Goddess*, she was beautiful even when she was angry.

He babbled on. "I had no way of knowing, of course, what exactly you'd been put through and when you buried your face in my chest I took that as a signal that perhaps you were not faring well—uh—mentally and emotionally. Do you understand? I would do nothing to offend you on purpose, my lady."

Another long uncomfortable silence.

He swallowed hard and continued on. "I had no way of knowing at that time that your abductors had also used odinroot on you and that by doing so once again would bring up the terrifying issue of your loss of control. Uh—do you understand?"

A ghost of a friendly smile passed over her well-shaped mouth. "I understand you had good intentions." She pursed her lips and leaned forward as if to stand. "But next time, ask my *permission* before you make such a decision for me." She stood and with a swirl of rose-colored skirts and sweet scent she was gone.

Tol leaned back in his chair and let out a pent-up breath. She had an air of commanding presence around her. Not unlike Gregor. They were a good match, he mused. Together, they'd be a powerful force.

A familiar laugh reached his ears. Tol looked in its direction. Speaking of good matches...

He watched Melandra float across the chamber with two of her friends. A green diaphanous flaxcloth gown swirled around her luscious body. Her blood-red hair was loose this evening and hung to her waist. Her blue eyes danced as she talked and laughed with her companions.

It took Tol about two seconds to leap from his chair and follow her. "Melandra," he called.

She hesitated, and then turned with a smile on her generous mouth. Her friends called out their goodbyes and continued on. "Tol," she greeted him warmly. Always there was affection in her eyes, but Tol knew well she held herself in reserve. She didn't want to grow too attached to him. Did not wish to invest her romantic interests solely in him.

Goddess, how it cut him every time—that look of cool reserve in her eyes when she gazed at him. But he also knew of the fire beneath that façade and how easily he could stoke it to a raging inferno. She was not immune to him. Far, far from it.

He wanted Melandra for himself, no matter if it was against both his and her own nature and against Nordanese culture. He wanted to be the only man sliding into her sweet pussy—the only one she kissed and cuddled with during the night. The only one she shared her heart with.

"Where are you hurrying off to?" he asked.

She gave a short laugh. "Why do you wish to know?"

He shrugged. "I have more than a passing interest in what you do, Melandra."

She glanced away. "I-I'm going to visit Aric, if you must know." Her gaze steadied and her eyes flashed in warning. "Do I need to ask your permission for that?"

Tol clenched his jaw and fought to keep his voice even. "Why are you going to see Aric?"

She lifted her chin. "You sound jealous."

Without a word, he grabbed her by the upper arm and pulled her down the corridor and into a shadowed alcove. He walked her back until she was pressed against the wall. His hard chest rubbed her nipples into stiff peaks, so perfect for sucking. "Of course I'm jealous. I want you, Melandra. Only you." He lifted her dress and he grazed her clit with his fingertips in a gesture of possession. "And I want you to want only me."

She flinched, then let out a low sigh. But she didn't move away from him. "You have no claim over me or what I do. I should leave right now," she forced out.

Ah, but he did have a claim. Tol knew well the power he wielded over her body. She could never resist his touch. He had a need to remind her of that and to mark her as *his*. He rubbed her clit back and forth. She moaned and spread her legs just a little, allowing him better access.

He pressed his mouth to hers in a deep, possessive kiss. Then he pulled back and set his forehead against hers. "But you know you won't leave." He slipped two fingers into her pussy and thrust. *Goddess*, she felt so good—warm and wet. Her vaginal muscles rippled and pulsed and he wished his cock were within her.

She tipped her head back and closed her eyes. He lowered his head to kiss his way over her throat and collarbone. At the same time, he teased her clit with his thumb.

Her breath caught and she shuddered in pleasure. He placed the heel of his hand to her clit and rubbed as he stroked his fingers in and out of her. She tossed her head back and forth. "What you do to me," she murmured, "it's incredible."

He trailed his lips up to nuzzle her ear. He kept up the play at her pussy, driving her higher and harder. His tongue flicked out to trace the delicate whorls. "Come for me, Melandra. Come hard."

"Tol," she said in a low, breathy voice and then she cried out. The muscles of her core spasmed, and he covered her mouth with his and caught every one of her sweet moans against his tongue.

Breathing heavy and aroused beyond all belief, he snaked both hands around her waist and held while she relaxed in the aftermath of her climax. She dropped her head to rest on his shoulder.

"Ah, Tol," she murmured. "If only I could be certain you'd get me pregnant, I'd give you my life." She lifted her head and gazed up into his eyes. They glimmered bright with unshed tears. She pressed her lips to his in a long, sweet kiss. "You already have my heart," she murmured against his lips. Her voice broke on the words.

She pushed her way past him. Stunned, Tol let her. Melandra hesitated just outside the alcove. "Know that every man I take to my bed I pretend is you, but I beg you not to make this any harder than it already is."

And she was gone.

Chapter Nine

Haeffen scowled down at the nearly destroyed text and squinted. He could barely read the smudged and aged print scribed on the pages of the ancient and dusty tome. He'd scoured the libraries in the bowels of all the lorddoms since Nordan had defeated Sudhra, looking for the records of Ecasia, the land Nordan and Sudhra had once been. Now he found himself in the cold, musty depths of Adal's Lorddom, in the northernmost part of Nordan.

He skimmed a finger over the text as he read the ancient historical account.

In Ecasia, they'd worshipped the God Anot and the Goddess Ariane in tandem and in balance—the male and female. Harmony and wellbeing abounded for their people. The women and men had been fertile, so there had been no threat to their survival.

Soon the culture of Ecasia shifted. Bloodline, paternity, power, and hierarchy became increasingly important and valued. Women began to be treated as chattel and were traded in strategically planned matings to secure political alliances, power or land. Love ceased to be important in couplings, and the desires of the females stopped being considered. Their worth lay only in their ability to provide children to their lord.

Haeffen sighed. He knew all of that. He ran his finger over an interesting passage, skimming it.

It was soon after this shift in Ecasia's culture that the rate of fertility decreased dramatically. Some decreed it was a curse from the Goddess Ariane in retaliation for the abuse her daughters were enduring from her sons, and she'd cursed the seed of the men that it would take root but rarely. Soon, the population of Ecasia was greatly endangered.

Some men realized they had displeased the Goddess by treating her chosen sex so, and saw the error of their ways. They proposed changes in their social system and an improvement of the way they treated their women. But others had grown so drunk on power and control that they only grew angry with the Goddess that she dared to curse their seed. They turned to the God Anot solely and denounced the Goddess and her life-giving force. Why should they bow to a female deity?

And the balance was destroyed.

A long and brutal war had broken out between the followers of the God and Goddess. The followers of the God took up in the southern half of Ecasia and called it Sudhra. The followers of the Goddess stayed north and called their country Nordan.

Haeffen trailed his finger down several paragraphs. This was history he was already familiar with. He was looking for something else, something far more useful to the present than the past... His heart skipped a beat as he found a passage with the information he was looking for.

According to these ancient accounts, the Goddess Ariane's curse could be broken if the lands were merged and there was a representative from each willing to become a vessel for the supreme beings. A ritual was described as a way of communicating with the higher powers. A way the goddess might be reasoned with.

Haeffen read it over quickly and then slammed the book shut, sending up a cloud of dust.

He had to get this information to Gregor.

*****

The sack over her head cut off her air supply and chafed the skin of her cheeks. Her hair was stuck to her face in sweaty masses of tendrils that snaked their way into her mouth from time to time. The rope binding her wrists and ankles dug into her flesh until she could feel a hot viscous substance run down her skin – her blood. The blood flowed nonstop until she felt herself grow pale and still.

She screamed and screamed until she lost her voice, but no one came. Then she felt him enter her awareness. He was like a dark cloud in her mind consuming her sanity. She went silent and still and waited for him. Every breath brought him nearer, nearer.

Finally, he stood over her. He reached down, took her by the shoulders and shook her...

"Anaisse, wake up!"

Her eyes came open and she gulped air. She struggled against the arms that held her for a moment before she realized whose they were. "Gregor," she breathed in relief.

His arms tightened around her and she molded herself against his body. "You were whimpering and crying in your sleep," he said in a strained voice. "Another nightmare?"

She shivered and nodded. "It was a bad one."

He kissed the crown of her head. "Lay back, love."

She let him ease her back onto the pillows and cover her with the blankets she'd likely kicked off while she dreamt. She squeezed her eyes shut and tried to banish the remnants of the nightmare.

Beyond her nightmares, she sometimes experienced the sensation of being observed. From time to time as she walked through the keep she felt as though she was being watched – stalked. It always made a cold shiver run down her spine, made the hairs on the back of her neck stand on end.

Because of her nightmares and her feelings of being watched, Gregor had doubled the number of guards in and around the keep. He'd told her he was not worried that anyone would seek her out, but he'd ordered it done just to make her feel safer. Anaisse knew better. The Ganotte had not all been captured and she was, after all, the link between Sudhra and Nordan.

She'd feel much better if they caught Vant. However, so far they'd had no luck locating him.

Gregor kissed her temple. "Are you all right?" he asked.

She snuggled her face into his chest, laid a kiss to one of his nipples and smiled at his answering shudder. She fit so perfectly against him. "I am now. I can always count on you to save me from the dark."

Anaisse watched the shadows cast by the firelight dance over the walls as Gregor stroked her hair and soothed her with gently murmured words. The servants had moved the last of her things from her chamber into Gregor's that afternoon.

At some point she'd relented on the issue of keeping separate rooms, but she wasn't sure when. It must've been at some moment when she'd realized she was deeply in love with her husband and powerless to stop herself from being that way.

She snaked her hand down between them and found his cock. It lay large and soft against her palm, but began to respond when she wrapped her hand around it and slid the foreskin back.

His body came to full attention. "What do you think you're doing?" he purred into her ear.

She let out a sigh and stroked him to delicious hardness in a matter of moments. "It's comforting to me. Your arousal is like a talisman against the dark. Something—uh—solid for me to hold onto." She smiled. "You don't mind, do you?"

He growled and pressed her underneath him. "You're asking for trouble, love."

"Mmmm...I know. Trouble of the very best kind."

He moved his hand to her pussy and teased her clit. She caught her breath. "Come inside me, Gregor. Fuck me until I can't remember the nightmare anymore. Remind me that I'm warm and alive."

"Yes, I'll always save you from the dark, Anaisse." He covered her body with his.

Chapter Ten

"Where are you taking me?" Anaisse pulled her pelisse tighter around her throat against the chill wind. The biting promise of winter in the air practically stole her breath. He'd woken her early that morning, ordered her horse ready and then brought her out into the middle of the woods for some mysterious reason.

"You'll see," answered Gregor.

She sighed and tucked her head down to the horse's neck to clear a branch. Her mount cracked twigs beneath his hooves. Beyond the creak of the leather of her horse's saddle, it was the only sound she could hear. Even the birds had more sense than go out today.

She was freezing!

"What did you say?" asked Gregor.

"What? I didn't say anything."

He turned and flashed a smile at her. "You muttered something."

"Oh." She narrowed her eyes. "Probably that *I'm freezing*!"

He laughed. "Anaisse, this isn't Sudhra. We do have cold weather here."

"I noticed," she bit off.

"You need to get used to it. Anyway, we're almost there."

Gregor led her over a rise and through a leafless copse, then into a stand of evergreen. A large blue pool of water stood in the center of the secluded area. Anaisse walked her horse to the edge and saw that it was lined with rock and was so clear you could see to the bottom.

Gregor climbed off his mount, took a blanket and some linens from where they'd been secured to his saddle and set them by the side of the pool. Then he took off his shirt. Her breath caught at the sight of his chest. She never grew tired of seeing his magnificent body. He stepped toward the pool. "Come in with me, Anaisse."

She gaped. Had he lost his wits? "Didn't you hear what I said? It's freezing out here! It's nearly winter!"

"Yes, but the water is warm. It's fed by a hot spring. Come, feel it with your hand."

"A *hot* spring?" The word hot definitely held appeal. She dismounted, knelt and dipped her hand into the water. It was indeed warm, almost uncomfortably so.

"You see?" asked Gregor.

She looked up, saw he'd removed the rest of his clothing and tried not to swallow her tongue. He stepped down a series of graduated rocks leading down into the water. "I-I guess I could come in," she answered.

Because of the cold, it took her less than a heartbeat to make it from her the pile of her shed clothing to the pool. She sank down into the water with a grateful sigh. "Ah…it's so good to be warm again." A tingling sensation sunk into her muscles, almost like a full-body massage. She let out a low sound of satisfaction and closed her eyes.

"You're feeling the minerals. Wonderful aren't they? This is the first part of the gift I have to give you today. This pool will loosen your muscles. Relax you as you've never been relaxed. The effects will last for over a day and night and will prepare you."

She opened her eyes. "Prepare me? Prepare me for what?"

"That is the second part of your gift and it is a surprise."

She scowled. Surprises she didn't need. "A surprise? I really don't—"

"Anaisse?"

"Yes?"

"Come here."

His voice was a silken rasp moving over her skin even from a distance. She took a couple steps toward him and he grasped her wrists, pulling her through the water the rest of the way and flush up against him. The water against her bare flesh felt wonderful, but he felt better.

His gaze ate her up hungrily from head to toe through the clear water. "Play with your breasts for me, love," he purred in his dark silk voice.

She smiled seductively and trailed her hands over his upper arms to her breasts. She cupped and massaged them, then focused her attention on playing with her nipples. They hardened under her attention and she sighed with pleasure.

Gregor stared at her, his gaze growing passionate and dangerous. The muscles of his body were visibly tense. He reached out, moved her hands away and palmed her breasts. Her nipples stabbed up, demanding attention. He rubbed over them with the pads of his thumbs, making her moan. Her pussy was plumped, aroused, and her clit had distended and was now swollen. It begged for his attention. Biting her lower lip, she dropped her hand and rubbed her fingers over it. She tipped her head back and closed her eyes and a wave of pleasure enveloped her.

When she opened her eyes, it was to find Gregor's gaze full of erotic promise. His pupils were so large his eyes looked black.

He leaned back against the stone wall behind him and laid his hand on her lower stomach. She could feel the heat his palm gave off even in the water. She bit her lip to keep from moaning.

"Spread your legs for me, Anaisse," he said.

She moved her feet further apart and waited with anticipation for the touch of him against her. He placed a hand to her breast and stared into her eyes as he trailed his fingers slowly down over her skin to her pussy. First he teased her lips, and then he circled her clit.

"Do you like that, *karisama*?" he rasped.

She closed her eyes and nodded slowly, losing herself in sensation. "Mmmm." Her fingers found her nipples and caressed them.

"So do I."

Gregor leaned forward, put a hand to the small of her back and pulled her toward him. He lowered his head and placed his mouth to her breast, then flicked his tongue over her nipple as he slid his hand down and thrust two fingers in and out of her pussy.

Anaisse moaned long and low, reveling in the wonderful friction he exerted over her body. He nipped at her nipple with his teeth and she nearly came undone.

He kissed his way over her throat and sucked on her earlobe. Her hands tightened on his shoulders, then she moved them down, aiming for his cock.

"No, love. Not now. I would like to keep the control I have," he whispered into her ear. He added another finger to the play at her pussy and thrust.

"Oh, yes," she cried. Oh, God. She was going to go mad. "Gregor, make love to me, please."

"No. Not now. Tonight."

She started to protest, but he covered her mouth with his thrust his fingers into her again. He pumped her hard and fast, just like how she wanted his cock. His fingertips found and rasped over the sensitive concentration of nerve endings within her that he'd told her was her pleasure point.

She came undone. Spasms of pleasure shook her body and she cried out under the force of them. He drew her orgasm out until she thought she'd die from pleasure. Finally the tremors eased and she drew a long, shuddering breath.

She pushed away from him. "Why wouldn't you—"

"Shhh… Ask no questions. Let yourself soak in the water and allow the minerals to do their work." He grasped his erection, tipped his head back and groaned. "Believe me, I don't want to deny you, but you'll understand why I did soon enough."

She pushed back from the edge and let the comforting water cradle her. Her mind turned over possibilities for that night.

* * * * *

Later that afternoon, Anaisse wandered down the main corridor that led through the children's part of the castle. Here the few children that were born to the castle's inhabitants lived with their mothers and male caregivers. It was rare that a woman knew which man had sired her offspring, so all the men took turns coming in and spending time with the children. The raising of children was, overall, a community effort in both Nordan and Sudhra.

This part of the keep was kept well-secluded from the rest of the castle, so as not expose the children to open sex play before they were old enough to understand it. This wing of the castle was very spacious and was furnished more richly than the rest of the keep. Thick, soft carpet covered the stone floors, where rushes normally sufficed in most of the castle. Bright tapestries covered the walls and far more candles and windows provided light. Anaisse knew that a door on the end of the corridor led into a large garden where the children could run. Toys scattered the floor and sounds of children laughing and playing filled the air with a joyous resonance.

She her eyes and breathed in deeply, absorbing the sights, smells and sounds of the young. She wished for a child of her own more than anything. To have a child of Gregor's would be bliss beyond imagination.

Something brushed her hand and she looked down. A little girl with dark brown curls slipped her hand into Anaisse's. She looked to be maybe five or six.

"Hello," the little girl greeted her shyly. "My name is Lyssa."

Anaisse sank down to the carpet in order to look her in her eye. She smiled. "My name is Anaisse. Where is your mother, Lyssa?"

Clouds formed in Lyssa's eyes. Anaisse was immediately sorry she'd asked. "She isn't here anymore," replied the girl.

She wondered what she meant. Was her mother gone from the lorddom? Or had she died, perhaps? "Oh. I'm sorry, Lyssa. Would you like to walk with me in the garden?"

The little girl brightened and bobbed her head up and down.

Anaisse stood and began walking down the corridor holding the little girl's hand. A concerned young woman with dark red hair appeared in the doorway. The lines of her face eased when she spotted Lyssa. Anaisse deduced she must be a caretaker. "I'm taking her outside for a turn in the garden, but I'll have her back in soon," said Anaisse.

The caretaker gave a little curtsy. "Of course, my lady. I am Melandra. I often take care of the children at this time of day."

"Very nice to meet you, Melandra." So this was Tol's love, she mused. Gregor had told her about how Tol cared deeply for her and wished monogamy, but she wished so much for pregnancy that she would not commit to it.

"Lyssa is feeling sad today," said Melandra. "Her mother has recently left the lorddom and has not yet returned."

Anaisse paused. "How long has she been gone?"

Melandra frowned. "Over a moon's cycle, my lady." She faltered and glanced at Lyssa. "We are still waiting, but we fear that..." she trailed off meaningfully.

"I understand," answered Anaisse. "Come Lyssa."

They entered the bright sunshine filled day and amused themselves by walking around and smelling the various late-blooming flowers and collecting leaves from the trees. They finally found themselves sitting in the grass at the foot of a tree. Anaisse stuck a large purple cotas bloom behind Lyssa's ear and made her laugh.

The sound of scampering feet met their ears and a small boy appeared from around the trunk of a tree. "Come on, Lyssa. We're playing," he said. His cheeks were rosy and a smile lit his cherubic face.

Lyssa looked from her to the boy and back again, obviously unsure of what to do.

"Go on," Anaisse urged. "Go play."

Lyssa landed a quick kiss on Anaisse's cheek, then shot to her feet and followed the boy. The cotas bloom fell to the ground as she rushed away. Anaisse leaned back against the tree and stared at it. Bittersweet emotion filled her. She would likely never know the beauty of motherhood.

A large masculine hand picked the bloom up and Anaisse's gaze flew up to see Gregor standing above her. "Melandra told me you'd be here," he said.

She smiled. "This part of the keep is very nice. It's...relaxing."

"Relaxing?" Gregor laughed and settled down beside her. He gave her the bloom, then drew her into his arms. She was happy to snuggle against his chest. "You obviously haven't spent much time around children."

It was true, she hadn't. The highborn women of Sudhra weren't encouraged to spend much time in the children's wing. There were servants to see to such responsibilities. It was even more rare that a man should spend much time around them. She bristled. "Well, have *you* been around them much?"

"Yes, of course. I visit the children's part of the keep daily." He laughed again. "Believe me, it's not always a relaxing place to spend time."

"Still, I'd like a child," she said softly.

He arms around her tightened. "Yes, so would I. Perhaps the goddess will bless us."

"Perhaps."

"And there is always adoption. I was going to wait to tell you of Lyssa. I wanted to make sure there was not a chance her mother would return, but I see Lyssa found you."

Anaisse lifted her head. "She is a wonderful child. But what of Melandra? Doesn't she wish to adopt her?"

"I believe that's likely. There are many in the keep that will want her if her mother doesn't return. However, as rulers of this lorddom, we say who she will go to in the end."

"Hmm…maybe that would be a way for Melandra and Tol to be together? She'd have a child then and perhaps she'd be content to agree to be his monogamous mate?"

"Maybe." He paused. "I thought you didn't like Tol. Now you're figuring out ways to make him happy?"

"I never said I didn't like him. I just wanted him to be sure he understands the importance of allowing a woman to make her own decisions."

"Aye, well, I think Melandra is teaching him that, love."

"I suppose," she answered.

Anger flashed through Anaisse. "How could Lyssa's mother leave her child so easily when they are so hard-won?" she asked.

Gregor shrugged. "I do not have the answer to that."

She pursed her lips. "Well, while we wait to see if her mother returns, I will continue to visit Lyssa every day."

Gregor her pulled her toward him and laid a bone-melting kiss to her mouth. He pulled away a little to look at her and brushed the hair back from her face. "I believe Lyssa would like that very much. I know I enjoy looking at your pretty face every day."

The man did know how to sweet-talk her.

She played with a blade of grass and cast him a sidelong glance. "Gregor, what's my surprise this evening?"

He only laughed, stood, and pulled her to her feet. "The key word in that last sentence was *surprise*, love."

Autumn Pleasures: The Union

* * * * *

The rest of the day was a pleasurable anticipation. Finally, that evening, she entered their bedchamber and stopped short, staring at the bounty before her.

"Remember I said I'd make all your fantasies come true, Anaisse," said Gregor.

Apparently, Gregor had made good on his promise to bring another man to her bed. *This* is what he'd spoken of earlier that afternoon. Tol and Gregor now stood before her, watching her with dark, erotic promises in their gazes.

Gregor walked toward her slowly. His boots clicked on the stone floor with every step he took. He circled her with a predatory look in his eyes, reminding her of a jungle cat stalking its prey. Heat rolled off his muscular body and his gaze was just as hot as it roved her body, catching at her breasts and the patch of hair between her legs. "Good evening, Anaisse," he purred. "You're looking mouthwatering, as usual."

She closed her eyes for a moment, unsure if she could actually follow through on this. Two months ago, she'd had only contempt for sex acts like the one Gregor now offered her. Now her body hungered for them, needed them. Desire flamed through her alongside a small current of guilt. But the lust overshadowed her misgivings, drenched them in dark shadow.

Tol moved toward her and she watched him warily. "I know you were angry with me, Anaisse. I want a chance to make amends. In our culture sometimes rifts are healed by sex. The giving of pleasure from one to the other."

"Will such an act as this not also bring you pleasure?" she asked.

He stopped and looked her up and down. Tol was a handsome man, with long black hair and piercing blue eyes. A slow smile spread over his well-formed mouth. "Oh, aye. Yes, it will."

Gregor stood in front of her and traced her lower lip with his thumb. Anaisse's eyes fluttered shut at his touch.

"Tol, together, you and I will make her cry with pleasure," Gregor murmured, in a voice laced with passionate heat. "I will enjoy watching her face contort with the ecstasy of two men within her. I cannot wait to hear her moan and whimper."

She heard the heavy click of Tol's boots on the floor as he slowly walked to her. He bent his head down and spoke near her ear, making her shiver. "I have watched you ever since you came to the lorddom and thought you beautiful and desirable. When Gregor offered this opportunity to pleasure you this evening, I agreed right away. Will you accept me?"

She only hesitated for the length of a heartbeat. "Yes."

He smiled. "See, I asked your permission, my lady."

Tol dropped his head and ran his lips down her jaw line. He placed his fingers to the strap of her nightdress and pushed the thin strip of fabric of her shoulder. "I wanted to rush in and kill those men who held you captive along with Lord Gregor."

"Why would you risk your life for me?" she asked in a shaky voice.

From behind, Gregor nuzzled her ears and throat. "You forget we are Nordanese. We do not like to see women treated the way you were. We want blood on our blades for those crimes." He laid a line of kisses along her shoulder and pushed the other strap of her nightdress off her shoulder. Tol and Gregor held themselves away from her, allowing the gown to slither down her body and pool at her feet, leaving her bare between the two still clothed men. It made her feel vulnerable and highly aroused.

Gregor turned her toward him. Anaisse put her arms around Gregor's neck and let him pull her into an embrace. He kissed her deep, his tongue stroking against hers hard. At the same time his hand snaked between their bodies and trailed down to the apex of her thighs. He found her clit and rubbed at it. "Tonight you have us both to pleasure you," he murmured into her mouth.

Her flesh pebbled in the cool air and she whimpered under the sweet demands of his lips and tongue, and the spell his words seemed to weave around her.

Behind her, Tol brushed her long hair to the side and let his teeth and lips play along her shoulder, kissing, nipping and tasting, and awakening every last nerve. He slipped his hands around her front and played with her breasts with practiced ease, palming them and tweaking her nipples.

The sensation of four hands on her body caused her knees to go weak. She could not imagine more pleasure than this. She reached out and grasped Gregor's upper arms, feeling his biceps flex beneath her fingers.

From behind, Tol ran his hands from her shoulders and down her sides. "Part your legs," he commanded. She spread her legs and he slipped his fingers inside her from behind and thrust. She gasped and instantly soaked his hand.

"She's ready, Gregor," Tol said softly. "She is very wet."

Gregor pulled away from her. "Well then, let's her bring her to the bed."

They each took her by the hand and led her across the floor to the bed. She sat down on the edge of the mattress, made quick work of Gregor's trews and slipped her hands inside to stroke his long, thick phallus. Then she did the same with Tol.

Tol's shaft was long and almost as thick as Gregor's. She followed the thick vein running from the head of his cock to its base with her fingertip, drawing a ragged sound from Tol's throat.

She closed her eyes for a moment, savoring the feel of two cocks before her, one for each hand. She wrapped her hand around each, exploring the smooth, silky heads, and stroking down their hard lengths. Her smile widened when both the men tipped their heads back on a groan.

Dear Anot...this was power. Her smile widened.

She slipped Gregor's cock into her mouth and pushed him in as far as she could. At the same time she caressed and stroked

Tol's shaft. Gregor's hands fisted in her hair as she licked and sucked on him. She purred like a cat, deep in her throat, reveling in the feel of them, the sounds of arousal they made.

Tol covered her hand with his. "You kiss Gregor there, I should get to kiss you here." He dropped his hand and ran it over her mound.

Gregor moved then. She made a small sound of dismay at the loss of him. A low, deep chuckle rumbled through him. "I'm coming back, love." He stripped off his clothes and went to kneel on the bed.

Tol also stripped. His body was warrior shaped, like Gregor's. Strong muscles marked him from head to foot. His hair was darker than Gregor's and he had slightly more of it scattered over his chest. His cock rose strong and long from a nest of hair a shade darker than that of his head.

Gregor crooked a finger at her and she climbed onto the mattress after him. "Get on all fours, my love," he told her. "It will allow Tol to pleasure you as you pleasure me."

She did so in front of him and took him back into her mouth, worshipping his cock with passion until Gregor was groaning. She felt Tol arrange himself underneath her. He eased her hips down so she straddled his face. The first lick to her clit had her moaning around Gregor's cock. Tol sucked and laved her sex, proving he had a very skillful tongue and lips. His fingers slipped inside her as he bathed her pussy with his tongue, and his mouth fastened around her clit, sucking and rasping his teeth gently against the sensitized bit of flesh. Then he reached up and stroked and pulled on her nipples at the same time. She moaned against Gregor's shaft.

"*Enough!* I must touch her," growled Gregor. He pulled her away from him and flipped her onto her back. Both Gregor and Tol rose over her. Her body quivered with anticipation. Then their mouths and hands began to work magic over her. Tol dropped his mouth to her breast and laved and sucked her nipples each in turn. Her fingers knotted in his thick hair.

Autumn Pleasures: The Union

Spreading her thighs wide, Gregor settled between them. He laved over her pussy with the flat of his tongue and teased her vaginal lips. Then he circled her nether entrance at the same time with a fingertip, awakening all the tiny nerves there and causing her to moan. Anaisse now understood the purpose of the mineral bath. It had loosened all her muscles and would make it easier for one of them to enter her anus.

Gregor licked over her labia and then thrust his tongue into her pussy. She reared up, pressing her swollen sex into his face. His finger traced around and around her anus like a dark promise, teasing her. He half groaned, half growled into swollen, damp flesh, vibrating her.

Anaisse reached down between her body and Tol's to find his cock. She took the hardened length against her palm and worked it, drawing a low groan from the man. A bit of moisture had pooled on the top of his shaft. They both shifted a bit, bringing his cock to her mouth, and she licked up the bead of come he'd secreted. Tol tipped his head back on another groan as she engulfed the head of his shaft in her mouth. He reached down and palmed her breast and they submerged themselves into an ocean of mutual pleasure.

She had never felt so aroused in her life. Her mind was a cloud of feeling and emotion. It was so thick that rational thought seemed unable to penetrate it. Her world now was all about Gregor's mouth on her, his tongue laving over her sex. It was about Tol's cock in her hand and under her tongue and his work at her breast. Her world was all about pleasure—sweet, deep, dark and overwhelming.

Gregor nipped gently at her clit with his teeth, causing her to cry out in maddening ecstasy and bringing her attention back to him. He plunged his fingers within her pussy and thrust deep and hard, drawing over her pleasure point within. He growled low in his throat, and sucked hard at her clit.

With a sharp cry, she came. She thrust her hips up as pleasure washed over her in intense waves. Hot liquid trickled down her inner thigh. Gregor drew out her peak by laving her clit and making low sounds of approval in his throat that made her shiver and shake in ecstasy. As soon as her climax ebbed away, her clit swelled insatiably once again, wanting more of the incredible sensation.

She wanted, *needed*, to be well and thoroughly fucked. She also needed to return some of the pleasure she'd been given. Anaisse sat up and pushed at Gregor's shoulders. He let her press him down onto the mattress beneath her. Feeling suddenly ravenous for his body, she lowered her head to his chest and closed her lips around one of his flat, round nipples. She laved it and bit it, loving it with her mouth.

"Anaisse," Gregor murmured, brushing her heavy hair out of her face and over her shoulder. "How lovely you are."

He reached down and cupped her chin bringing her face up to look into his. His dark eyes were heavy-lidded. She moved up his body and straddled him, then lowered her mouth to his. He set his cock to the entrance of her passage, and pushed himself inside. He pressed his hands to her hips and thrust up hard, until he was sheathed within her to the hilt. He groaned, a deep, reverberating sound.

She gasped and arched her spine, throwing her head back. She was seated on him to the hilt, completely impaled on his long hard cock. "Yes," she hissed.

Tol sat on the bed, stroking himself and watching them. "I can wait no longer, Gregor," he bit off.

Out of the corner of her eye, Anaisse watched Tol take a vial of something from a nearby table and come back with it in his hands. He put a little of whatever fluid was in the vial on his fingers.

He straddled Gregor's legs and pressed his chest to her back. "I am going to prepare you for my entry," he murmured. "Though I think you're more than ready." She could hear the gentle smile in his voice. "Aren't you?"

"Oh, yes."

Autumn Pleasures: The Union

He pushed her head down, so her rear was exposed to him and she practically rested on Gregor's chest.

Tol covered her back. His warm flesh teased her sensitive body and he caressed her lower hip, moving slowly toward her nether entrance. When he reached it, he rimmed her anus with the fluid—she guessed it was a kind of oil—while nipping at her neck. The liquid was slick and warmed her skin.

She tensed.

"Shh...it will feel good," whispered Gregor as he palmed her breasts. "I'll be within your passage and Tol will be within your anus at the same time.

Tol breached her nether entrance with a finger and thrust. Gregor moved beneath her, driving his cock in and out of her so slowly she thought she'd go mad. Then Tol added another finger, widening her. Her body felt as though it would explode from all the sensation. She shuddered and closed her eyes.

"Do you like that, love?" purred Gregor.

"Yes," she breathed.

Tol removed his fingers and Anaisse felt the smooth, velvety head of Tol's cock pressed at her nether hole. He circled it, and then entered. She gasped as his full, broad length filled her. It was slightly painful, even though her muscles were relaxed from the mineral bath. The slight pain she felt, however, seemed to only inflame her lust.

"Oh, *Anot*," she cursed under her breath. The feel of two cocks within her, possessing her was beyond description. She couldn't stop moaning as the men started to shaft her slowly...so very, very slowly. She opened her eyes and looked down at Gregor. He held her gaze, watching the play of pleasure across her face.

Gregor shifted his hips and the angle of his thrust changed. Now the tip of his cock rubbed across the pleasure point every time he drove into her.

Tol and Gregor both placed their hands to her waist and drove her on their shafts, hammering into her. Anaisse let a low, primal moan rip from her throat. The feelings she experienced now were like nothing she could've ever imagined. The hot, hard chests of the two men braced her. Their thick cocks surged in and out of both her openings relentlessly, driving her pleasure hard and high. A second climax ripped through her body and pulled a long cry from between her lips. It was so exquisite she almost wept.

Both men groaned at the same time. Sweat sheened Gregor's body. She bent her head down for a kiss and he found her mouth and slid his tongue in to play against hers as her third peak washed over her. He consumed every passionate sound she made.

Behind her, Tol cried out and she felt his hot seed flood into her. He withdrew from her body and collapsed onto the bed, breathing hard.

Pressing a hand to the small of her back, Gregor flipped her so he was on top. He plunged into her over and over. The tip of his shaft massaged her pleasure point deep within and pressed her hips deep into the mattress with every hard, deep thrust.

She closed her eyes. "Oh, yes, Gregor. Yes," she breathed. She'd never felt anything better in her life than his shaft hammering into her.

Emotions passed like swift moving over his face as he looked down at her. Love shone so strongly in his eyes that recognizing it almost made her climax. Responding emotion bubbled up within her fast and hard, meeting his love and mating with it as sure as their bodies came together. She felt completely and undeniably his in this moment.

On her fourth climax, Gregor yelled out, pinning her hard against the mattress and injecting his seed into her. She hoped he'd given her child.

They clung to each other, breathing heavy. She clasped her legs around him and he lowered his head to bury his face in her neck. He remained deep within her. Their bodies, minds, and emotions were one.

As if from far away, she heard the sounds of Tol gathering his clothing and then the click of the door closing as he discreetly left them alone.

Finally she let out a laugh. Joy suffused her from her head to her toes. Gregor raised his head and looked down at her. He found her lips with his. "Anaisse," he murmured against them.

"Gregor," she murmured back, smiling.

His arms tightened around her. "I love you, Anaisse," he whispered. "I want you to be mine."

"I am yours. I'm your wife."

"No, that does not make you mine. Only your love makes you mine."

She lowered her gaze and swallowed hard. Then she looked up him. Her voice shook with emotion when she finally spoke. "I *do* love you, Gregor." She paused and looked up at him. "I love you," she repeated. Her heart swelled with the truth of those words. "I *am* yours."

He smiled. Then he moved to the side, his cock sliding from her passage. He pulled her back flush up against his chest and pulled a blanket over them. She snuggled into the heat of his smoothly muscled chest and sighed.

"As I am yours," he murmured into her hair.

* * * * *

Vant watched from the darkened corner of the chamber where he'd hidden himself behind the wardrobe and fisted his hand so hard his fingernails gouged his palms, breaking skin and drawing blood. It ran hot though his fingers, but he barely noticed.

He'd been there the whole time, watching his pure, sweet Anaisse sully herself with these pagan barbarians. He grimaced. Not one, but two of them.

At the same time.

She was lost forever to Anot now with such wanton behavior. She was soiled and dirty and in need of cleansing. His one and only purpose now was to punish her for what she'd done. It overshadowed all his other plans.

Punish her for the whore she'd become.

He'd abduct her and make her bow her head in supplication to Anot. Make her beg for forgiveness before he split her veins wide and made her blood run until they were empty and her body was cold.

Anyway, his other plans were so much dust. Tonight, he'd intended to make it appear as though Gregor had murdered her in a passionate rage, but that was no longer an option. Gregor and Anaisse were in love now and too many people had witnessed that love for anyone to believe Gregor would do her harm. He himself had watched them at dinner just that night. They'd acted in love, kissing and feeding each other bits of meat from their plates. The tension he'd seen between them before in the garden was virtually nonexistent.

Aye, they may have only declared their love tonight, but it had been apparent not only to him but to all others long before.

Frustration stabbed through him. That would make his plan more difficult to carry out, but not impossible. He could still use her death to break the alliance between Sudhra and Nordan. He could still induce the Sudhraians to rise up against those who now occupied their land. She was the official link after all.

All he had to do was sever it.

Chapter Eleven

Anaisse awoke and felt first the hood over her face, restricting her airflow, then the bonds wound painfully tight around her wrists and ankles. It was a feeling to which she was accustomed. Shock ripped through her. Was she dreaming now? Nay…she would not be feeling the biting pains of her bonds were this a dream.

Not again! *Not again! Not again!*

Anot, it was just like her nightmare.

"No," she whispered and swallowed hard. Tears pricked her eyes. "*No!*" she wailed. She thrashed hard against her bonds and screamed long and loud.

"Hush now, my lady."

She stilled, recognizing the voice. "Vant."

"It is I, Lady Anaisse. I know you must remember me well."

"Of course I do. We've known each other since we were practically child—"

"*Do not speak of such things now.*"

She went silent. Oh, if he allowed it she'd speak of such things long and loud in an effort to make him remember she was a human being and once had been a friend. "Take off the hood, Vant, so I may see you," she requested softly.

Silence.

She could hear his breathing, harsh in the otherwise quiet air and her low shallow fight for breath against the burgeoning panic she felt. Where were they? Where had he taken her this time? She counted her heartbeats to stay calm. One after another until it became the only thing she was aware of—the hard, heavy thump of her own heart.

Finally, the hood was drawn over her head. Her tangled and snarled hair fell into her face and tickled her nostrils. A wall behind her braced her back. At least she was sitting up and not sprawled on her back or her side. She wore a dirty shift she didn't recognize and her feet were bare.

She took a deep breath of cool air and smelled herbs. She glanced around. He'd brought her to a cottage. The hearth was cold and it looked abandoned save for the drying herbs hung in bundles from wooden rafters. She lay among the rushes on the floor and Vant stood above her, looking down. Her heart stopped when she glanced behind him. Two bowls and several thin, sharp looking knives lay on the floor among the rushes.

She squeezed her eyes shut and counted her heartbeats again in an effort to force down the cloying dread that was currently trying to climb up her throat.

"Anaisse, open your eyes. You wanted to see me."

She opened them. "How did you get me out of the castle, Vant? How did you get me out without Gregor or the guards noticing?"

He gave a loose shrug. "You and Gregor were easily drugged while you slept. I got out easily since the guards knew me as a servant. I've been coming and going for weeks now. To get you out I disguised you as a sack of weed clippings from the garden to be dumped in the forest."

Coming and going for weeks now. He'd been watching her with Gregor, with the Nordanese. He likely felt she'd betrayed Sudhra. She now knew with certainty that the knives and bowls behind him were meant for her.

He bent down and looked her in the eyes. The smile that spread across his mouth was chilling. "You've been a bad girl, Anaisse." Madness shone in his gaze. "I've seen it all."

She swallowed hard. "Why would you say that, Vant? I've done nothing but fall in love and integrate myself into the culture of my lord's people."

He grimaced. "You mean you've fallen in love with your enemy and given in to their debauched way of life. You've comprised yourself and whored for their culture."

"I only want what's best for Sudhra, Vant. It's best they ally with Nordan. It's best we unite the countries as they were once united. It is the only way we will survive ultimately, by breaking the curse on our fertility."

He straightened. "You've been twisted by them," he roared and began to pace back and forth over the rushes. "They've turned your mind to their will, their agenda. I should've known it would happen. You're a woman, therefore your mind is weak."

"Vant—"

"Silence! It's partially my fault. I should not have waited so long to take you. I should've carried out my plans immediately, the very first day I saw you in the gardens with him. That was before he'd taken you to his bed and seduced first your body, and then your mind to his way of thinking. Instead, I waited and I watched." He shook his head back and forth violently. "Too long. Too long."

Ice ran through her bloodstream. At some point, he'd lost his sanity. He'd be so much more difficult to deal with this way. He'd be so much harder to reach. "Vant," she said softly. "Please, sit down. Let's talk. Let's talk of home and of the past. Please."

He stopped in the middle of the floor and looked down at her. "You don't understand, Anaisse. I'm going to have to kill you."

She forced her fear down, though she could taste it right behind the back of her tongue. It was a metallic-flavored growing thing. It was something alive—a monster ready to consume her at any moment. "I know," she forced herself to say. She tipped her head to the side and forced a gentle smile. "But do me the courtesy of sitting with me and talking for a while first."

"I suppose we have a little time."

"Good," she cooed, as if talking to a child. "Sit down and talk with me."

He hesitated, then settled himself cross-legged on the rush-strewn floor.

She studied the wild look in his eyes and forced a smile to her lips. "Remember when we were children and we would sit cross-legged in the great hall before the fire? We'd talk and share pastries from the kitchen."

"Yes, I remember. Gingerbread was always your favorite."

"Yes, that right." Her false smile broadened. "It still is. Maybe we could go back to the lorddom now and share some." Dark clouds rolled over his expression and she spoke quickly to divert the storm. That had been the wrong tact. "Remember sometimes how we would play *sarendice*?" she asked.

His eyes glazed over. "Yes, I remember. I used to let you win."

She forced a laugh. The sound was shaky and harsh and made her shiver. She swallowed hard and steadied herself before speaking. "And I used to let *you* win sometimes. Remember riding horses through the priestdom woods?"

He smiled and nodded slowly. Suddenly rage twisted his features. "I see what you're doing!" he shouted. He shot to his feet.

The barely restrained monster that was her fear reared its head. "W-what do you mean?"

"You're trying to make it more difficult for me to kill you and you're stalling for time, hoping Gregor will come to your rescue." He shook his head at her. "He's not coming, dear Anaisse. There's no possible way he could know where we are."

"Vant, I—"

He stood and yanked her up by one of her bound arms. Pain shot down from her shoulder to her elbow to her wrist and she cried out.

He dragged her to the opposite wall and what she saw there made her shiver in dread. Two shackles were inset into the wall. He dropped her between them. Her buttocks made contact with the floor and her back hit the wall hard enough to knock the wind out of her. He picked up one of the knives and walked toward her.

Her breath caught in her lungs as he bent over and cut the rope binding her hands. He grabbed her forearms and she twisted and fought against him. With far superior strength, he forced her wrists into the shackles and locked them.

"Don't do this!" she screamed. Tears ran freely down her cheeks. "Please, Vant, *please*. Don't do this!"

He cupped her cheek and gazed into her. "You're making this sacrifice for your country, Anaisse. It's the least you can do since you've betrayed it so badly."

She sobbed now. "I've betrayed no one, Vant!"

He ignored her, stood, and picked up the bowls. The panic she felt as she watched him walk toward her rocked her to her very core. She pulled and strained against her bonds and screamed and sobbed until her throat felt raw.

He set one bowl beneath her left hand and the other bowl under her right. His hands shook as he brought the knife to her left wrist. Tears streamed down his face. "I'm sorry for this, Anaisse. I loved you once."

"Please," she whispered.

The blade was so sharp that when cut into her flesh it didn't even hurt. Her blood began trickling from the split he'd made in her vein and dripped into the bowl. The sensation was very strange, hot and cold at the same time. After he'd made the incision in her other wrist a bizarre calm stole over her. She stopped fighting against the shackles and went silent.

Gregor. How worried he must be by now. How terrible would he feel when he could never find her? Never know what had become of her? Would he think she'd run away from him?

She'd miss him so very much.

She watched Vant through the tangled veil of the hair that had fallen over her eyes.

He stood and looked down at her for a long moment. "Goodbye, Anaisse," he said. "Fare well in the Underworld." Then he turned and walked out of the cottage.

She heard the sounds of his horse leaving the area and then there was near silence. Only the *drip, drip, drip*, of her blood into the bowls. Outside the birds sung in the trees, sounding so normal and strange in her ears.

Her heartbeat grew loud in her ears until it was the only thing she could hear in all the world. Then it grew fainter and she grew colder.

Fainter and colder.

Her teeth chattered and her eyelids fluttered closed.

Gregor…

Chapter Twelve

"She's definitely gone, my lord," said Tol. The guards at the front gates believe she left with a man they thought was a servant. He was supposed to dump some refuse in the woods, but he never returned to the castle."

Gregor grit his jaw and fisted his hands. He needed to stay in control. Anaisse counted on him now to remain controlled and together. That morning he had awoken to a cold, empty bed and had known instinctively that something was wrong. He'd searched the castle for Anaisse and come up empty. Somehow he knew she was nowhere in the lorddom. He couldn't *feel* her anywhere close.

"Do you suspect the Ganotte, my lord?" finished Tol.

"I don't know. It could be the work of the Ganotte, yes. That would seem likely."

"We never did locate Lord Vant."

Gregor fought the enraged roar burbling up his throat. "I am aware of that," he forced out in a low, dangerous voice. "Bring me Haeffen. He may be old, but he is the best tracker we have. I will gather the men and wait for you at the front gate. And do it *quickly*."

"Yes, my lord." He turned and left.

Minutes later they were assembled outside the walls of the castle and examining all the tracks that led away from the front gates.

It was necessary to follow every fresh set away from the castle in order to find the ones that led off in directions that were completely unique and unusual. It was tedious and time consuming work and every second that ticked by had Gregor more agitated. When they'd determined which were the most likely sets of tracks, Gregor broke the soldiers up into small groups to follow each and every one.

Gregor took his time deciding which set he would trail. In the end, he ordered his group to follow the set that he had the strongest instinctive feeling about and took Tol and Haeffen with him.

They set off into the woods. Haeffen rode lead, watching and reading the trail as only he could. At the same time, Haeffen told him about the ritual that had the potential of capturing the attention of Anot and Ariane.

Gregor only hoped Anaisse still lived and would be able to play her part in it.

Every moment that passed made the cage of fear around Gregor's heart grow tighter. He gripped the reins of his horse until he couldn't feel his fingers anymore. His jaw was clenched so tight he doubted he'd ever be able to open it again.

Dark images and thoughts swarmed through his mind as he fought a rising feeling of dread. He would not, *could* not, lose Anaisse now…or ever.

The feel of her soft skin against his filled his mind as surely as the sweet scent of her hair suffused his nostrils. She completed him now in so many ways. Her absence was like a piece of himself gone.

It was late afternoon when they glimpsed a cottage nestled in among the trees. Gregor's heart rose into his throat. He knew somehow that he'd find her inside. Her presence filled his awareness with a screaming need. Aye, she was within and all was not well. He kicked his heels into his horse's sides and raced to the small, dilapidated building. Not waiting for his men, he swung off the horse and raced inside with his sword drawn. The door slammed against the wall, echoing through the one-room cottage.

He glanced around with wild eyes. Sunlight filtered in through a hole in the roof and dust motes floated lazily through the wide beam of light.

His heart skipped a beat when he caught sight of her. Her arms were flung out to her sides and secured by shackles, her bare feet and legs smeared with grime. Her head was bowed and her hair lank.

She was so very, very pale.

His mind took a moment to register the blood. *All* the blood. When it finally did, he let out a roar and ran to her. "Anaisse!" He knelt before her, tipped her face up. Her eyes were closed.

His hands shook as he undid the clasps on the shackles and released her wrists. Very gently he took her into his arms. She was heavy, limp, and cold. Her head lolled to the side.

Hot moisture marked his face. Something salty ran into his mouth and he realized he was weeping. "Anaisse, please, love. Please," he pleaded. He smoothed her hair away from her face. She gave no response.

Gregor heard noise at the doorway of the cottage and looked up to see Tol and Haeffen standing there. They both looked shocked. "Bandages. Hot water. Healing herbs," he demanded in rapid-fire succession. When they hesitated he bellowed, "*Now!*"

Tol moved, but Haeffen remained. Deep lines of grief marred Haeffen's already deeply lined face. "My lord—"

"Don't say it. Don't even think it!" Gregor raged, holding Anaisse closer to his chest. Her blood-smeared arm flopped to the side. A long, deep cut marred her from her wrist halfway to her elbow. The bastard had sliced her veins wide open.

Haeffen took careful, measured steps toward him. The rushes shifted softly under his boots. He knelt in front of Gregor and laid his hand to Anaisse's cold cheek. "Please, my lord. I know this is difficult. Will you please allow me to—"

"Check to see if she lives?" His voice sounded raspy and wild to his own ears.

Haeffen eyed him warily. He nodded once.

Her bloodied hand twitched.

Hope ripped through him. Her eyes fluttered open and her breath came shallow and hard. "Gregor," she rasped.

Gregor smiled at her. "You're going to be fine, love. I'm going to make sure of it." He shot Haeffen a look of challenge. "See, she's fine."

Haeffen glanced at the bowls that Gregor had been trying not to truly see. They overflowed with her blood. When the old man looked back at him his expression was grim.

"Vant," she breathed. "It was him."

"And so he will pay, love," said Gregor.

Tol raced into the cottage, his arms overflowing with the items Gregor had requested and dropped to his knees before Anaisse.

Haeffen took her into his arms. "I will bandage her and we will perform the ceremony."

Gregor shook his head. "She's not strong enough for it. We need to concentrate on healing her."

Haeffen stared at him. "We must do it while she still lives, Gregor. It may be the only chance we have to break the goddess's curse."

"No!"

Anaisse made a small sound in her throat. Her lips and cheeks were near white. "Break...the curse?" she rasped in a halting voice. "Whatever it is. Do it."

"Love, we need to make you well," said Gregor.

"Ceremony...do it," she repeated.

With Anaisse's consent given, Haeffen and Gregor cleansed and wrapped her wrists while Tol and the rest of the men cast a circle with stones on the cottage floor under Haeffen's directions.

Gregor gathered Anaisse into his arms and knelt in the center of the circle with her.

"Everyone, out," commanded Haeffen. All the men filtered out of the room, leaving only Gregor, Anaisse and Haeffen.

Gregor bent his head to Anaisse and kissed her lips for the hundredth time since he'd found her. "Stay with us," he pleaded softly.

Her eyes fluttered open and then closed. "I love you, Gregor," she murmured. "But I don't know how long I...can...stay. Hurry, please."

Gregor looked up at Haeffen with tired, sad eyes.

Haeffen opened the book in his hands and began to read the words to the ritual aloud in ancient Ecasian.

In the name of the people of Ecasia
We call upon the caretakers
Those who create, benefit, and reprimand
In equal measures of punishment and love

May the power of Anot fill the room now
Infuse this vessel with power
Drawn from the blessed male who rules above
with equal measures of punishment and love

May the power of Ariane fill the room now
Infuse this vessel with power
Drawn from the blessed female who rules above
with equal measures of punishment and love

A very faint buzzing began in the room, making Haeffen's words falter. The buzzing grew louder as Haeffen continued.

Gregor's skin tingled and a sense of strong presence filled the small cottage. He felt it watching them, assessing them. It moved around the room, and into the circle of stones where the sense of presence grew stronger and the buzzing became louder.

We beseech the God Anot and the Goddess Ariane

Fill these children.

Take solid form to allow communication.

The buzzing grew so loud Gregor could barely hear Haeffen's words. The presence stepped up to Gregor's back, causing all the small hairs on the back of his neck to rise. The presence entered him and he drew a surprised breath as the energy filled him. He felt like himself, and yet...*not*. The buzzing ceased.

In his arms, Anaisse took a deep gulp of air and opened her eyes.

Gregor glanced up at Haeffen. "Anot wants to know why you summoned him." He didn't understand how he knew that, only that he did. Anot had become a part of him.

Anaisse sat up. "This one is very damaged and unable to communicate well with me. She is not fully present," she said.

Gregor immediately understood that Anaisse was too far gone to share her body with Ariane as he currently shared his body with Anot. Ariane overpowered Anaisse's personality completely.

Anaisse/Ariane turned to him. "Did you do this to her?"

He shook his head. "No. I would never harm her. Another did this to Anaisse."

She put her hand to her temple. "She will not live," she murmured to herself. She looked up at Haeffen. "Speak quickly. I do not wish to be in this body when it dies. It's a most unpleasant sensation."

Anger tore through Gregor. He opened his mouth to reprimand her for her callousness but Anot closed his mouth for him. *Allow me to deal with her*, came a voice within his mind.

Inwardly, Gregor relented and was able to once again open his mouth. "This one called Gregor truly loves that one called Anaisse. As you and I love each other, my Ariane."

She turned to Gregor. Her face lit with hope and love. "Anot?"

"Yes, my love."

"It's impossible they share such love. Men do not love women anymore. They treat them as chattel. They abuse them and neglect them."

Haeffen cleared his throat. "How long has it been since you've taken a close look at your children, my goddess? We have couples here in Nordan who love deeply to exclusion of others and have bonded as you are bonded with Anot."

She shot a piercing look in Haeffen's direction. "Do you mean to gainsay me? What do you want of me? Why have you summoned us?"

"We've joined Nordan and Sudhra, my goddess," said Haeffen. "We are working now to create Ecasia once more. But to do that we need for you to break your curse of infertility."

"Why should I? I've seen no evidence that anything has changed with those to the south."

"I love Anaisse, my goddess. I am Nordanese and she is Sudhraian," said Gregor.

She breathed in deeply and closed her eyes. "I *do* feel the love this one has for you." She smiled. "It is warming and overwhelming."

"Not only have they joined in love and in marriage, they have created a union between Nordan and Sudhra," said Haeffen. "They want once again to unite the lands and bring the worship of Ariane and Anot back together again. In tandem. Separate no longer."

Anot forced Gregor to speak. "They want to bring *us* back together again, my love. It has been so long."

"That would be nice," she murmured dreamily. Her eyes opened. "But this one is the link and she dies. Your plan will not succeed. Therefore there is no reason for me to bring fertility once again to the land."

"What do you have to lose in the trying, my goddess?" asked Haeffen. "Give us a chance to do as we say and if we fail you may take the fertility back."

She only scowled at him in reply.

Gregor closed the distance between himself and Anaisse/Ariane. He drew her into his arms and kissed her deeply. "They want to bring us back *together* again, my love," Anot repeated meaningfully through Gregor.

She pulled away and her lips were swollen from the kiss, her eyes half-lidded. "I've missed you," she murmured. She kissed him again, hard. Her fingers threaded through the hair at his nape.

Tears pricked Gregor's eyes. He intensely wanted to believe this was Anaisse kissing him, not just her barely alive body animated by the goddess's energy. Gregor slanted his mouth over hers with new fervor and gave into the fantasy. He realized this might the last time he ever kissed her.

Hot tears fell freely from his eyes. They broke the kiss and Gregor set his forehead to hers. "I love you, Anaisse," he repeated over and over. "I love you so much."

"I feel your love through Anot, Gregor," she said with a smile. She cupped his cheek in her palm. "Please know that I will do right by her. She is not suffering now, nor shall she. I give you my word."

"I don't want your word," he said angrily. "I want *her*."

"I know." She smiled and for a moment Gregor saw pure Anaisse once again in her eyes. "Goodbye Gregor," she said.

Anot's energy left him in a whoosh and at the same time, Anaisse's body buckled and went cold. He caught her before she collapsed to the floor.

"No!" cried Gregor.

He lowered Anaisse to the floor and pressed his lips to hers. Her eyes were closed, her body cold, and no breath flowed through her. The beating of her heart had ceased.

I'll always be there to save you from the dark. He'd vowed that to her.

His tears stopped and pure, near controllable rage replaced his sorrow. He bowed his head over her and when he raised it again, his jaw was locked, his eyes were narrowed and the untainted drive for revenge flowed through his veins.

"Bring her back to the lorddom, Haeffen. I have something to see to." He stood and stalked out of the cottage.

"But where are you going, my lord?" called Haeffen from the doorway.

He ignored his question. Instead, Gregor swung up onto his mount. The animal beneath him sensed his rage and pranced beneath him, tossing his mane. He controlled the beast and circled the cottage, his eyes intent on the ground. He picked out the trail that led away from the cottage and into the woods toward the south—toward Sudhra.

Gregor looked up at Haeffen, who watched him silently. All his men stood around regarding him as though he'd gone mad. "I won't return to the keep until I've found Vant," Gregor stated.

He reined the horse toward the forest and kicked his heels into the beast's flanks. The horse jolted forward into the forest, on the trail of the one he planned to kill before sundown.

He rode as hard and as fast as he was able while still keeping the trail. Gregor had the advantage. He could tell by the depth and pacing of the tracks that he was much swifter than the one he stalked. Eventually the tracks traveled out onto a dirt road, one Gregor knew led to Sudhra.

Around mid-afternoon, a cold and driving rain began. It pummeled Gregor and began to muddy the road he traveled. He quickened his pace, unwilling to allow the rain to slow him.

Gregor did not think of anything save for what he would do to Vant once he found him. He'd tortured and killed him twenty different ways by the time he finally caught up with Vant at twilight. His prey rode at a leisurely pace ahead of him, as though journeying without a troublesome thought in his mind. As though he hadn't just murdered an innocent woman.

Gregor slowed his pace and kept well behind him, deciding which of the ways he'd fantasized was the best way to kill him.

Unexpectedly, Vant stopped his horse and dismounted. He stood in the middle of the road, facing Gregor. "What do you want?" he called through the rain.

Gregor kept riding toward him. "You killed Anaisse," he growled.

Vant sighed. There were deep lines around his eyes. "Is she dead?"

Gregor advanced. "Yes, you bastard."

"It was...very painful for me. I loved her."

"*I* loved her," Gregor roared. His hands clenched bloodless on the reins and he forced himself to relax his grip and dismount. With the reverberating ringing hiss of metal on metal, he unsheathed his sword from the scabbard attached to the saddle and stalked toward Vant. "Why did you do it?"

"For Sudhra." Weariness shone in his eyes.

Gregor stopped in front of him. Vant still hadn't drawn his sword. "You're going to die now," he stated simply.

Vant went for his scabbard, but before he could get his blade unsheathed Gregor nicked his left arm neatly. The cloth rent and blood welled. Vant cried out and clutched his arm, but made no move to defend himself.

"That's for Sania," Gregor said, then nicked his right arm. "That's for Lilane."

Vant finally backed away and drew his sword, but Gregor made sure he had no chance to use it. Gregor's sword swirled around him so quickly that Vant had no hope of hindering him.

Gregor's blade took nip after nip, slashing at him unmercifully until the man was a mess of blood and shallow wounds. "That's for all the other women you've tormented."

Gregor's blade bit Vant deep into his shoulder of his sword arm and pulled it out. Vant screamed in agony. "That's for Anaisse," he said, his voice breaking.

Vant's face went slack. He dropped to his knees.

Gregor hefted his sword to make the deathblow but Vant dropped his blade into the mud and covered his face with his hands, sobbing like a child. Softly, he began babbling to himself under his breath.

Gregor's sword hung limp in his hand. Of all the ways he'd imagined killing Vant, this was not one of them. It was as if Vant had been waiting for him to catch him. As though Vant longed for death. His mind was clearly not stable. How could he kill a man who'd gone daft? It was already a punishment worse than death. A mortal prison for the mind.

"You disgust me," Gregor said simply and spat on the ground beside the sunken man.

Vant's state of sanity was of no matter. Gregor simply couldn't leave him alive. Not after what he'd done. He raised his sword once again.

Too fast for Gregor to react, Vant drew the dagger sheathed at his side. "*This* is for Anaisse," Vant said, and then thrust the dagger into his own heart.

Vant gurgled and looked oddly surprised. Then he slumped to the ground. With a long sigh that seemed to come from the depth of his soul, Vant went silent and still. Gregor lowered his sword and watched Vant's blood pool with the mud around his boots.

So that's how it would end, Gregor thought with a grimace. No victory for either of them.

He stayed that way for a long time, letting the rain pound down on him. Not only was he soaked through with the rain, but by deep, deadening sorrow. When he returned to the keep, it would be an empty sleeping chamber and a grief-filled existence.

Images of Anaisse flashed through his mind and then were gone. Her hair tickled his nose as she rested her head on his shoulder. Her eyes flashed with mirth as she teased him. He felt her lips moving against his, warm and full of demanding passion.

Then he felt them as he'd felt them today, slack and cold.

He collapsed to his knees beside Vant. "*No!*" He put all his emotion into that one word. It ripped through the forest, torn from somewhere deep within him. He wanted her back. He covered his face with his hands.

Goddess, how he wanted her back.

He raised his face from his hands. The goddess. She'd let her die, coldly, inhumanely. The goddess didn't even care his heart would be ripped out of his very chest to see Anaisse die. He turned his head to the heavens and screamed, "I renounce you!"

Nothing greeted his declaration. The rain continued to fall. The cold mud continued to soak into his trews where he knelt on the ground. Vant continued to bleed beside him. The goddess hadn't heard him and didn't care what he thought of her. She paid no attention to dealings of mortals, except to curse them from time to time. He understood that now.

Gregor stood and picked up his sword. Then he located Vant's horse and took the reins in hand, in order to lead it back to his lorddom. He mounted his horse, looked back at Vant's body one last time, then headed home.

Chapter Thirteen

Anaisse knelt in a patch of lush green grass and inhaled the sweet scent of growing things wafting on the air. A long blue gown sheathed her body. She glanced at the clear sky and the green stretch of grass before her. She felt strong and healthy. Better than she'd ever felt before.

Realization hit her hard and fast. "The Afterworld," she breathed.

"Yes, my child."

Anaisse shot to her feet and whirled. A woman so beautiful she was difficult to look at stood there. Her thick black hair tumbled to her waist. The glossy length framed a face with a generous mouth and high cheekbones. Her complexion was of darkest morning before the dawn. A black so black it was nearly blue. To look into the pupils of her eyes was to fall into eternity. Stars twinkled in the depths of each, surrounding a flake of silver shaped like the crescent moon. She was shadowed mystery. Night to Anot's day.

Anaisse blinked rapidly. A sense of peace overtook her—a pleasurable numbness. She glanced around at the lush surroundings. She felt so good here, so relaxed and *right*. On some level she realized she could have anything she wanted in this place, could create her wildest dreams and live them.

But...a niggling of something teased the back of her mind. She grabbed for the thought but it slipped from her like a fast-fading dream in the morning. Anaisse frowned and shook her head once hard, as though to jar her memories back in place.

She'd left someone important behind, hadn't she? Something of great magnitude had just happened?

Hadn't it?

"You look confused," said the goddess. She walked toward her and her silken white gown moved over her skin making a shushing sound.

"I-I'm forgetting," she stammered, putting a hand to her temple.

"Yes, I provide forgetfulness to all those die. Especially those who die so violently as you. Remembrance can wait until you've had a chance to heal a little. Later you will remember your past life as if it were a dream. You will be detached from the brutal memory of your death and from those you left behind. There is no grief in the Afterworld."

"No! I can't forget." She shook her head again. "There was someone—" An image slipped through her mind and then out. She looked up at the goddess. "Stop it!" she yelled.

"Most are happy to let go of the anguish." Ariane shrugged and waved her hand. "But as you wish."

The memories crashed into Anaisse's mind. She grabbed her head with both hands and fell back onto the grass. Pain and sorrow rolled over her until she couldn't think or breathe. Finally, she acclimated herself to the sensations and memories relentlessly pounding at her and drew a long, shaky breath. She looked up at Ariane. "I must return."

"I had a feeling you would ask that of me. I felt the love you shared with the one called Gregor. It was like a pure sweet note singing through your bloodstream. I've felt that kind of love very rarely."

"Please. It is not only for Gregor that I need to return. My motivations are not all selfish," Anaisse pleaded. "If I die, Vant might get the uprising he sought. I link Sudhra and Nordan. Without that alliance, Sudhra may try to break the fragile truce that is now in place."

"Hmm." The goddess walked around Anaisse as though deep in thought. "I have been doing this since the beginning of time and, believe me, you are not the first to ask to go back. I have very rarely said yes."

Anaisse got to her feet and discovered she now wore a long violet gown. Hadn't it been blue before? Anaisse dropped her head in defeat. "Please. I cannot leave now," she sobbed.

Long moments of silence descended. Anaisse choked back a sob. She hung her head. "Do you not wish to see Ecasia again? Don't you wish to be reunited with your consort, Anot, in the minds and prayers of your children?"

"Of course I do."

Anaisse looked up at her. "Then give us the chance to make it so. Let me go back."

The goddess sighed. "I am compelled to grant your request. I know you ask for life not only for yourself, but another as well. Even if you do not understand that."

Hope surged through Anaisse. It overwhelmed the question she had about what the goddess had said. She asked for life for another besides herself, but she did not know it? What did that mean?

"I do not think this alliance between Nordan and Sudhra will be successful. That aside," the goddess smiled and her eyes sparkled, "even though you were near death, I felt something within you. Something amazing. It is for that reason and also for the love you and this man, Gregor, share that I feel compelled to soften."

"What did you feel within me?"

Ariane ignored her question. "But you must realize, you are going back to great pain. I can heal you somewhat, but you will still bear the scars, internally and externally for what that man did to you."

"I will endure anything."

"You are strong and very willful. Definitely one of my children." Ariane smiled again, a flash of dazzling white against black. She lifted a brow. "Fare well, my child. I will give you a brief gift along with your new breath."

Relief flooded through her. "Thank you." She opened her mouth to ask about the *gift*, but the goddess spoke first.

"Time flows differently here. Only minutes will have passed in the other space." The goddess waved her hand again.

Darkness overtook Anaisse.

She found herself on the floor of the cottage. She took huge gulping breath of air.

And felt the gift the goddess gave her.

* * * * *

It was full night by the time Gregor entered the keep. All but the guards were sleeping. His body felt beaten as though from battle, and he could barely move his legs to get up the stairs to his room.

His emotions were numb, frozen. As if his grief was so complete it had overwhelmed him and shut him down. It made him feel heavy.

He carefully made his way down the corridor toward his chamber, glad he had not run into anyone since he'd arrived. He pushed his door open and walked within. The servants had stoked the fire in his chamber, though they had not known when he'd return. Even *if* he would return. That was odd. The firelight flickered over the table and chairs flanking the hearth.

His gaze seized one of Anaisse's nightdresses that hung over the back of one the chairs. He looked at nothing but that article of clothing and went to it. Scooping it up, he brought it to his nose and inhaled the scent of her. He closed his eyes and breathed her in as his mind rapidly turned over ways to keep the scent in the material for the longest time possible.

"Gregor."

His eyes popped open. *Her voice.* But it couldn't be.

"My love," came the voice again. It was filled with heartbreaking emotion. He could feel her love reach out and touch him just from those two words.

He whirled. Anaisse stood in front of him, the firelight licking over her form. She wore a long white gown that was a little too large for her. The neckline slipped down over one shoulder, revealing her creamy skin. No blood marred the smoothness of her flesh or her clothing.

Was she an apparition?

He closed the distance between them and pulled her to him. He lowered his mouth to hers and kissed her. She felt warm, solid, *real*. And she kissed him back with a vengeance. Wetness touched his cheek and he pulled away. Tears streamed down her face.

Apparitions didn't cry and kiss, did they?

He touched her cheek and rubbed her tears between his fingers. "I don't understand," he whispered. "I watched you die. You lay lifeless in my arms."

"I *did* die. But my heart ceased beating only for a handful of minutes." She held up her arms and showed him her wrists. By the light of the fire, he could see two long, thin scars where she'd been cut. They looked old and faded, not fresh like logic said they should appear.

"When I awoke," she continued, "my wounds were healed and the cottage was empty. I heard you outside, and Haeffen stood in the doorway watching you, but I was very weak and couldn't get up or call for attention. When Haeffen came to gather me, he found me breathing."

He hugged her to him and rained kisses on her face, neck and shoulders. "I don't understand why the goddess let you come back and I don't care. I'm just so happy you're here," he murmured into her hair.

She wound her arms around his neck and laughed. "I was so afraid I'd never see you again." She kissed him long and hard, then pulled away. "What of Vant?"

"Gone. Finished. He will not be returning. If it's of any consolation, he truly regretted what he'd done to you."

He watched her expression harden. "It's not."

Gregor scooped her up into his arms and carried her to the bed. "Let's not talk of him anymore." He tossed her onto the bed and she laughed. It was the best sound he'd ever heard.

He lay down beside her and pulled her into his arms. She snuggled against him and sighed in contentment. "The goddess said she felt the love I had for you and also that she felt something else. Something she'd never experienced before. She said that because of these things she'd give me my life back, along with a gift."

"A gift?"

"I didn't understand until I awoke and also felt it, just for a moment. Then I understood." Anaisse reached up and cupped his cheek in her hand. "I felt a spark of life burning steady in my womb. I'm pregnant, Gregor. That's what the goddess felt."

Gregor was speechless. All he could do was kiss her. The worst day of his life was now the best. He placed a hand to her lower abdomen and stared in wonder.

"I was pregnant before Vant abducted me. I'm not very far along, maybe only a few days, but still the goddess felt the life within me and knew pregnancy as we experience it while she was inside my body."

"Amazing," was all Gregor could manage.

"Amazing," she agreed.

Silence enveloped them. They both went still. The crackling of the fire was all Gregor could hear. All he could see were the shadows dancing on the walls. Calm joy filled him. It left him bereft of thought and afraid that if he moved or said something, it would all vanish. He couldn't believe how lucky he was.

"Gregor," Anaisse said finally. "Aren't you going to say anything besides *amazing*?"

He flipped her to her back and covered her body with his. He fit perfectly against her, molding himself to all her curves. "I love you."

Her white teeth flashed in the darkness as she smiled. "I love you too."

He kissed her long and deep and when he pulled away, her breathing was erratic, following the pattern he'd come to recognize meant she was excited.

She licked her lips and his cock hardened. "I want you inside my body almost as much as I want you in my life," she said. "I *need* to feel you within me now, Gregor. Make me feel alive."

"Are you well enough?"

"Yes." She sat up. "Will you make love to me now?"

They met in the center of the bed and fell at each other wildly. As though this would be the last time they'd ever be able to feel each other. The last time they'd ever make love. They tore at each other's clothes while they pressed their mouths together in a kiss. Their tongues tangled again and again.

Finally, after fumbling and bumping into her arms several times, he got her gown over her head and off. She was nude beneath it. That was lucky. He didn't think he could handle trying to get her undergarments off, too.

He was so hard his cock hurt.

He helped her get his clothes off and then she crushed up against him. Her soft, silky, warm skin slid along his. Ah, there was nothing better in the world.

"Gregor," she breathed against his mouth. She kissed her way down his chin, down his chest and stomach. When her hot mouth closed around his cock, his hips jerked forward. He curled his fingers into her hair. By the light of the fire he watched his shaft disappear into her mouth as she sucked on him. Her tongue smoothed over the crown and licked up and down the shaft as she cupped and massaged his sac in her hand.

Dear goddess, he'd come if she didn't stop and he wanted to climax with her. He gently pulled her away from him, although it pained him to do it and pressed her back into the pillows.

He spread her thighs and positioned himself between them, readying himself to feast on her sex. He licked from her inner kneecap to the crease where her thigh met her torso. Then he lowered his mouth to her pussy. It was ripe for his tongue, begging to be licked and worshiped with his mouth. With his thumbs, he spread her pussy lips apart and licked from her anus to her clit. She let out a sigh of pleasure and her back arched.

He licked around her folds, drawing them into his mouth and sucking on them. From time to time, he'd delve down and slip his tongue into her passage, wringing moans of pleasure from her. Then he settled on her clit, drawing it into his mouth, laving it with his tongue and sucking on it. Her body tensed and Gregor knew she was ready to climax. He slipped two fingers into her passage, found her pleasure point and rubbed against it. It pushed her over the edge. She came against his mouth and her juices coursed over his fingers. He pulled his mouth away, still savoring the taste of her on his tongue. She grasped his arms and pulled him down on her, and moved her hips until the head of his cock pressed against her pussy. He teased her clit with it and she moaned and arched her back.

He slipped down and pushed the head of his shaft into her passage. Then with one long, hard thrust that sent her buttocks into the mattress, he impaled her on his phallus. Her soft, warm heat surrounded him. He pounded into her, his flesh slapping against hers.

"Yes," she moaned into his ear. "Gregor, oh, yes."

He kissed her hard, his tongue slipping in and mating with hers. Then he braced his hands on her waist, falling to the serious task of fucking her. He thrust into her with abandon, the muscles of his buttocks flexing and releasing with every deep stroke. She felt soft and warm, slick with the juice of her excitement. Her vaginal muscles tensed and rippled around his length with every thrust.

She tipped her head back and shouted out her climax. He came with her, releasing a groan of satisfaction as pleasure emanated out from his groin and overwhelmed him. He thrust into her to the hilt and let his hot seed fill her.

He held her close, remaining sheathed inside her. They were both breathing hard. Finally he shifted to her side and pulled her toward him so they could laze in the aftermath of their shared orgasm.

She snuggled back against him and gave a contented sigh. "Does life get any better than this?"

He kissed her temple. "I don't know. Let's find out."

* * * * *

Tol watched Gregor hand-feed bits of food to Anaisse. She looked flush with both health and happiness. Tol had been relieved to discover that Anaisse was alive. He'd grown very fond of her and had mourned when she lay dying.

He was filled with joy for the couple he now watched, but at the same time, jealousy haunted him. Like Gregor, he also wanted a woman with whom to spend his life. Someone to hand-feed bits of food during dinner.

He took a long drink of his wine and stared down at his plate. Suddenly, he didn't feel very hungry.

"Tol."

He looked up at the sound of Melandra's voice. Had she come to profess her undying love and agree to give up all her other men for him?

Nice thought, but he doubted it.

"Melandra," he answered. "Come to spear me in the heart again, my love?"

She sank down beside him and burst into noisy tears.

Tol froze in shock, and then took her into his arms in an effort to comfort her. She shook against him as she sobbed and buried her head into the crook of his neck. *Goddess*, she smelled wonderful. She felt wonderful. The woman simply *was* wonderful.

It broke his heart to see her like this. Was it what he'd said? "Melandra, you can spear my heart over and over if only it will prevent your tears, love." He groped for his napkin and handed it to her.

She cried harder. "S-stop being nice to me," she sobbed.

"Why are you crying?" he asked.

Finally, her tears receded into a soft hiccupping and tearful melancholy. She raised her head. Her eyes were red and puffy and her nose was swollen. Tearstains tracked her pale cheeks. "I can't do it," she rasped in a tear-laden voice.

"What can't you do?"

She shook her head. "I can't pretend that I can be with other men when the only one I want is you."

Another shock. Had he heard her correctly? "Really?"

"I don't even know if you want me now, but I'm telling you that even though I long for a child, I'm ready to commit to one man—*you*." She looked away and sniffled. "It will hurt, but I'll understand if you won't have me."

He stilled for a moment, registering all her words. Then he pulled her toward to him and kissed her. "Melandra, I've been dreaming you'd say those words to me. Of course I want you."

She let a soul-shuddering sigh. "I was so afraid you'd reject me."

His arms tightened around her. "Never."

"Oh, I'm so relieved. I'm so sorry for what I put you through. I promise I'll make it up to you." She raised her head and quirked an eyebrow. "I really do want a baby, though, Tol. There is much work ahead of us."

He grinned. "Love, you've come to the right man." He kissed her.

Chapter Fourteen

Anaisse watched Lyssa, Tol and Melandra playing together in the common room of the children's wing. The little girl's mother had never returned and she and Gregor had made the easy decision of allowing Melandra and Tol to adopt her.

She sat back on the bench and rubbed her swelling abdomen. She was not very large yet, although she was sure that in just a few moon cycles, she would be.

She, along with scores of women all over both Nordan and Sudhra.

The goddess had broken her curse, it appeared. More pregnancies were being reported every day. Sienne, Lord Marken's monogamous mate, had announced only just yesterday. Anaisse's child would not lack for playmates, that was for certain.

Anaisse fancied the goddess had broken the curse because she'd felt the life spark burning within her on that fateful day in the cottage.

It appeared to both the people of Sudhra and Nordan that it had been her match with Gregor that broken the curse. Things had all but quieted in the other country and relations and goodwill had flourished since the women had begun conceiving. There was still much work to be done, but it was a start.

It was definitely a start.

Vant had brought about the success of the very thing he'd striven to stop. It was poetic in a way.

Gregor walked into the common room and went to a window. Anaisse watched him for a few moments, taking advantage of the fact he didn't realize she was in the crowded room.

Aye, she'd lost all control to him and he'd consumed her fully.

And she wouldn't have it any other way.

She stood and walked to him. At his side was the only place she wanted to be. He smiled when he spotted her. Wordlessly, he wrapped an arm around her waist and pulled her close. She rested her head on his shoulder.

Together they watched the first snow of winter gently fall.

Enjoy this excerpt from
Ordinary Charm
© Copyright Anya Bast 2004

All Rights Reserved, Ellora's Cave Publishing, Inc.

She walked back to the entryway where she'd seen a table with a phone. "It's here." The message light blinked five messages. Cole came to stand beside her. She hit play.

A sultry, breathy female voice filled the foyer. "Darling, this is Monique. Call me. I'm missing you." Pause. "Darren is out of town on business this weekend. Come see me. *Please*."

Serena rolled her eyes. The woman sounded like she needed a fix. Maybe Cole *was* a drug dealer...of the carnal variety.

Beep

A perky cheerleaderesque voice was up next. "Hey, Cole, baby. This is Cynthia. I had a fantastic day with you last Saturday." Pause. Her voice lowered, got huskier when she spoke next. "Saturday night was even better. Wanna repeat? Call me back."

Beep

"Yeeeech." Serena turned away and walked toward the living. She couldn't take any more. It was nauseating.

"I guess I have a few women," Cole said, sounding mightily pleased with himself.

Was it any surprise? The man was stunning. Serena looked back in time to see him push a hand through his hair. The action defined his biceps perfectly and made hunger twist through her body. She looked away. "Yeah. Guess it hasn't really been a long time, like you said."

He frowned. "Guess not. Sure feels like it, though."

There were two hang-ups. Blessedly, the next message was not from a woman. Instead, it was an older sounding man. Serena wandered back to the answering machine.

"Hey, Cole, just wanted to let you know that we received *Fire of the Ancients*. We love it and only want a couple changes. You did a fantastic job on this game. You're the king of adventure games, man. We'll be getting back to you with more details, but you've done it again. This'll be a hit!"

"Well." He slanted her an unsure look. "I'm the king of adventure computer games, I guess."

"Apparently, that's not all you're the king of," Serena muttered.

He appeared to not have heard her. "So," he said to almost himself. "I design computer games. That explains all the equipment in the living room." He frowned and glanced at her. "Designing computer games is kind of geeky. Do I seem like a geek to you?"

"What?" She turned toward him. "First of all, there's nothing wrong with geeks. I happen to be one myself. Second of all—" She took him in from the top his head to his feet, every luscious well-defined muscle in-between, and tried not to swallow her tongue. "No, you don't look like one." Suddenly uncomfortable, she turned away. "Anyway, what the hell does a geek look like?" she finished, irritably.

"Let's explore the rest of the apartment." He turned and walked into the living room.

"Don't you want to call *Monique* and *Cynthia* back?" She mimicked their voices when she said their names. It was childish, but she couldn't help herself.

He turned back toward and fixed her with suddenly hooded and heated gaze. It was the calculating and measured gaze of a predator. Like shark that had just scented blood in the water, or a lion on an African plain that had spotted a wounded zebra.

Shit.

She took a step back involuntarily and bumped into the telephone table. "Are you jealous, beautiful?" he purred as he came closer.

"Uh." Oh, *that* was an intelligent response. Mentally, she smacked her forehead with her open palm.

"Because you sound jealous," he murmured. He reached her and cupped her cheek in his hand. "Maybe I should kiss you again and reassert the fact that I desperately want you in my bed, Serena. It was *you* that balked, remember?"

"I-I'm not jealous," she replied, tipping her chin up a little. "I just don't like to see women make idiots of themselves over a man." *Just like she was doing.* "I just don't…shit—"

His mouth came down on hers, completely stealing the rest of her thought. He seduced her lips to part and kissed her deep. All the while he rubbed his thumb back and forth over her cheek. He broke the kiss and set his forehead to hers. After making a little purring sound in the back of his throat, he closed his eyes and clenched his jaw. "Your skin's so soft," he murmured thickly. "I can't help but wonder if you're as soft all over."

Serena's breath caught. She used the table behind her to take some of her weight because her knees weren't doing a very good job of it.

He set his hands on either side of her, resting them on the table, and gazed into her wide eyes. "You need to leave, Serena. I mean it. You're not safe around me…for so many different reasons. I want to lead you to my bed, lay you out and take you over and over until the morning light breaks the night. I want to strip you, beautiful. I want to sink myself inside you."

A whimpering sound reached her ears and it took her a second to realize it was coming from her.

He pushed away from the table and turned. "If you don't want any of that, you should leave now. Because you're tempting me something awful."

Serena glanced at the door and back at Cole. He stood with his back to her. Suddenly, he shot a hand out toward the door and it opened.

She stared at the open door, her ticket out of here, out of this whole dangerous mess. If she left now, she'd be free of the whole Ashmodai thing, presumably.

But she couldn't seem to move.

She did want Cole. Of course, she did. She was just surprised, and more than a little wary about the fact that *he* wanted *her*. In her mind, she was still the fat girl in school all the boys ignored. It was hard for her to wrap her mind around the fact that this perfect, beautiful specimen of manhood—this man who could have any woman he wanted—found her attractive. No. Not even that. Cole professed to find her *irresistible*.

How could that be?

She wanted to find out if it was true, however, so instead of walking to the door and out of it like she *should*, she stood staring at Cole's broad shoulders, his tight ass and the back of his head. She *liked* this man as well as found him attractive. He was compelling, mysterious and more than a little dangerous. She found *him* irresistible.

But…what would happen when he got her clothes off and he discovered her overweight body naked? Would the fire in his eyes dim? Serena shuddered. That was something she *didn't* want to find out.

Something Brian had told her once came back in a rush, *You'd be so pretty if you just lost some weight.*

She glanced at the door, then back at Cole. She *should* leave. It would save them both some pain and anguish. She moved to take a step toward it.

He flicked his wrist. The door slammed shut.

Crap.

Suddenly, her mid was awhirl. What kind of bra and underwear had she put on this morning? She flushed as she remembered donning the serviceable blue briefs that sported tiny pink flowers and the boring white cotton bra. Not exactly alluring lingerie.

She just hadn't expected to be seduced today.

A wild laugh rose up in her throat, but it was choked into submission by the look on Cole's face as he turned toward her. A dark, predatory light graced his brown and green-flecked eyes. "You're mine now, beautiful," he murmured.

Enjoy this excerpt from
Blood of an Angel
© *Copyright Anya Bast 2005*

All Rights Reserved, Ellora's Cave Publishing, Inc.

His muscles and mind protesting the movement, Charlie pushed off from the ground and launched himself at the woman with an anguished roar. She cried out in surprise, as he slammed full-force into her midsection, driving them both back into the door of a garage behind them. A hot slickness coated his stomach and chest and it took him a moment to realize it was his own blood. She struggled against him, waving that hawthorn stake dangerously close to his back.

Hawthorn wood was highly toxic to the Embraced. The wound made by a hawthorn stake not only poisoned their blood, it wouldn't close up. Ironically, most Embraced died of blood loss if someone staked them. So the fact that the hawthorn was now scraping his shoulder didn't make Charlie feel exactly warm and fuzzy.

He shifted to the side and grabbed the wrist of the hand wielding the stake. His whole body screamed from whatever it was she'd done to him. The wound made him weak and she was exceptionally strong. *Way* too strong for a human female. The result made them almost evenly matched in a fight. *Almost.* He suspected he was still the stronger one.

There was something off here. What was it?

With single-minded intensity, he pushed her down the garage door to the pavement. She shrieked in rage, but she couldn't stop him from pressing that wrist down to the ground. The woman might be faster than him, but it turned out that, even injured, he was still stronger. He wrested the stake from her grasp and threw it to the side. It ended up behind a row of trashcans that stood nearby.

She kicked, coming dangerously close to his balls with her knee, and slammed her fist into his jaw. His head snapped to the side under the force of the punch. Pain blossomed through his skull.

Damn, she was strong. She *couldn't* be human, but she didn't feel like an Embraced.

What the hell was she?

He needed to further control the woman, and he needed to do it fast. Using his inner thighs, he pressed in, pinning her legs together. He also grabbed her other flailing arm at the wrist and pressed it down to the ground.

She shrieked again and Charlie wondered when someone in one of these nearby houses would call the cops. They didn't need that. The police would call in the local SPAVA unit—Squad for Paranormal and Vampiric Activity—and they'd give both Charlie and Anlon absolute hell. Any conflict between a human and an Embraced—if *human* really was what this woman was—got extra special attention from the local law enforcement, always at the expense of the Embraced, no matter which party was truly at fault. Prejudice against the Embraced was alive and well in the United States.

But more important than avoiding SPAVA was finding out if Vincent was all right. He hadn't moved or made a sound since the woman had knelt over him with the stake in her hand. The fact that Charlie had wrested the hawthorn away from her before she'd had a chance to strike Vincent gave him hope that he was probably okay.

The woman went limp beneath him. Charlie was thankful, since the blood he'd lost was making him feel weak and the *sacyr* was rising hard and fast as a result. Plus, the closeness of his peculiar woman and her violet scent, combined with his own rage, was fueling his blood hunger.

She stared up with him with complete and utter animosity in her eyes.

Gone were the glasses. Gone was the illusion of bookishness and fragility. Completely gone was the impression that this woman was *angelic*. She felt delicate beneath him, but the way she'd kicked his ass contradicted that image.

"You should have let me kill him. He deserves to die," she spat.

Charlie's brow furrowed. Vincent was harmless. He was one of the most harmless Embraced he'd ever met. Vincent was almost *naive*. What could Vincent have done to gain this woman's wrath? The question posed on his lips was *why* in the moment the woman suddenly pushed up hard. Caught off-guard by the jolt of inhuman strength, Charlie toppled to the side.

The woman sprang to her feet, eyeing the dark corner behind the row of trashcans where Charlie had thrown the stake. She lunged in that direction, but he stretched out quick as a striking snake and caught her by the ankle. He toppled her to the ground face-first and pushed to his feet.

The *sacyr* roared within him, overwhelming his weakness. It screamed in his head. He needed to feed. He needed to feed *now*.

Too bad for the woman in front him. She was about to become a meal.

With an intense gaze, he watched her flip to her back and spot him. He was the predator now. He might be injured. He might be weak. The rising *sacyr* didn't care about any of that. It just wanted the blood of this woman. Her gray eyes widened as she realized the tables had suddenly turned. Charlie watched her crab-walk back a few paces, then lurch to her feet.

Charlie lunged.

The woman spun to the side, kicking her booted foot up and around in a roundhouse kick. Her heel caught him hard in the solar plexus, right where she'd wounded him. He grunted, but the *sacyr* held him upright, made him push through the intense pain. The *sacyr* was unstoppable now. He had no say in his actions and was a slave to its whims. She threw a punch, but he blocked it. He took a step forward; she took a step back. It was like a dance, but one wholly without romance.

She turned to run, but he grabbed her by her upper arms and dragged her back flush up against his chest.

He lowered his head to her ear, scenting the violet in her hair and the blood that ran through those delicate veins under her pale, soft skin. He inhaled and closed his eyes, letting her aroma infuse him. His breath left him in a groan of ecstasy. "All the gentleman's been beaten right out of me," he murmured into her ear. "You're in trouble now, angel."

She stilled. Her breathing sounded harsh in the suddenly quiet air. It was as if the whole world had fallen away and only this alley, only he and this mysterious woman, remained.

Charlie dipped his head to the place where her shoulder met her throat and rubbed his lips against her skin. The woman shivered. From fear? He didn't know. He didn't smell any fear on her, but by rights she *should've* been afraid. Charlie only knew that her shudder increased the pull and strength of the *sacyr*.

He had to have her...*now*.

He flicked his tongue out and tasted her skin, tasted the hard pulse under her earlobe. So sweet. So soft. So perfect. He stifled a groan. His fangs extended and he brushed them across her vulnerable throat. At the same, he readied his glamour. Charlie was exceptionally good with glamour. The woman would feel nothing but pleasure when he bit her.

It was far more than she deserved.

The sudden scent of arousal filled the air, delicately musky. The woman whimpered in her throat. She relaxed against him and the tang of her sex, plumped with excitement, teased him.

That sound, along with the fragrance of her, gripped him and wouldn't let him free. Feeling drugged, he grazed his fangs along her shoulder. He felt the skin slice open in a thin, neat line and tasted just a drop of her blood on his tongue.

Somewhere in the *sacyr*-controlled, pain-fogged back of his mind, Charlie noted that she didn't taste like a human. Her blood was smoother, silkier on his tongue. It reminded him of milk flavored with a bit of sugar.

So, delicious.... He lowered his mouth to take another taste.

Suddenly, the woman thrust her elbows up hard and twisted to the side. Charlie tried to maintain his grip on her, but she was gone in a blur of speed.

An angelic tinkle of laughter was all he heard from the mouth of the alley. Then, nothing.

The *sacyr* wailed within him at being denied sustenance. His wound overwhelmed him. Charlie groaned, dropped to his knees and knew nothing more.

About the author:

Anya Bast writes erotic fantasy and paranormal romance. Primarily, she writes happily-ever-afters with lots of steamy sex. After all, how can you have a happily-ever-after WITHOUT lots of sex?

Mary Wine welcomes mail from readers. You can write to her c/o Ellora's Cave Publishing at 1337 Commerce Drive, Suite 13, Stow OH 44224.

Why an electronic book?

We live in the Information Age—an exciting time in the history of human civilization in which technology rules supreme and continues to progress in leaps and bounds every minute of every hour of every day. For a multitude of reasons, more and more avid literary fans are opting to purchase e-books instead of paperbacks. The question to those not yet initiated to the world of electronic reading is simply: *why?*

1. *Price.* An electronic title at Ellora's Cave Publishing runs anywhere from 40-75% less than the cover price of the <u>exact same title</u> in paperback format. Why? Cold mathematics. It is less expensive to publish an e-book than it is to publish a paperback, so the savings are passed along to the consumer.
2. *Space.* Running out of room to house your paperback books? That is one worry you will never have with electronic novels. For a low one-time cost, you can purchase a handheld computer designed specifically for e reading purposes. Many e-readers are larger than the average handheld, giving you plenty of screen room. Better yet, hundreds of titles can be stored within your new library—a single microchip. (Please note that Ellora's Cave does not endorse any specific brands. You can check our website at www.ellorascave.com for customer recommendations we make available to new consumers.)
3. *Mobility.* Because your new library now consists of only a microchip, your entire cache of books can be taken with you wherever you go.

4. *Personal preferences are accounted for.* Are the words you are currently reading too small? Too large? Too...ANNOYING? Paperback books cannot be modified according to personal preferences, but e-books can.
5. *Innovation.* The way you read a book is not the only advancement the Information Age has gifted the literary community with. There is also the factor of what you can read. Ellora's Cave Publishing will be introducing a new line of interactive titles that are available in e-book format only.
6. *Instant gratification.* Is it the middle of the night and all the bookstores are closed? Are you tired of waiting days—sometimes weeks—for online and offline bookstores to ship the novels you bought? Ellora's Cave Publishing sells instantaneous downloads 24 hours a day, 7 days a week, 365 days a year. Our e-book delivery system is 100% automated, meaning your order is filled as soon as you pay for it.

Those are a few of the top reasons why electronic novels are displacing paperbacks for many an avid reader. As always, Ellora's Cave Publishing welcomes your questions and comments. We invite you to email us at service@ellorascave.com or write to us directly at: 1337 Commerce Drive, Suite 13, Stow OH 44224.

Discover for yourself why readers can't get enough of the multiple award-winning publisher Ellora's Cave. Whether you prefer e-books or paperbacks, be sure to visit EC on the web at www.ellorascave.com for an erotic reading experience that will leave you breathless.

www.ellorascave.com

Printed in the United States
49201LVS00001B/130-144